Some Great Thing

Some Great Thing

Lawrence Hill

Turnstone Press

Turnstone Press
607-100 Arthur Street
Winnipeg, Manitoba
Canada R3B 1H3

Turnstone Press gratefully acknowledges the assistance
of the Canada Council and the Manitoba Arts Council.

Cover illustration: Scott Barham

Cover design: Marilyn Morton

Text design: Manuela Dias

This book was printed and bound in Canada by
Hignell Printing Limited for Turnstone Press.

Canadian Cataloguing in Publication Data

Hill, Lawrence, 1957-

Some great thing

ISBN 0-88801-167-9

I. Title

PS8565.I44S6 1992   C813'.54   C92-098127-5
PR9199.3.H544S6 1992

To my parents, Donna and Daniel Hill

"What! discouraged? Go do some great thing."

Crawford Kilian
Go Do Some Great Thing;
The Black Pioneers of British Columbia

Acknowledgements

I couldn't have finished this novel without the help of many people. In particular, I want to thank:

Joanne Savoie, my wife, for loving a writer; my sister and brother, Karen and Dan Hill, for encouragement of every kind; Paul Quarrington and Shirley Sharzer, generous in too many ways to describe; Silvana DiGiacomo, Hope Kamin, Irène Léger and David Steen for reading early drafts; Tom Goldstein for putting me up in Winnipeg; Christie McLaren, Cecil Rosner and Wilf Slater for details on journalism; Wilson Brooks, Harry Gairey and Cyclone Williams for details on railroad porters; James Finlay and Patrick Riley for details on welfare; Terry Moore and Frances Russell for details on bilingualism in Manitoba; Wayne Tefs of Turnstone Press for editing the manuscript; the Ontario Arts Council for financial assistance; and, finally, my writing group friends Paul McLaughlin, Kim Moritsugu, Oakland Ross, Ronald Ruskin, Mark Sabourin, Bert Simpson and Christine Slater for commenting on the manuscript.

PROLOGUE

His SON WAS BORN IN 1957 AT THE MISERICORDIA HOSPITAL IN Winnipeg, before men had to start watching their wives give birth. Asked about it years later, Ben Grafton replied, "What's a man to do in a place like that, except grow all bug-eyed and wobbly and make a shining fool of himself?"

On that windless January night, Ben Grafton didn't enter the delivery room. He didn't consider it. He waited until Louise was "finished," poked his head in the door and shouted "atta way Lulu!" Wearing a blue woollen cap that stopped short of his huge brown ears, he followed two nurses who took the infant to the nursery. Ben Grafton was not invited. Nor was he self-conscious. He was a forty-three-year-old railroad porter who had coped with all sorts of nonsense in the past and had long stopped wondering what people thought of his being this or that. They turned to tell him he couldn't stay in the nursery. He said he wanted to look at his little man.

"So cute, this little baby," one nurse cooed, turning the brown face toward Ben.

Ben touched a tiny cheek. He didn't understand all this hospital nonsense. Why couldn't the nurses just leave the boy with his mother? Or with him? But he wasn't going to raise a ruckus. He was going to take it calm and easy. But then something happened. The nurse crossed the baby. With her thumb. She actually touched his forehead and made a sign of the cross. Then she started mumbling a prayer. "Hey," Ben said.

The nurse continued.

"No praying." Gently, but firmly, Ben poked the woman in the ribs.

She turned on him, eyebrows raised. "Please," she hissed.

"No praying," Ben repeated.

The woman's jaw dropped. The nurse beside her stared at Ben.

"That's right," Ben said, eyeballing both of them. "This little man is a Grafton. And Graftons don't go in for devils and angels and heaven and hell. This little man will believe in humanity. Humanity and activism. You can leave him here till his mother wakes up but I don't want any more of those rituals. Is that clear?"

The praying nurse nodded, the other one blinked. Neither spoke. They lay the baby in his bassinet. Ben backed out of the nursery but watched through the window. He stayed there for an hour or so. He had some thinking to do. Thinking about a name. A *good* one. This child was destined for great things. No ordinary name would do.

PART ONE

ON HIS WAY TO THE MEN'S ROOM, WHICH HE CONSIDERED A refuge, since in all his years at *The Herald* nobody had run in there to dispatch him to the scene of an accident, Chuck Maxwell spotted a memo from the managing editor. "*Mahatma?*" Chuck muttered. Staring at the message board, he read the news again: "I am pleased to announce that Mahatma Grafton of Toronto will join our reporting staff on July 11, 1983." Chuck let out the news with a shout. Colleagues surrounded him. They found the recruit's résumé appended to the memo. Mahatma Lennox Grafton. Age: twenty-five. Education: B.A. double honours, History and French, Université Laval. M.A. Economics, University of Toronto. Languages: English, French, Spanish. Marital status: single. Work experience: reporter for *The Varsity,* U. of T. Interests: literature, languages, squash.

"What kind of name is Mahatma?" Chuck asked.

"Indian," someone said. "East Indian."

"Maybe it's Spanish," Chuck said. "Hispanic or something."

Reporters argued about it all afternoon. One said he had heard the new reporter was a Pakistani, but Helen Savoie challenged him. "Who told you that?"

"Don Betts."

Helen snorted. Don Betts was the city editor. "What does he know?"

"Somebody might have told him," Chuck said. "Maybe the guy is a Pakistani. Maybe he's coming to live with his family here."

"Do you know how many Pakistanis there are in Manitoba?" Helen said. "Hardly any. But Betts is such a pea-brain, he'd call every East Indian a Pakistani."

"How can you say there's hardly any Pakistanis?" Chuck said. "There's tons of 'em."

"What do you mean, tons?"

"Thousands."

"Thousands in Manitoba?" she asked.

Chuck held Helen in high esteem. Sure, she was stagnating at *The Herald* just like him, never getting a decent assignment, but the woman knew more than anyone else on staff. Still, Chuck went after her on this one. "They're everywhere you look."

"Where, exactly, have you been looking?" Helen asked. "Do you see any on the police force? In politics? Delivering mail? You see three driving cabs and you say they're everywhere."

Chuck said, "I'll bet you twenty bucks the new guy is Pakistani."

"You're on."

A white bungalow. A closed-in porch with yellow trim six steps off the ground. Tyndall stone exterior. A living-room window looking out on American elms on Lipton Street. His old bedroom window faced a garden plot, an alley, trash cans, electric wires and, further back, the rear ends of houses on the next street west. Mahatma Grafton took the stone path by the south end of the house. He set down his suitcases and dug in his pocket for a key that he hadn't used in six years. He wouldn't stay long with the old man. A few weeks, maybe. Then he'd find an apartment. A cheap bachelor that he could abandon easily if the job didn't work out. The doorknob turned all by itself. The old man must have been watching from the window. He swung the door open, smiling. Wearing the same burgundy bathrobe, the same heel-beaten slippers. He was not a tall man. Five-seven, maybe. Mahatma was surprised. He had remembered his father as being taller.

"Welcome home, son."

"Thanks."

They shook hands. Mahatma gripped loose flesh around old bones. Dark grooves slanted down his father's cheeks, and others cut across his forehead. Mahatma glanced at his father's mahogany irises. Ben asked, "So you're going to work for *The Herald?*" Mahatma started to tell him about it, but Ben cut him off. "Let me take one of those bags. Is your old bedroom okay?"

Magazines and newspapers covered a chair in the living-room. A cherry desk, which Ben had bought at a garage sale fifty years ago, played host to scraps of paper—phone messages, memory prods, shopping lists. Mahatma tugged up the old blanket on the couch and saw boxes on the floor. The same old boxes stuffed with documents. Documents Ben collected. ("Did I ever show you this?" Ben had asked a thousand times. "What?" "This picture of your mother. . . . This picture of your mother's mother. . . . This picture of railway porters. These are history.") Mahatma wondered if the old man had touched the boxes in years. Did he still log details about the family, lecture about race consciousness and think Mahatma had forsaken his people? Ben asked, "You had lunch?"

"On the plane." Mahatma felt six years of silence rising between them. "But thanks, abuelo."

Ben smiled. Mahatma watched the dark lips lifting. He studied the ears: huge half-hearts running from eyes to jaw. The old man still liked to be called *abuelo*. It reminded him of union days; it reminded him of long-ago lessons from father to son: *hermano* means brother, *libertad* freedom, *papá* father, *abuelo* grandfather.

Uno dos tres cuatro cinco: one two three four five. I'm your papa
but you can call me *abuelo.* Our little secret. What'll you call me,
Daddy? Mahatma. No, something else! *Gran alma,* then. What's
that, Daddy? It means great soul, it means Mahatma. Ben said,
"Glad to have you back, son."

"Glad to be back."

They didn't touch. Mahatma managed a smile. "I'm going to
have a nap."

"Good idea." This surprised Mahatma, who had expected the
old man to squawk, "Nap? I'm three times your age and I don't nap."

Mahatma closed the door. He sighed. Ben had dusted the
window ledge, swept the floor, stuffed four boxes into the closet.
Mahatma flipped one open and saw pages and cards and
brochures and hand-kept journals. He dropped the box lid back
in place. He lay back on his old bed. There was a desk in the room.
A new desk and a lamp. Nice of the old man, that. Mahatma would
have to keep in touch after renting an apartment. It had been
understandable, not writing or calling from Toronto. His father
hadn't written or called, either. But it would be wrong to return
to Winnipeg and fall out of touch again. He wouldn't do that to
his father. No matter what had come between them.

Mahatma chose to walk. He remembered the way. It was on the
east side of Smith Street, just north of Graham Avenue.

Lyndon Van Wuyss, the managing editor, had confirmed it all
three weeks ago by long distance. But Mahatma still found it hard
to believe that he was going to work for *The Winnipeg Herald.* An
establishment newspaper. He and his friends had poked fun at it
when they were in high school. *The Winnipeg Hare-Brain,* they
called it. Mahatma's father used to call the newspaper racist. By
the time Mahatma was old enough to understand the word, he
had stopped listening to his father. But he could still remember
the old man's complaints: *The Herald* ignored the Indian
community, except for its criminals; it ignored Martin Luther
King, except for his death. . . . Mahatma hadn't consulted his
father about the job with *The Herald.* He merely sent a three-line

letter, saying when he'd be arriving and why. 'Why' was a question Mahatma had asked himself a lot. The first thing in life was to be true to oneself. And there was no reason for Mahatma to be a journalist. He could think of a million places he would rather be than at a political convention, deafened by the dim-witted ranting of five thousand Young Conservatives. He felt no urge to report the bloody details of a court case, or to interview brokers about the stock market. And isn't that what reporters did?

Well, why not? The fact was, he had nothing better to do. Mahatma was an intellectual bum. No. He was worse than a bum. He was an M.A. graduate over his head in student loans. He had no particular job skills and no goals in life. What thinking citizen would place his life, or his liberty, or even his bank savings in the hands of an economics major? What Mahatma had discovered about journalism was this: it was the only pseudo-profession left in the world that still hired bums. Mahatma found it scandalous that one of Canada's biggest newspapers would hire a reporter—him!—on the basis of a ten-minute interview that focussed neither on Manitoba's fiscal deficit nor on its tensions over French rights, but on the nocturnal carousing of one of Mahatma's professors, a friend of the managing editor. Sure, he was on a four-month probation. But Mahatma wasn't worried. He was putting them on probation too. Giving journalism a try.

Here goes freedom for twenty-five grand, Mahatma sighed, pushing through the revolving doors of *The Winnipeg Herald*. Three people were ahead of him. All of them walked by the security guard and waited for an elevator. Mahatma got stopped. "Sir," the guard said. Mahatma looked at him blankly. This sort of thing happened twenty times a year. Store detectives suspected him of shoplifting, border officials thought he was carrying contraband and security officers believed he came to foment trouble. The guard asked, "Where are you going, sir?" Mahatma detected a note of sarcasm in the word 'sir'.

"Fourth floor."

"For what purpose?"

"I work there."

"You work there. Funny. I've never seen you before."

"Funny. This is my first day."

"Name?"

"Mahatma Grafton."

"What?"

"Grafton," he repeated. "Tell them it's Mr. Grafton."

The guard picked up a phone. He spoke, waited, listened. Then he hung up the phone. He didn't apologize. He just said, "Fourth floor."

"Is that a fact?" Mahatma rode the elevator alone. He rushed a pick through his curls, which held close to his angular head. He saw his own dark eyes in the mirror, gauged the shade of his copper-brown face, stood tall to straighten his tie and lingered on a depressing thought: he was going to have to read *The Herald*. Regularly.

When Mahatma entered the newsroom, he saw a rectangular work space with two long columns of eight desks each. He also saw twenty or so filthy orange and yellow computer terminals, Styrofoam cups smelling of cold coffee, garbage cans as big as oil barrels and blinds that barred all natural light. The blinds were caked in dust. They blocked the windows as if life outside were a military secret. It could have been 100° outside, and not one reporter would have known. But the newsroom did have one good point. It seemed like an acceptable shelter in the event of nuclear attack. Mahatma saw phone books on the floor. Reports. Filing cabinet drawers yawned wide and leaked letters, envelopes and pencils. He didn't see one clean desk. Nor did he see a receptionist. Nobody greeted him as he stood there. Nobody noticed him at all. Mahatma walked up an aisle, past a switchboard operator, and toward the biggest desk in the room. A police radio babbled but nobody listened. Messages had been jammed onto a spike anchored in a block of wood. A telephone rang. Nobody answered it. A man sat with his feet up, leaning back in a swivel chair, talking on another phone. He was forty or so. His sandy blond hair gave way to advancing columns of baldness. He had blue eyes and thin lips, and didn't appear to be discussing newspaper business.

"I don't care!" he shouted into the receiver. "You said those stocks would go up but they've gone down. I want you to sell 'em before they sink." Slamming down the receiver, he leaned back a little further, eyed Mahatma and said, "Can I help you?"

"I'm looking for Don Betts."

"You've got him."

"I'm Mahatma Grafton."

"Mahatma Grafton!" Betts swung his feet off the desk. "You're fucking Mahatma Grafton?"

"You could put it that way," Mahatma said with a grin.

"What happened to the Pakistani guy?"

"I beg your pardon?"

Snickering broke out among editors working around a long, horseshoe-shaped desk.

"Don't mind those cowboys," Betts said. "They thought . . ."

Again the men broke into laughter. So did Betts. When he calmed down, he shouted across the newsroom, "Hey, Chuck, you sharing that desk with anybody?"

A man in his mid-thirties shook his head in the negative, staring at Mahatma. He then yelled at a woman typing at a computer terminal, "Hey Helen! I owe you twenty!"

"Chuck," Betts called out again, "could you show, uh, uh . . . ," he said, turning to Mahatma, "what should I call you, anyway?"

"Mahatma. Hat."

"Good enough. Chuck, show Hat around, would you?"

"Sure."

Chuck guided Mahatma by the elbow, as if they were old friends. "Welcome aboard." Before Mahatma could answer he added, "Could you hang on a minute? I've got to finish something." He began typing on a computer keyboard. "By the way, what's 'acronym'?"

"Beg your pardon?"

" 'Acronym,' " Chuck said. "What's it mean?"

"It's a set of letters that stands for the name of an organization, like NATO or FIRA."

"Thanks." Chuck typed a little more. "You must be a brain.

Knowing a word like that, straight off—I admire that in a person.
I always use the dictionary. Betts says I oughta use it more." Chuck
turned to face Mahatma. "Can I ask you a question?"

"Sure."

"Are you black?"

"It's hard to say," Mahatma said. "My heels are pink."

"I mean, I know you're black," Chuck said, "but from where?
You're not from Pakistan?"

"Do I look like I'm from Pakistan?"

"Just checking," Chuck said. "There was sort of a disagreement
about all this yesterday. Anyway, lemme show you around."

Chuck gave Mahatma a brief tour of the library. "I try to spend
as little time in there as possible, but you'll probably be different.
You're an intellectual." They visited the cafeteria. It was as ugly as
the newsroom: fluorescent lights; tables stained with coffee;
armless, plastic chairs; steam tables and vending machines. They
returned to the newsroom. "We've got forty reporters on staff,"
Chuck said. "About half do city news. See that guy? That's Norman
Quentin Hailey. But we call him No Quotes. You see his copy,
you'll know why. B-O-R-ing! And watch out! He chews garlic. Calls
it a natural antibiotic. Takes all kinds, eh? And that's Helen Savoie.
She's French but she spells her first name the English way. You
know, she dumped the accents and the extra 'e'. And her last
name? You gotta pronounce it Savoy, okay? Very touchy!"

Don Betts approached them. "Hey, buddy, let's have a chat," he
said to Mahatma. They entered the office of the managing editor,
who was apparently out of town. "So," Betts said, "where are you
from, anyway?"

Mahatma tried not to stiffen. He kept his legs crossed, casually,
at the ankles. "Winnipeg. The Wolseley area."

Betts frowned. "Yes, but your nationality?"

"Canadian."

"Yes, but you know. Where were you from? Before that?"

"Before that?" Mahatma fought back a lump of anger in his
throat. He met Betts' stare blankly.

"You know, your origins."

"Origins," Mahatma repeated, aware of the tension in his voice. "I originated in Winnipeg. Misericordia Hospital." He said that a touch too smartly. His father had been much more skilful in dealing with fools. The old man knew how to play dumb.

Chuck Maxwell walked into the office. "Sorry, Don," he said, "but there's a phone call for you. Say, you guys almost finished? There's some reporters who want to meet Mahatma."

It wasn't more than a twenty-minute walk to work. Mahatma crossed the Osborne Bridge and ducked behind the Manitoba Legislature, passing by American elms topping the banks of the Assiniboine River. It was a hot, sunny Tuesday morning, the start of his second day at *The Herald*. He passed between the green lawns of Government House. A statue of Louis Riel stood high in the park alongside the riverbank. Some people thought it was grotesque but he preferred the looming, naked man with an ugly head and bold genitals to airport music and corporate boardroom art.

Mahatma turned up Kennedy Street and right on Broadway, which was one of the most attractive streets in Winnipeg. It boasted the Manitoba Legislature and the Fort Garry Hotel, with rows of tall trees and a wide boulevard running between them. Just yesterday, Mahatma had seen hot dog vendors on Broadway. That would be something, being a hot dog vendor. Ever since he had read *A Confederacy of Dunces*, Mahatma had considered such vendors with a curious eye.

A curious eye. That was one thing he hadn't had too much of this morning, trying to force himself to read through *The Winnipeg Herald*. It had been tough. It had drained the taste right out of his coffee. There was a story about a group home—one of the tenants had pissed on a neighbour's lawn, provoking a neighbourhood clamour: move the home elsewhere, far from women and children. Women and children, Mahatma scoffed. They, presumably, were to be protected at all costs from retards and urine. That story had been written by Chuck Maxwell. Also on page three were two police briefs, one rape, one purse-snatching. Mahatma skipped over them. There was a story about pensions for City Hall councillors. It carried Norman Hailey's byline. It was deadly serious and devoid of quotes, except for one remark by an actuary. Who in his right mind would quote an actuary?

Mahatma turned up Smith Street, made a quick right and headed into *The Herald*. He saw Don Betts send Chuck Maxwell running into the library. Betts had another reporter trying to phone City Hall. Betts told Mahatma, "I've got one helluva story cooking and I don't have time to talk. Hang around and watch. I might need you." The phone rang. Betts hit a button. "City desk," he said, without having to pick up a receiver. A deep male voice came through a speaker in the telephone, asking if this was *The Winnipeg Herald*. "Yeah," Betts said. He whispered to Mahatma, "This guy's a complete dingo. I can tell 'em a mile off." The man asked if Christine Bennie worked there. "Yeah," Betts said, "but she's in Nicaragua."

"Nickar-what?"

"She's out of the country," Betts said. "Okay?"

"Wait! Wait!"

"What is it?" Betts said.

"I'm Jake Corbett."

"So?"

"She was gonna do a story on me. A whole big number. Page one!"

Betts shook his head and grinned. He ran a palm over his forehead. "She said that, did she? Well, I'll tell her you called."

"She said I had a good case. The welfare people are stomping on my rights and she was gonna look into it."

"Did you say you're on welfare?" Betts said.

"Yes. And—"

"Then get a job." Betts hung up. "I've gotta deadline in one hour," he said while dialling long distance. Through the telephone speaker, Mahatma heard someone answer at the Hotel Managua.

Betts asked for Christine Bennie. The hotel receptionist didn't speak English. Mahatma offered to help, since he spoke Spanish, but Betts declined. He raised his voice until someone else came to the phone. He said he was calling from a newspaper in Winnipeg, Canada, that it was a question of life or death, that he had to speak to Christine Bennie, and that if she wasn't in her room could they please check the goddamn bar? As it turned out, Bennie was in her room. Sleeping.

"Sleeping? How come you're not tailing our mayor? Why do you think we had you follow him all the way to Managua?"

Christine Bennie's voice came through the speaker. "Piss off. I filed a feature three hours ago."

"Yeah yeah," Betts said, "we got it. Where's the mayor?"

"At a reception," she said.

"Hustle over there and tell him to call us."

"Yeah, sure."

"Then ask him these questions and get right back to me. The mayor's name is on a blacklist used by the United States Immigration and Naturalization Service. They use this list at the borders to keep out unwelcome visitors—commies, anarchists, you know. Ask him three questions. One: Does he know he's on the list? Two: Does he think being a communist is preventing him from doing his job? Like, how is he gonna fight U.S. duties on our hog exports if he can't even go down there? And three: Is he going to resign over the matter? Call me back pronto. Bye."

Betts sent Mahatma to the library. "See if Chuck has anything on the mayor. Tell him to move it."

Mahatma found Chuck Maxwell thumbing through a wad of clippings without letting the newsprint touch his sleeves. He sat with perfect posture. Chuck shifted in his seat and turned his head to the side, glancing at a newspaper on his table. Mahatma walked up to him. Chuck didn't hear. Mahatma, standing behind Chuck, looked at the paper. It was today's *Herald.* July 12, 1983. Opened to the Lifestyles page. Chuck began underlining a horoscope entry:

> If Today Is Your Birthday: You are a simple person with simple goals. You refuse to accept injustice, and that is your greatest strength. But you must hone your working skills to survive.

"Chuck?"

Chuck looked up as if he'd been caught reading dirty magazines. "Hey, man, don't sneak up on me like that. My nerves are really shot."

"Sorry," Mahatma said. "Betts wants to know if you're done."

Chuck dried his forehead with an initialled handkerchief. He got up. He stood six feet tall, and had a good body. Slender. Athletic shoulders. A square, cleft chin. He smoothed his jacket. "That man's really on my case, you know that?"

"Giving you a hard time?"

"I only had like five minutes to go through three years of clippings!"

"What's Betts want?" Mahatma asked.

"To know if the mayor's ever been turned back at the U.S. border."

"Has he?"

"S'far as I can see, no."

Betts marched in. "Nothing?"

"Nope," Chuck said.

"So when was he last in the States?"

Chuck said, "He went to Minneapolis in 1979."

"Christ, Chuck, nothing more recent?"

"Gimme a break! It's not my fault if we've got nothing on him."

Betts glared at the reporter. "Thirty-five thousand dollars a year and you can't get the mayor's wife on the phone, you can't find his assistant, and now you can't dig through files. You know something, Chuck? You couldn't handle a news story if it ran up and bit you!" Betts stormed out of the library.

"When he thinks he's onto a big story, he writes it himself," Chuck scoffed, "to see his byline all over page one. Don't let him impress you. It'll be a one-day wonder. Here today, forgotten tomorrow."

Betts shouted at Mahatma, "Sit here at city desk and handle the phone! If Christine Bennie calls, I gotta talk to her."

Mahatma nodded, glancing around the newsroom at the rows of computer terminals, the mounds of trash and notepads and pens and government reports piled on desks. He noticed a cigarette butt floating in an old cup of coffee. He watched Betts bash out a sentence with the middle fingers of each hand. The editor glanced up to see how it looked on the computer screen, then bent down to pound out another sentence. His hands bounced high off the keys, nearly striking his face. Mahatma read the screen.

> Winnipeg Mayor John Novak has been barred entry to the United States by the United States Immigration and Naturalization Service, *The Herald* has learned.
> Documents obtained by *The Herald* show that Novak—the only communist mayor in North America—has been blacklisted because of political activities incompatible with American interests.
> Border officials at airports, roads, train stations and ports have been equipped with a 'lookout book' containing names of unwanted foreigners.
> Novak has been barred under Section 28 of the 1952 McCarran-Walter Immigration and Naturalization Act, which aims to keep out communists.

The telephone rang. Mahatma said, "City desk."

A voice jumped out of the speaker. "This is Jake Corbett. I want you to do a big story on the cruel and unusual punishment the welfare people are doing to me. Section 12 of the Charter says they're supposed to be cutting that out. And—"

Mahatma took down a long message. But when the call ended, Betts crumpled the message and grinned. "Drop that dingo and take a look at this." Mahatma read two more paragraphs on the screen.

> Informed yesterday by *The Herald* of the American move, three city councillors said they planned to call on the mayor to resign.
> "Who's going to defend our farming market south of the border if our own mayor can't get down there and lobby for Manitoba hog farmers?" said Councillor Jim Read.

Christine Bennie called back. She told Betts the mayor denied being barred from the States. He had no intention of stepping down over a non-issue. "Get back to him," Betts said. "Ask if he's *ever* been barred entry."

She told him to forget it.

"Why?"

"He's gone off to meet villagers who've been brutalized by contras."

"You are one useless tit, Bennie."

"I love you too, Betts."

"I'm gonna have you suspended for insubordination."

She hung up on him.

Betts finished off his story:

> Reached in Managua where he is to meet Marxist leader Daniel Ortega, Novak said there was "no substance" to the charge that he was a persona non grata in the United States. He refused to resign, claiming that the information obtained by *The Herald* was "a non-issue."

Betts added a few more details. Then he sent the story through the computer system. He walked over to the slot man and said, "It's all yours."

The slot man spoke hesitantly. "You know, Christine Bennie has filed a good feature about contras mutilating villagers. It's twenty-five inches long."

"Hold Bennie's feature! I'm talking spot news. You'd better use this before someone else gets it."

"Let's see it," the slot man said. He hit some keys. He waited. Then he stared at the screen. "How'd you get this?"

Betts bellowed out in laughter. "None of your business who my sources are. Good, isn't it?"

"I'll see if we can cut Bennie's feature."

"Now we're talking!" Betts said, slapping the slot man on the back. Then he shouted across the newsroom. "Hey Chuck! C'mere." Chuck wandered over, taking his time.

"No offence about what I said earlier, pal," Betts said. "I got the story anyway. Wanna see it?"

Chuck looked at the screen. "Yeah, good, Don, good work."

"You feeling okay?"

"I'm all right."

"Today's your birthday, right? Why don't you leave early?"

"All right."

"No hard feelings?"

"Nope." Chuck slung a leather jacket over his shoulder and walked toward the exit.

"See you, Chuck," a copy editor called out.

"See you, Bill," Chuck said.

"Happy birthday, Chuck," another editor called out.

"Yeah, Chuck," a third editor said, "happy birthday."

"Thanks guys." Chuck Maxwell waved and turned out of the newsroom.

"The man's heading toward a breakdown," Betts told Mahatma. "He's lost his balls. Lemme tell you something. A reporter needs balls. No balls, no scoops."

The story by Don Betts ran on Wednesday. The retraction ran on Thursday.

Helen Savoie had worked for eight years at *The Winnipeg Herald*. She had never been promoted. Actually, for a brief period, they had given her the labour beat. But she angered her editors by refusing to cross picket lines and, in 1976, she joined a one-day national workers' strike to protest against government controls on wage increases. She had tried to get Chuck Maxwell to join the protest. "You kidding?" he said. "They'll can my ass."

"You have to believe in something," she told him.

"I do," he said, "I believe in my pay cheque."

They pulled Helen off the beat and put her back on general assignments. She asked for work as a copy editor. They turned her down. But after several years, they cut her reporting back to three days a week. The fourth and fifth days, they had her edit the Lifestyles page. It contained horoscopes and gossip columns.

Editors disliked Helen because she displayed no enthusiasm and minimized the importance of her assignments. However, she was the best-read reporter on staff, and could be counted on to put good questions to foreign dignitaries, business executives, famous writers and scientists who visited Winnipeg. Editors used her to cover complex stories but had little else to do with her. Reporters consulted her on points of fact, but, although desks were shared at *The Herald,* Helen Savoie ordinarily sat alone at the back of the newsroom.

Thursday the 14th of July, however, was no ordinary day. It was the day *The Herald* published its retraction of the Don Betts scoop. It was also the day that Christine Bennie resigned. Helen knew a fair bit about these things, and reporters, for once, had been approaching her all day. Late in the afternoon, Chuck Maxwell slipped into the seat next to hers. The setting sun had pierced a few cracks of the dust-covered window blinds. Dust particles floated in streams of light cutting across the newsroom. Chuck heard Helen relate how Christine Bennie had phoned from Managua to tell the assistant managing editor that she was quitting and not coming in to clean out her desk so why didn't he just send her the last cheque in the mail? Helen asked Chuck if he wanted to know the kicker. Chuck nodded. The kicker, Helen said, was that Christine Bennie had just been hired by *The New York Times.* Chuck asked all about that. Then he asked what Helen thought about Betts' so-called scoop. Helen uttered one or two expletives and offered to rewrite Betts' lead, just to see how dull the truth looked. Chuck glanced at the computer screen as Helen typed.

Winnipeg Mayor John Novak visited the United States before his recent trip to Nicaragua despite claims that American immigration authorities had listed him as an unwelcome alien.

"Betts is pissed off at me for not telling him that the mayor had been in the States before going to Nicaragua," Chuck said.

"You didn't write the story," Helen said. "He did. So it's his problem."

"Would you pull him out of a burning car?"

Helen said, "That's a hypothetical question."

"Would you or wouldn't you?"

"It depends," she said.

"The car is burning. You happen to come along. Yes or no?"

"He's watching," Helen said. "And he's got ears like a hound dog."

Chuck glanced over a column of desks and heads. He saw Don Betts at the front of the room. "Big deal. Just answer me."

"Of course I'd pull him out. Wouldn't you?"

"No way," Chuck said. "I'd let him roast."

"And his family?"

"Better off without him."

Helen grinned. "His car's on fire. He's screaming. He has a fractured leg. And you won't pull him out?"

"Not a chance," Chuck said.

"But you oppose capital punishment."

"We're not talking punishment," Chuck said. "We're talking fate."

"Say he's bleeding to death," Helen said, "but the car isn't burning. Then would you help?"

At that moment, Mahatma Grafton passed by. He heard Chuck say no, EN-OH NO! "What's going on?" Chuck explained. "If the car's on fire, then I'm not going near it," Mahatma said. "But if there's no fire, I'd have to yank him out."

They laughed together. Several heads turned.

Betts shouted, "Hey Chuck, I need you here!"

"He's got it in for me," Chuck said.

"Maybe he's got a good story for you," Helen said.

"Yeah, like rotten meat found in dog meat tins."

"But with a new twist today," Mahatma said. "Dog meat is tainted, but proves safer than canned tuna."

Ten minutes later, Chuck returned to his desk. He ran a hand through his curled hair, which was brown but streaked with silver. He asked if Mahatma were good for a walk. They rode the elevator downstairs. Mahatma saw skin twitching under Chuck's right eye. "I can't handle it," Chuck said. "I can't take it any more."

"Having a bad day?"

"You know how long I've been at *The Herald*?" Chuck said. Mahatma shrugged. "Twenty-one years. I dropped out of school to start as a copy boy." They headed north on Smith Street. "I'm a man, aren't I? An adult, right? I get up in the morning, wash my schlong, drive to work, pay my Visa, right? Then why this? Why this?" Chuck gave Mahatma a piece of paper. It was the size of a birthday card and entitled, in bold typed letters, Performance Appraisal—Chuck Maxwell. The appraisal had five categories: Accuracy, Speed, Story Initiative, Enthusiasm, and Dress and Demeanour. Chuck got a B for Dress and Demeanour, and Ds for the rest.

"They're trying to rattle you," Mahatma said.

"They'll suspend me if I screw up again. They blame me for Betts' errors in that story on the mayor. They say the story never would have run if I had found some library clipping about the mayor stopping off in the States before he flew to Nicaragua. Okay, I missed it. I missed one clip. So what am I, an axe-murderer?"

"Don't let it get to you," Mahatma said.

They walked back to *The Herald.* Chuck blew his nose, threw his head back and took three deep breaths. "It's okay. I'm all right now."

His name was Hassane Moustafa Ali, but friends called him Yoyo. To sharpen his journalism skills, he was working temporarily for a French weekly in Winnipeg. All his life he had dreamt about travelling outside Cameroon. Recently, he had won a scholarship to work for ten months in Manitoba. Since his school days in Cameroon, he had known it to be the fourth most westerly province in a huge nation of ten million square kilometres. Yoyo had longed for years to visit North America. Now, after several days in Canada, he was already counting the months remaining before he could return to his people.

Of the many things that confused him about Canada, one was most irksome. It had to do with a massive tree on Provencher Boulevard in St. Boniface. A tree with white letters painted sloppily on its bark. Yoyo considered the lettering poorly done. Unaesthetic. Unprofessional. If *he* were to name a tree, he wouldn't do so in such a slapdash manner. A great country like Canada and a great province like Manitoba could surely produce a sign on which the tree's name in English, French and Latin could appear in neat letters, as one saw in the botanical gardens of Yaoundé, his home town.

Who had made the decision to identify the tree in such a fashion? In his first days, Yoyo paused to look at the tree as he travelled to and from work. He planned to contact civic authorities to suggest another naming procedure. The name itself, sprayed on the tree, also troubled him. Yoyo, who had read a book on Canadian nature before leaving Cameroon, was sure it was an elm. An American elm. He recognized the leaves: oval-shaped with serrated edges and bold parallel veination. But he had never heard of this tree name. *Clitoris.* He checked the letters carefully. Canadian handwriting differed from that of his countrymen, but Yoyo felt confident after several examinations: the name painted around the bark was *Clitoris.*

Yoyo noticed something else. Whenever he stopped to stare at the tree, people stopped to stare at him. The problem became dramatic on the third day, when he attempted to question a woman passing by on the far edge of the sidewalk. "Excuse me, Madame," he said, pointing to the letters, "this is the name of the tree?" She coughed and began trotting down the sidewalk. Without even having the decency to reply. Yoyo was troubled by the manners of Canadians. Even if his French accent were strong, he saw no reason for the woman not to answer him. It was highly impolite. In his country, if a foreigner had stopped him to ask the name of the tree, Yoyo would have been honoured to provide the answer in English, French, Latin and in Bamileke, his maternal tongue. Then he would have befriended the foreigner and invited him to dinner.

When he returned home, he would tell his family and friends that Manitoba was a great land. But he might have to concede that its inhabitants perplexed him.

Today, however, he planned to straighten out at least one difficulty. He would ask a friend at his newspaper about the name of that tree.

It wasn't a great story. It wasn't even a particularly good story. But it wasn't a total sleeper. So Edward Slade, crime reporter for *The Winnipeg Star*, went after it. As a matter of principle, Slade pursued all tips about cemeteries. Readers devoured anything to do with corpses. This one was about some kid who quit halfway through his first day as a backhoe operator at the St. Vital Cemetery. He quit because he dug up a bone. That's what he was telling Slade on the telephone.

"How do you know it wasn't a stick?"

"It was a leg bone! A big one! Here I am digging my third grave and I come up with a bone in the teeth of the backhoe. I freaked out, man!"

"Did you take the bone home?"

"No! It belongs to God!"

Slade wrote, "Boy says bone belongs to God."

"Where'd you put it?"

"I hid it in the cemetery."

"What's your name?"

"Denis Fortin."

The kid met Slade at the cemetery entrance, but he didn't want to go inside. "I don't work here any more. They might charge me with trespassing."

"Nobody's gonna charge you," Slade said. "You and I are just visiting. What good's a boneyard without visitors?" Slade led the kid toward fresh plots of earth. "Is that where you dug?"

"Yeah."

"It's filled up now."

"Like I said, they were burying someone there."

"So there's no bones left."

"I guess not," Fortin said, shivering. It was cool, for a July afternoon.

"Where'd you hide the bone?"

"By the fence over there."

"Go get it." Slade unslung his camera. When the kid didn't move, Slade growled that he had discussed this case with the police and he hadn't driven all the way out here to piss around.

Fortin trudged over to some shrubs. "It's here."

"Lift it!"

Using a paper bag stuck against the fence, the kid picked up the bone, careful to keep his fingers from touching it. It was about one and a half feet long, covered in slime. It looked like a human femur. It had a head like a tennis ball, and a socket—like the inside of a giant tooth—to fit a knee joint.

"Kneel by that gravestone," Slade ordered. "That's it. No, you're too close to the flowers. Get back. Hold up the bone. Look serious. Don't smile. Don't move." The kid still held the bone with the paper bag. Slade lowered his camera. "Get rid of the paper." Fortin grimaced. He let the paper drop. "Okay now, both hands on the bone!" The kid inhaled deeply. He held the mud-coated bone in his bare hands. The camera shutter clicked repeatedly for ten seconds. "Okay," Slade said.

The kid ran back to the fence. He hid the bone again and wiped his hands on the grass. "Can we kinda get out of here?"

"Believe in ghosts?" Slade asked.

"Sorta."

Slade's story and photo ran the next day under the headline *Mystery Bone Spooks Gravedigger.*

Don Betts told Mahatma to match the story. Mahatma tried, but the cemetery manager claimed Fortin had dug up a stick. And Fortin wouldn't cooperate. Edward Slade had warned him he could face a lawsuit if he spoke to *The Herald*. Maybe even a jail term. It was against the law to speak to two newspapers about the same story, Slade had said. It was breach of trust and fraud. Mahatma wrote a brief story and hoped it didn't run. But it did run, on page three, and it carried his first byline.

During his first week on the job, Mahatma felt guilty about not doing anything substantial. He killed time by reading the paper.

The horoscopes amused him. After his cemetery story appeared, Mahatma checked Aquarius. It said: "When someone asks you to perform a foolish task, assume your responsibilities as a thinking adult. Refuse!" "Right," Mahatma mumbled to himself. "Refuse, and I'm out of a job."

Three times in as many days, Mahatma heard reporters arguing on the telephone, saying, "But the public has a right to know!" Once, Mahatma guessed that the information the reporter was demanding was somebody's age. To Mahatma, the most striking thing about journalists was not what they did, but that they seemed to believe in it.

Jake Corbett didn't like the letter from the welfare people.

"The Manitoba Social Assistance Allowance program has ruled against your request for an increase in benefits. Therefore, $8.90 will continue to be deducted from your monthly cheque of $178.10. The deductions will continue until they offset the $602.38 overpayment you received in 1976 as a result of an administrative error. . . ."

Jake threw the letter down. He sank onto his bed in his tiny room above Frank's Accidental Dog and Grill. His leg ached. On $169.20 a month, he wouldn't even have enough to buy a new bath towel. His only towel was seven years old. The words "Fort Garry Hotel," his last place of employment, were barely visible on the cloth. Jake propped his leg on a pillow. At least he had a place to stay. Some people didn't even have that. Jake had a feeling he would win this battle. He had no job, no family, no hobbies, no friends—and that made him lucky. He had nothing to do but fight the welfare people.

Jake wrote to his Member of Parliament. He complained about his overpayment deductions. He described his honourable discharge, For Reasons of Serious Bad Health, from his job as a doorman at the Fort Garry Hotel. Jake folded his letter into a stamped envelope. He even included his one-page Testament to the Good Character of Jake Corbett, which had been signed by the hotel manager. Jake hobbled downstairs, marched across Main Street and deposited the letter in a mailbox outside the entrance to Winnipeg City Hall. But the instant the letter slipped from his fingers, Jake recoiled in horror. He had included his only copy of the reference letter from the hotel manager. He needed that letter to fight for justice. He put his arm in the mailbox mouth but couldn't reach anything, so he hurried back into Frank's Accidental Dog and Grill, ignoring the pain in his leg.

"Frank," he called out, breathless.

"Whaddya want?" Frank emerged from the kitchen with hamburger meat on his hands.

"Lend me your vacuum, okay?"

"It's in the corner. Put it back when you're done." Frank disappeared back into the kitchen.

Jake lugged the vacuum across Main Street to the mailbox. Stepping into the foyer of City Hall, he ignored a crowd of people listening to a speaker at a podium, and found an electrical outlet by the door. He plugged in the cord and rolled the vacuum outside. Turning it on, he plunged the naked, sucking nozzle deep into the mailbox. It made an awful racket. Something flattened against the nozzle, making it rattle and buzz. He fished out four letters. None of them was his. He held them in his left hand and shoved the nozzle back down the mailbox. He got two more letters, but neither was his. Jake dived down again with the nozzle. At that moment, a large hand gripped his shoulder.

"Drop that vacuum! You're under arrest!"

A crowd formed while two police officers led Jake Corbett toward a cruiser. A black man identified himself as a reporter for *The Winnipeg Herald* and asked a lot of questions. Jake tried to explain about his overpayment deductions. The officers pushed him into the cruiser. They also seized the vacuum and put it in the trunk.

Mahatma was having an awful time writing the story. He had the name and address of the accused. He had checked with police to verify the charge. He had even learned that letter boxes were considered post offices according to the Criminal Code of Canada, which said: "Every one who steals anything sent by post, after it is deposited at a post office and before it is delivered . . . is guilty of an indictable offence and is liable to imprisonment for ten years."

Mahatma couldn't come up with a lead paragraph. He wrote one sentence, deleted it from his computer screen and tried another. Half an hour later, Chuck Maxwell came up to him and said, "The trick is to not think about details. Just write the sucker. Bing bang, put it out." Mahatma sighed. Chuck persisted. "Be like me, Hat. Let the story write itself. Stop looking at your notes!"

Mahatma ignored him.

"I've been doing this for years. Don't even look at your notes. Put 'em away! You've got a deadline to meet."

Mahatma thought Maxwell was crazy. Writing a story without notes!

"Just give it a try," Chuck said. "Okay?"

"Okay."

"Good," Chuck said. "Look at me. Now tell me just one thing. What happened today?"

"I was covering a speech by the mayor at a reception for Franco-Manitobans. The mayor talked about the historic place of French people here. He mentioned constitutional talks between the government and francophone leaders."

"Forget that stuff," Chuck said. "Tell me something unusual. Something weird!"

"In the middle of the reception a guy came out of the blue with a vacuum, plugged it in and began sucking letters out of a mailbox."

"All right! Then what?"

"The cops dragged him off."

"You get his name?"

"Jake Corbett."

"You get the charge?"

"Theft from the mail."

"So whaddya got so far?"

Mahatma showed Chuck a lead paragraph about the mayor urging the province to recognize the constitutional rights of Franco-Manitobans.

"Never mind the French stuff! Put the vacuum in the lead."

Mahatma wrote: "A civic reception ground to a halt yesterday when a man walked into Winnipeg City Hall, plugged in a vacuum and began sucking letters out of a nearby mailbox."

"Better," Chuck said. "Second paragraph you say the cops arrested the guy with a pile of mail in his hand. Third graph you name the guy, say he's on welfare and say what they charged him with. Then you get into the mayor's reception, toss in a graph or two about that French stuff, and bingo, your story's done!"

Mahatma produced a second and a third paragraph. Chuck stood behind him, watching the computer screen, keeping Mahatma on track. When he finished the story, Mahatma stood up. His legs were stiff, his neck ached and his eyes stung from staring for so long at electronic fuzz.

"Thanks, Chuck."

"You just needed a jump-start. You should have seen me when I started. You've got it all over me, Hat. I couldn't even spell when I started! I dropped out of school in grade ten."

Mahatma was too tired to listen. He'd been listening and thinking all day. He drifted out of the newsroom, ate two hamburgers in a greasy spoon, walked home and fell asleep on the couch.

Mahatma left home early the next morning to buy *The Herald* in a drugstore. Standing at the corner of Lipton and Portage, he let two buses come and go as he pored over his first page-one story. The headline ran across two columns below the fold: *Cops Stop Mailbox Theft.* The minute Mahatma arrived at work, Betts sent him to the cop shop to cover Corbett's hearing. "The cop shop?" Mahatma asked.

"The Institute of Public Protection. Opposite City Hall. Hurry."

The halls outside the courtrooms were packed with bikers,

hoods, women with black eyes and relatives of the accused. There were also lawyers and Crown attorneys. Mahatma saw a black judge walk by in his robes. Everyone looked at him. Mahatma heard one man advise another, "Stay away from that judge. If you're on his docket, tell your lawyer to get you another date. The man's crazy."

A clutch of men and women crowded around four sheets of paper taped to a wall. There was one sheet for each courtroom. Each sheet had a list of names and offences. Mahatma found what he needed on the sheet for Court B: Jake Corbett—Theft From Mail.

The dimly lit courtroom had no windows. In the back, divided by an aisle, were two sections of public seats, each with twenty-five chairs. Every chair was taken. Latecomers leaned against beige stucco walls. The Crown attorney and defence lawyers stood near the front, working at podiums. At the very front, the judge's chair rose above the courtroom, and higher still rested a portrait of Queen Elizabeth. To one side was the prisoner's dock. Behind the Crown attorney was a long desk marked Media Only. Reporters occupied four of the five chairs. Mahatma took the last place on the right. The man to his left was in his early twenties, but he looked to Mahatma like a schoolyard brat. He wore jeans and a purple shoestring tie. His ears seemed as big as satellite dishes under punkish needle-points of blond and yellow hair.

"You media?" the brat asked.

"Yeah," Mahatma said.

"Journalism student, I bet."

Mahatma smiled vaguely. The young man unfolded *The Herald* to scan the story on Jake Corbett and the vacuum. "You know this Mahatma guy?" he asked.

"How come?" Mahatma said.

"Well, if I didn't have to be following his story, I could be doing something interesting. And who has a name like that? Sounds like a goddamn saint."

A voice called out, "Order please, all rise." Everybody stood. The judge entered the courtroom.

The brat shoved the newspaper back under the table. "Old man Hill doesn't like me reading in his courtroom," he whispered.

Everybody followed suit when the judge sat down. He was the dark-skinned judge Mahatma had seen in the hall. He wore a black robe with red stripes running over the shoulders and down the chest in two lines. He was a short man with a slight build, but he had a big head with salt-and-pepper curls combed back.

"Let's get this going, Mr. Peters," Judge Hill said to the Crown attorney. "We've got a full house today." The first prisoner came to stand in the dock. His lawyer remanded the case to the next day. The prisoner was sent out.

"Call number 37, Jake Corbett," cried the court clerk.

A door to the adjacent prisoners' holding cell swung open; a guard shouted into it, "Corbett! Jake Corbett!"

In rumpled clothing and unbrushed red hair, Jake Corbett limped into the prisoner's dock and leaned on the wooden counter before him. The charge was read. Theft From Mail, contrary to Section 314(1)(a)(i) of the Criminal Code of Canada . . . Corbett pleaded guilty. Judge Melvyn Hill asked for details. The Crown attorney checked a file on his lectern. "It appears, Your Honour, that Mr. Corbett placed the activated nozzle of a Hoover vacuum cleaner into a Canada Post letter box and removed a quantity of mail by means of air suction."

"That is an indictable offence, Mr. Corbett," Judge Hill said. "It can lead to incarceration. What do you have to say for yourself?" Corbett embarked on an explanation about the Charter of Rights and his overpayment deductions. The judge cut in, "Get to the point. Why were you stealing letters?"

"I wasn't stealing, Your Honour!"

"The accused was holding six letters in his left hand when arrested, Your Honour," the Crown said.

Corbett protested, "But I was gonna put them back."

"Then why were you holding them?" asked the judge.

"I was just trying to get my letter back, and I'd a been cutting down my chances if I'd put back the letters I kept sucking up, Your Honour!"

"You were fishing for a letter you had just posted?" the judge said. "Can you prove it?"

"No, Your Honour, I never got it. I got arrested."

The judge cupped his chin in a palm. "I'd send you away for thirty days, were it not for the fact that I, too, have been tempted in the past to retrieve correspondence in the exact same fashion."

Mahatma and the reporter to his left both got that down word for word. The judge said, "Although I hasten to add, for the benefit of all those in the courtroom, I repeat, all those present, that I have never acted on such an impulse. So while I congratulate you for your ingenuity, I must warn you not to do it again. Is that clear?"

"Yes, Your Honour."

"I'm giving you an absolute discharge, Mr. Corbett, but I'm warning you that if I see you again within twelve months, you can expect harsh treatment. This court has no time for foolishness."

"Call number 91," cried the court clerk.

Whispering to the reporter next to him, Mahatma asked, "Don't the prisoners come up in the order listed on the page?"

"No, they come up random. Why? You lookin' for somebody?" Mahatma shrugged. "I'm waiting for the Dwight Matthewson case," the brat said.

"What'd he do?" Mahatma asked.

"Caused a public disturbance. But he's black."

"So what?"

"Everybody knows Judge Hill gives black guys a hard time. Say, who are you, anyway?"

The judge rapped his gavel on wood. The next prisoner stood taller than both guards. "That's him!" the brat whispered.

"State your name," the prisoner was told.

"Dwight Matthewson."

"Are you represented by counsel?" the judge asked.

"I don't want a lawyer. I want to get this over with."

"You're making a mistake," the judge warned him.

"I want this done with," Matthewson repeated.

"Read the charges," the judge said.

A clerk read out: "Dwight Matthewson, you have been charged in the City of Winnipeg, on or about the 18th day of July 1983,

30

with causing a public disturbance, to wit, screaming and shouting in the mayor's office. How do you plead, guilty or not guilty?"

"I was there," Matthewson said.

"Nobody asked if you were there," the judge said. "What we need, Mr. Matthewson, is your plea."

"I did what I feel is right. My plea is guilty. Sure I—"

The judge cut him off. "Guilty!" He turned to the Crown attorney. "What happened, Mr. Peters?" The Crown attorney said Dwight Matthewson had stormed into the mayor's office, brandishing a placard and hollering that racial minorities were barred from jobs at City Hall. Judge Hill cleared his throat. The brat elbowed Mahatma. "You listen to me, Mr. Matthewson. Wouldn't you agree that yours was an act of colossal stupidity? Waving a placard around and shouting like a child. There are more civilized ways to express one's beliefs, wouldn't you say? Hmmm? Speak up!"

"I need no lesson in civility from you."

"Don't be smart with me, Mr. Matthewson. I won't put up with it. You are a disgrace to your race. If everybody started busting into offices, waving signs and impeding business, we'd have anarchy! We'd have a nation of boors. Have you considered that? No! Well, you will now! Three weeks in jail ought to smarten you up, Mr. Matthewson."

Matthewson's jaw sagged. "Three weeks? I have a family, I—"

"Think about that next time, Mr. Matthewson."

The guards led Matthewson out. "Told you he was a bastard," the brat said. Mahatma finished writing and got up. "Who do you work for, anyway?"

"*The Herald.*"

"*The Herald?* You're not Mahatma Grafton?"

Mahatma raised his eyebrows in acknowledgement.

"No offence, man. You did a good story on that guy with the vacuum. That's why I was pissed off. I don't have anything against your name. It's just a little weird, that's all. You're not riled, I hope?"

"No."

"Good." The young man with ears like satellite dishes offered his hand. "Edward Slade. *Winnipeg Star.* I do cops and robbers."

"Whaddya got for page one?" Betts asked.

"Corbett got an absolute discharge," Mahatma said.

"No more than four inches. Anything else happen?"

"This judge called a black prisoner a disgrace to his race and jailed him for three weeks just for causing a public disturbance."

"I bet the judge was Melvyn Hill."

"You know him?"

"We call him Thrill Hill. We get a story every time he opens his mouth. Give it eight inches."

An idea came to Mahatma as he returned to his desk. He raced back to the Institute of Public Protection.

Judge Melvyn Hill sat at an oak desk in a small office. Several shelves of legal texts loomed behind him, as well as a portrait of the Queen and another of Prime Minister Trudeau. He was out of his robes this time, wearing a tweed suit. He had large temples and hollow cheeks. He removed a pair of reading glasses, held them in his left hand and said, "I don't speak to the press." Mahatma, standing at the door, wondered if that were a dismissal. "I have absolutely nothing to do with reporters," the judge said, examining papers on his desk. "They never get anything right. They shouldn't be allowed to work until they complete graduate studies at a reputable university. That would straighten them out. The number of times I've been misquoted would make your head spin."

The judge ranted on about the media. Then, suddenly, he stopped, lifted his head to aim hazel-green eyes at Mahatma and raised his chin a notch. "What did you say your name was?"

"Mahatma Grafton."

"Any relation to Ben Grafton?"

"My father."

"Well come in, lad. You should have told me so. Your dad's an old friend of mine. We go a long way back."

"I'll tell him I was talking to you."

"Yes, do that. Do that. Tell him Judge Hill sends his regards. Now, have a seat, young Grafton. What may I do for you?"

Mahatma sat down, fingering his notepad. He wondered if he

should open it. He had a feeling the judge would talk. "It's about the Matthewson case."

"I don't discuss particular cases. But I will say this: as a rule of thumb, I lean harder on Negro offenders than non-Negroes. I hold an extremely responsible position. People follow every word I say. I will have no one, and I say *no* one, accuse me of favouring people of my race. And, by the way, I don't approve of the word 'black'. 'Negro' sounds much more civilized."

Mahatma wrote as fast as he could, wincing with expectation. The judge would surely berate him, throw him out, insist it was off the record. But the judge kept talking. He said Negroes had to earn respect in the world. It was high time they did something for themselves. He had been born of illiterate parents and look what he had become—a respected citizen, a judge, a linchpin of democracy. No sir, he would not tolerate foolish acts by Negroes, for whom criminality was doubly shameful. Mahatma wrote so fast that the bone in the knuckle of his middle finger ached. This was a national news story! It would embarrass the hell out of the judge. But he deserved it. Listen to the pompous fool!

"Take me," the judge said. "How would I have advanced in this world if I hadn't displayed exemplary behaviour? My record to date has been spotless, but I still haven't been promoted."

"Promoted?"

"Appointed to a higher judicial level. With all my experience, I still haven't moved up. Not even to the Court of Queen's Bench." Mahatma asked how long Melvyn Hill had been a judge. "I've been on this bench longer than you've lived, I bet. I was appointed to this bench in 1960. When were you born?"

"Fifty-seven."

"See what I mean? So it irks me a little. I'm qualified. I've never been criticized. I deserve to be promoted and it's unfair that I've been overlooked."

"Why do you call it a promotion?" Mahatma asked.

"It's more power. More prestige. More money. I call that a promotion."

"But judges don't usually move from provincial to federal

courts," said Mahatma, who thought, I can't believe it, I'm actually using something I learned at university.

"It can happen," the judge said.

"But it hasn't for you because of your race?"

"I didn't say that."

"You said—"

"Let's say it's partly because of race. You journalists really can't accustom yourselves to nuance, can you?" Mahatma grinned. He felt a great story brimming. The judge rose to dismiss him. Mahatma was sure the judge would insist now that all this was off the record. But Melvyn Hill did nothing of the sort. He merely repeated his greeting to Ben Grafton. Mahatma went on to write the line story on page one for Wednesday, July 20. Canadian Press picked up the story and it landed in ten more dailies. Reporters from all over the country began phoning the judge. But Melvyn Hill refused to take any calls. He had his secretary advise Edward Slade to give Mahatma Grafton's article a close reading if he wanted information on the subject.

At *The Winnipeg Star,* Slade crashed down the telephone. "Fucking 'close reading,' " he muttered. "Grafton wouldn't even have picked up on that scoop if I hadn't told him about Matthewson!"

At *The Herald,* Chuck Maxwell was the first to congratulate Mahatma. "Stick by me, Hat. Follow my advice and you're heading for great things. You'll do better than me, in life."

Mahatma told his friend to shut up and took him out for a beer.

The Institute of Public Protection, where several provincial judges worked, and the Winnipeg City Hall, where the mayor worked, faced each other across a courtyard. About fifty yards long and wide, the courtyard had a fountain, a pay phone, three benches and five trees. The day after buying a $35 Blow-Joe megaphone,

Jake Corbett left Frank's Accidental Dog and Grill at 10:00 a.m., walked south on Main Street and turned right into the courtyard. Then he phoned *The Herald*. "I'm having a demonstration at City Hall. Guaranteed page one." A gruff voice mumbled "Damned dingoes" and hung up on him. Jake gave up on *The Herald* and turned on the megaphone. "Justice for the poor! Welfare is discriminating me to death! No more overpayment deductions! Justice for the poor!" Five people heading into City Hall paused to watch. Jake turned the volume button to max and emptied his lungs. He hollered for ten minutes. Then, resting on a bench, he saw a CBC-TV car on Main Street. Jake delivered another blast. His voice bounced off City Hall, ricocheted off the opposite building and came echoing back from behind him.

The mayor had gone south of the border to meet the mayor of Fargo, North Dakota. He had done this without any border troubles, despite *The Herald's* recent article about him during his trip to Nicaragua.

Sandra Paquette liked having the mayor absent; she got more work done that way. But today she had a splitting headache. That amplified whining came right through her window. She looked down at the courtyard. A few pigeons clustered near Jake Corbett. He took a heel of bread from his pocket and threw it to the birds. She had to credit the guy for his persistence. He probably did have serious welfare problems. Three minutes after Jake Corbett began hollering, the telephone rang in Sandra's office. A male voice, middle-aged or older, barked at her. "Connect me with the mayor."

"The mayor isn't in today. May I take a message?"

"This is Judge Melvyn Hill of the Provincial Court, and I won't stand for any run-around. It behooves you to connect me this instant with the mayor!"

Sandra rolled her eyes. Men! It behooves you to blah blah blah . . . "I'm afraid there's no way to reach him. He is in the United States."

"Who's speaking?"

"Sandra Paquette."

"Who is that idiot outside? I can't hear myself think!"

"That's Jake Corbett."

"I want you to march down there and have him cease that foolishness!"

"I'll see what I can do, but . . ."

"I want that commotion to cease this minute!"

Seeing a woman approach him, Jake Corbett stepped up the commotion. "Mr. Corbett! Can I talk to you a minute?" Jake kept bellowing. "Would you like an appointment to discuss this with the mayor?"

"Justice for the poor!"

Sandra sighed and walked away. Her phone was ringing when she entered her office. "Call the police," the judge demanded. "That man is causing a public disturbance."

"I'm not sure the mayor would approve of that," Sandra said.

"Silence that ragamuffin! This minute!"

Sandra found it pleasing to stonewall the judge. "I'm afraid I can't do anything about it. If you wish to leave your telephone number, the mayor will get back to you—" The dial tone buzzed in her ear.

Jake paused. His lips and throat were dry. His leg was sore. But the megaphone was holding up. He was admiring a white stripe on the bell horn's red surface when somebody called his name. Twice. He turned around and looked up at the fourth floor of the building opposite City Hall.

"Hey, you! Jake Corbett! Cease that commotion this instant!"

Jake stared up at the brown-skinned face of an older man leaning out a window. It looked like the judge he had seen in court. Grateful for the attention, Jake directed a blast at the Negro. Funny how there seemed to be a lot of Negroes around Winnipeg these days.

Don Betts had been listening to the police radio. "Hey," he shouted, "something's going on at City Hall!" Surveying the empty newsroom, he groaned. No Quotes Hailey was out. Helen Savoie was out. Chuck Maxwell was in, but he was useless. "Mahatma!" Betts ran up to him. "Get off the phone. I have something for you."

Mahatma Grafton saw Jake Corbett put down his megaphone. "Hi," Jake said, "they're gonna arrest me." A police cruiser pulled up on Main Street. Mahatma saw Judge Melvyn Hill confer with the driver. Jake Corbett jumped up and shouted again into his megaphone. He shouted in the name of dignity. He shouted in the name of justice. He shouted until he was put in the police cruiser and driven away. Judge Melvyn Hill returned inside his building. Mahatma strolled over to a young woman standing near the doors to City Hall.

"Hello," he said, "I'm with *The Winnipeg Herald*."

"I know," she said, smiling. "Mahatma Grafton, right? You were here the other day, when the same guy broke up a reception with his vacuum cleaner."

"I remember seeing you there too," Mahatma said, "but I don't know your name."

"Sandra Paquette," she said. "I'm the mayor's assistant."

They shook hands. She stood about five-five, had a slim figure and long brown hair parted in the middle. She had a generous smile, with a touch of blue-eyed humour that seemed to say, Welcome to the funny farm. The introduction relaxed Mahatma. "So what happened?" he asked. "Why was everybody out here? I even saw Judge Hill out here."

"Got a minute?"

"Sure."

"Then come up to my office. I'll tell you about it."

Jake Corbett got his name on page one of *The Winnipeg Herald* two days later, but it bugged him that the story came out all wrong. All Mahatma Grafton wrote about him was that a lady judge had given him a suspended sentence for making a racket in the courtyard. And the rest of the article talked about the Negro judge. People quoted in the article were saying judges weren't supposed to call cops on people. But there was nothing about the welfare people docking five percent from his cheque every month. Jake had some big thinking to do. He was going to have to drill it into the public's brain and judges' brains and reporters' brains that the welfare people were chopping five percent off his necessaries of life!

The day after he had Jake Corbett arrested, Judge Melvyn Hill turned on his TV twenty minutes ahead of time. He had told his secretary he might be on the news. He had also told his neighbour. Melvyn would certainly have told his ex-wife to see the news, if he knew her telephone number. But she had left him with no indication of her whereabouts. His first wife had done the same thing. First Eileen and then Doris had left him without notice, in the middle of the day, while he was working. Both had cleared out his furniture.

Melvyn sighed and lay back in a chair, waiting for the news. Earlier that day, when Mahatma Grafton had phoned to ask why he had ordered the arrest of Jake Corbett, Melvyn had been feeling lonely. It was a slow day at work. He wanted to call up old friends to say hello, but he had no such friends. Except maybe Ben Grafton and Fat Harry Carson. And Melvyn hadn't seen them for years. So Melvyn was happy to hear from Mahatma Grafton. He was happy to talk. He said he saw nothing wrong with calling the police on Jake Corbett. The noise had been driving him crazy! No, he had no comment about whether judges should intervene in such a way. By the way, was this likely to be in tomorrow's paper?

When he saw he didn't make the 6:30 news, Melvyn Hill turned off the TV. He had no appetite. It had been a horrible day. Leaving the office at 5:00 in the afternoon, the judge had been stopped by a pimply Indian on Main Street.

"Hey, mister, I just lost my job, can you spare some change?" Melvyn kept walking, keeping his head up. "I say, mister, got a spare quarter?"

Melvyn stopped and looked into the lad's sullen face. "I'll have you know that I don't give money in the streets. I am a judge!"

"You're no judge."

"Yes I am. I'm one of the highest people in this province, and I don't hand out money on the street. But I will buy you a sandwich if you wish."

The kid was chewing gum. He looked at Melvyn Hill curiously, up and down. "What kind of sammage?"

"Whatever kind you like. Egg salad. Tuna salad."

"Fucking egg and tuna salad! No fucking way! You're no judge. You're just a cheap old nigger."

Melvyn felt as if he'd been slugged in the solar plexus. His midriff caved in; his shoulders sagged. "How can you say that?" he gasped. "Being an Indian, how can you use such a word? Don't ever call people hurtful names, son. Mind my words. I'm a Provincial Court judge!"

"Gimme a break." The kid spat and turned away. "Judge, no judge, you're a fucking nigger just the same."

Melvyn spent Friday night alone, feeling depressed. But he brightened in the morning when he saw *The Herald*. There it was! Ben Grafton's kid had put him on page one again.

> Provincial Court Judge Melvyn Hill has admitted to ordering Wednesday's arrest of a welfare recipient who was complaining about his financial woes by shouting into a megaphone in a Winnipeg public square.
>
> Judge Hill told *The Herald* yesterday that he demanded that police arrest Jake Corbett, 45, in the courtyard outside City Hall.
>
> "The noise was driving me mad. . . ."

Melvyn considered it a fair and accurate article. He was proud of it. Of all the people whom he hoped would see this article, as well as the earlier story about him, he thought most about Fat Harry Carson. In fact, whenever he had accomplished something noteworthy in life, such as getting into university, and then law school, and then joining the Manitoba Bar, and then the Provincial Court, Melvyn thought more about impressing Fat Harry than his peers. In the past, Melvyn had thought he would always detest Harry. How many times had Harry humiliated him publicly? Once, at a reunion many years ago, Harry had attempted to beat him up. Melvyn had always feared Harry, and he still did. He feared Harry's geyser of hatred. True arterial hatred. Harry had hated Melvyn from the start, hated every atom in his body. *A judge? You think you can be a judge? You're nothing but a blackassed porter, just the same as me.* Despite his accomplishments, Melvyn feared it was true. That he hadn't amounted to much. Often he felt no happier about himself than he had felt forty years ago, working the trains. So he felt hatred for Harry Carson, and fear, but something else. Desire. Desire that Harry Carson see what he, Melvyn, had become. He heard that Fat Harry ran a café above the old clubhouse at 795 Main Street. In recent months, Melvyn had often considered looking the man up. He wondered what Harry would say, after all these years. He wondered if Harry knew that he, Melvyn, had been on the front page of *The Herald* twice in recent weeks. He clipped out the stories about himself in the extra newspapers he had purchased and mailed them one day to Harry Carson, Porters' Club of Winnipeg, 795 Main Street, Winnipeg.

Harry Carson studied the letter with mixed emotions. It stunk. Nevertheless, it was for him. Harry had mail! He closed the letter box, ensuring that his old, thick digits made no contact with the bird dropping that clung to a spot below the stamp. He took the letter up to the café where he worked alone. It was hard climbing those stairs. Harry was old. As old and plain out of date as a steam engine. He had no customers. No coffee percolating. No flapjacks cooking. Harry noticed, as he opened the envelope, that it said Provincial Court, Winnipeg, Manitoba on the upper left-hand corner. Who-all was sending him this material? Hunh! There was nothing inside but two newspaper clippings and one half-sized sheet of paper saying Compliments of Judge Melvyn Hill.

Harry unfolded the clippings. Someone had underlined the judge's name each time it appeared. Underlined it in red ink. Harry Carson, who never read the paper, took the trouble to read each article. Certain things confused him but he got the general picture. Melvyn Hill was messing up! Lookit right here, it said: "Civil libertarians expressed outrage at Judge Hill's statement that he handed out stiffer sentences to blacks than to whites." My, my! The old judge was giving black folks a fit. In this other article, Melvyn Hill was phoning the police on some welfare dude. Harry studied the little piece of paper again. *Compliments of Judge Melvyn Hill.* Hunh! Why was Melvyn sending this stuff? What that man needed was to have his black ass kicked. Harry made coffee. He reread the clippings. He still had no customers. He wondered how old Melvyn Hill was making out, anyhow.

Yoyo airmailed this report to his newspaper in Yaoundé:

Dear Reader:

Your correspondent's first month in Canada has proven full of surprises. In this communiqué, he wishes to examine the issue of poverty among white people. Cameroonians believe that it does not exist, but nothing could be further from the truth. Poverty does exist among white people, some of whom live as miserably, in their own way (necessarily in their own way, Dear Reader, since human misery is a relative affliction, and as yet unquantifiable by Any Scientist), as any other inhabitants of this troubled planet. Let This Author proceed by way of microcosm, offering a description of the life of the Quixotic Jake Corbett.

Mr. Corbett resides in Winnipeg, Manitoba. His predicament may puzzle Cameroonians who have observed white adults in Yaoundé, but have never seen one lacking employment.

Here are the astonishing facts of Mr. Jake Corbett's life: 45 years old, unmarried, red-haired and possessing a deathly white skin that burns when exposed to the sun, Mr. Corbett suffers from deep vein thrombophlebitis, which is a vein inflammation malady. He is unable to work because of a painful blood clot in his lower right leg. A victim of the disintegration of the North American kinship structure, Mr. Corbett has no family. He depends on the state for support.

Mr. Corbett was recently arrested for broadcasting his predicament in a public place. Canadians apparently believe in free speech, but not by means of volume-enhancing machinery. However, Mr. Corbett was exonerated in court. This Author visited him subsequently.

Let it not be said that only peoples of nut-coloured complexion live in hovels. Or that only we are undernourished. This Author contends that many Africans enjoy better housing than Mr. Corbett, and eat better food too.

As for the staple of Mr. Corbett's diet, This Author shall withhold details for Another Report. At present, suffice it to say that Mr. Corbett suffers from a lack of funds and proper food, and lives in cramped quarters atop Frank's Accidental Dog and Grill, a business establishment serving meals of dubious nutritive value. Despite the humiliation of his recent arrest, Mr. Corbett vowed, in his interview with This Author, to continue his struggle for an acceptable level of monetary assistance from his government. "I worked 15 years, until my legs gave out," he said. "Now I plan to bug the welfare people until their legs give out."

To Mr. Corbett's consternation, local newspapers have neglected to describe the details of his case. Yet these details are arresting. The Manitoba government publishes a yearly booklet entitled "The Social Allowances Program." This booklet sets out the cost of "basic necessities" of life. In Mr. Corbett's case, this amount has been calculated at 178.10 Canadian dollars a month. However, authorities have been deducting five percent of this amount every month from Mr. Corbett's cheque because of an ongoing dispute with him. But a penetrating question has been raised by Mr. Corbett: If $178.10 is required to meet his necessities of life, how can he do without five percent? Mr. Corbett, who appears well versed in his nation's Constitution, said he is initiating legal action to resolve the issue.

This Author respectfully predicts that Mr. Corbett, although of little education and failing health, will achieve greatness in his life. He will become a figure of world stature. He will become a symbol of the defeated working man abandoned by the wealthy. He will galvanize the downtrodden in countries developed and developing, of skins black and white, although, it must be conceded, Mr. Corbett is not generally recognized in Canada as bearing such potential. Watch for his name in future reports by This Author in Winnipeg!

Respectfully Yours,
Hassane Moustafa Yoyo Ali

La Voix de Yaoundé, the Cameroonian paper to which Yoyo filed weekly reports, ran the story on the front page. It sparked thirty-five letters to the editor. Most expressed disbelief. A white man? In dire poverty?

PART TWO

"BRAVER TO SLAY A CHARGING LION THAN A SLEEPING COW."
Mahatma Grafton reread his horoscope. What the hell did that
mean? The horoscope got him thinking again about his stories on
the judge. Chuck Maxwell assured him he was bound for stardom.
"Sniff out more ethnic stories," Chuck told him. "They'll land you
on page one for sure." Don Betts also showed his delight. "Got
any more dirt on the judge?" he asked. The stories had been
picked up by all the Winnipeg media. Mahatma heard his second
story on the judge read almost verbatim on CFRL Radio. And
Edward Slade at *The Winnipeg Star* came up with a scoop of his
own by obtaining transcripts of Melvyn Hill's recent court
hearings and quoting the judge's most outlandish comments.

The judge took no calls and granted no interviews. The media
coverage made him look idiotic. But the more foolish the judge
looked, the more uneasy Mahatma felt. And his discomfort was
heightened by the behaviour of his father, who had barely spoken
to him in days.

Mahatma finally asked, "Something wrong, Dad?"

"Not a thing."

"You've been quiet lately."

"What's there to talk about?"

"How about Melvyn Hill? He says he knows you."

"Is that a fact?"

"Since I wrote about him, you've barely spoken to me."

"Do you know that Melvyn used to be a railway porter?"

"So that's how the fool started out."

"Mahatma Grafton! Is that how you speak of your own people?"

"Who can deny that he's a fool?"

"He is *not* a fool!" Ben barked. "It's because of men like him that doors are open for you today. At one time, portering was the only job he could get. It was the only job most blacks could get. But he went on. He kicked and scratched and got himself a legal training."

Mahatma grumbled, "Legal training or not, the man's a fool."

Ben clenched Mahatma's wrist. "Tell me what's more foolish, leaving the railway to become a Provincial Court judge, or wasting a university education by taking pot shots at easy targets?" Mahatma gaped at his father, but Ben continued. "Don't you have anything more important to do than expose the silly habits of an old black judge?"

"Silly habits? He jailed a man for three weeks because he was black!"

"Dig enough and you'll turn up dirty laundry on anybody. I dare you to do the same number on the chief judge of the province. I dare you to go out and try to make him look like an idiot. But no, you can't do that. So you pick on someone who can't fight back."

"He seems to like the attention."

"You're still ridiculing him." When Mahatma said nothing, Ben added, "You think you've got Melvyn Hill figured out. But you don't know a thing about him."

"Like what?"

"I'll tell you when you're ready to listen!"

It is one of Mahatma's earliest memories. He is playing in front of his Lipton Street house. Girls are skipping. He tows a friend in his wagon. Elms form an endless tunnel over the street when he looks south, past Westminister and Wolseley avenues. He is towing his friend Albert down the street, into the tree tunnel, toward the banks of the Assiniboine River. They're halfway down the street when his father calls from the house. Ma-*hat*-ma! Ma-*hat*-ma! He deserts the playmate and climbs into Daddy's car. "We're going to see how the men are making out," Ben says.

"What men?"

"You'll see." They swing up to Portage Avenue, seem to drive miles east, then north on Main Street. They enter a world of trains, train yards, train tracks, the train station. Ben gives his horn two friendly taps. "Every time I come up here I see more coloured people on the street," he says, waving out the window. They arrive at a house on Annabella Street. The house has peeling pink paint, two storeys and steps leading up to a wide porch. Several big, dark men get up from chairs to clap Mahatma's father on the back.

"I want to go back to the car, Daddy," Mahatma says.

"Don't be afraid, son. These men ride the trains with Daddy."

Mahatma clings to his father's pant leg. The men tousle Mahatma's hair. Someone lifts him high onto a pair of shoulders. "Look Daddy!" Ben smiles, shakes several hands, disappears into the house. Mahatma pleads to be let down and runs after his father. In the kitchen, food-covered dishes cover the counter. A garbage bag overflows. Down the hall, a television blares and somebody is showering with the door open. Mahatma enters the bathroom, pulls the curtain back and asks the tall, fat, dark man what his name is.

The man says, "Harry Carson."

"Hey son, you bothering Fat Harry in the shower?" Ben scoops up the boy and removes him from the bathroom. Mahatma protests; it was warm and misty and pleasant in there. He also protests when it is time to go; he likes the noisy home, with its smells, its misty shower, its men. One has given Mahatma juice, another has offered him beer.

Later, back home, Mahatma says, "Can we go back to the house with the misty shower?"

"The misty shower?"

"The misty shower on Annabella Street." For years, Mahatma will refer in this way to the home his father rents out to railroad porters.

"Soon, son."

"Today?"

"Soon."

Mahatma whines. Ben tells a story. At first, Mahatma absorbs every word. In later years, he tires of these stories. And he grows conscious of his mother objecting, "Ben, stop lecturing. You sound like a church minister!" Ben, who refuses to give up, turns Mahatma completely off the subject. By the time he is a teenager, Mahatma tunes Ben out. Despite the lectures about discrimination on the railway, the struggle to unionize porters, black pride, Martin Luther King and Mohandas K. Gandhi, Mahatma learns little more of these things than how to shut them out.

Mahatma came home at 9:00 p.m., after a twelve-hour day. Ben, who had been looking out the window, waiting for his son, had already eaten. But he had also prepared a meal for his son. Now he reheated it. "You go rest on the sofa, I'm plenty used to working this kitchen solo," Ben told him. Mahatma smiled, looking into his father's brown eyes and his deeply wrinkled face, which was the colour of roasted almonds. This was the old man's way of saying that he bore his son no hard feelings, despite their argument about Melvyn Hill. Mahatma felt a sudden tenderness toward Ben. It didn't matter about the argument. Mahatma had thought it over and decided that his father had been right, in large part. Melvyn Hill had been an easy target. And Mahatma had taken advantage of that. The old man sang a spiritual as he banged around in the kitchen. This made Mahatma smile, lying on an old sofa and following his father's gravelly melody. Ben was the only atheist in the world who hummed spirituals. And he only sang when he was happy. When he wanted somebody to hear. Mahatma was there, listening. And thinking.

"Say, son," Ben said, "how long do you plan to stay here?"

"I'm not sure."

"No hurry about finding an apartment," the old man said. "No hurry at all. You comfortable here?"

"Sure."

"Good." Ben brought out the food. "Son," he said, "do you keep clippings of the articles you've written?"

"Yes."

"Then I'd like to have them when you don't need them any more."

"Sure. You even want the clippings about the judge?"

"Even those." Ben grinned. "It doesn't matter whether a broken down old ex-railway porter agrees with them. What matters is that those clippings are family history. I'm putting them in my files. You're the first Grafton to write for a newspaper."

After the meal, Mahatma pulled one of Ben's boxes out from under the sofa, dusted it off and lifted the lid. He found an old binder with his father's writing on the cover: "Negro History Appreciation." Inside the binder, he found Ben's clippings and notes about "Personnages of Import to the Negro People." Mahatma flipped the binder open to the section G. G for Garvey. Marcus Garvey. Born Jamaica 1887, died London 1940.

Mahatma scanned the details: Advocated back-to-Africa movement. Believed God was black. Promoted racial pride among Negroes. Founded Universal Negro Improvement Association, 1914, sought economic power for blacks. Paved the way for black power and black pride movements to emerge decades later. Convicted of mail fraud and jailed two years in U.S.A. Deported 1927. Presided over the International Convention of Negro Peoples of the World, in Toronto in 1936. Died in obscurity. Mahatma turned back one page. Gandhi, Mohandas Karamchand. Born 1869, Porbandar, assassinated 1948, Delhi. Known as the Mahatma, or Great Soul . . .

Mahatma paused. As a boy, he had been told countless times about the life of Gandhi. And about famous blacks. Booker T. Washington. Marcus Garvey. Harriet Tubman. Langston Hughes. Ben had talked about them daily. But Louise, Mahatma's mother, always cut the sermons short.

"Stop filling that boy's head with nonsense," she often said.

"It's not nonsense," Ben would reply. "It is the story of his people."

"He can learn about people in school! Don't go filling his head with mumbo-jumbo."

Ben would grumble and back down. Increasingly, he would try to educate Mahatma during his wife's absence.

Mahatma remembered a certain day, when he was eleven or so. He was watching TV. His mother was ironing. Ben came into the room and tried to turn off the TV, but Louise wouldn't let him. He said there were better things to do than look at the boob tube. Why didn't they read, study about their people? Did she know that the founder of modern Russian literature was a Negro?

"I bet," Louise said.

"He was!" Ben brought a thick volume to his wife.

"Alexander who?" his wife said, reading the cover.

"Pushkin. Alexander Pushkin."

"Doesn't sound like a Negro to me," Louise said.

"He wrote poetry. He wrote prose. He wrote *The Queen of Spades!* He wrote an unfinished novel about his great-grandfather, called *The Negro of Peter the Great.*"

"Didn't finish it, hunh?" Louise said. "Now *that* sounds like a Negro. So tell me, if he's Russian, how come he's black?"

"His great-grandfather was from Abyssinia," Ben said.

"From where?"

"Ancient Ethiopia."

"You're saying he had one ancestor from Africa?"

"That's right," Ben said.

"And the rest were Russians? Regular white folk?"

"Yes. But . . ."

Louise turned back to her ironing. "Then he didn't have much coloured blood left in him, you ask me."

Ben lost his temper. Who was she to deny black heritage? One drop of coloured blood made you black, and that was that.

"Don't pay him any mind," Louise told Mahatma. "Twisting and yanking the truth out of shape, he'll fill up your head with confusion. I say, better to have your head empty and see clear."

"Don't pay *her* any mind, son," Ben countered. "If you keep your head empty, you'll see clear all right. You'll look clear at mediocrity all your life!"

Louise had wanted to name her son Paul. Paul James Grafton. Ben would have nothing to do with it. Who ever heard of a world leader named Paul? This was no ordinary baby. He was a Grafton! The baby, the story goes, started to cry. Louise rocked him protectively. That husband of hers was insane. He read too many books. Lately, he'd been reading Greek mythology. Walking all around the house spouting crazy names: Prometheus, Zacharia, Euripides, Homer. She wished he would shut up about all those books of his. He carried on as if he were a scholar, and not just a plain old railway porter.

"And how do you want to name him?" Louise asked.

"Euripides Homer Grafton."

Louise put the baby in its room, closed the door and went to the kitchen cupboard. She launched a teacup at his head. It missed and exploded against a wall. "You're not naming my baby after any Greeks," she said between clenched teeth. "And none of your Negro pride names, either." With her next missile—a teapot—she nicked one of Ben's massive ears. Years later, Ben would show the scar to Mahatma. *See that? Your mother gave it to me.* Cupping his bleeding ear, Ben consented. It was agreed that he would find the name, but that Louise retained veto rights over anything sounding Greek or Negro. There was to be no Euripides Homer Grafton. No Marcus Garvey Grafton, no Booker T. Grafton. Ben accepted his wife's conditions, because he knew that otherwise she would oppose him at every turn. She would call the boy Paul no matter what Ben called him. Ben needed her cooperation. He didn't want the boy confused about his name.

Ben found the name for his son by a devious route. Mahatma Gandhi was a great man. A man of great thoughts and great action. A credit to his race. True, he was an Indian, from India. But he had brown skin. Call him an Indian, call him what you wanted, as far as Ben Grafton was concerned, the man was coloured. Brown-skinned just like Ben's son. Mahatma it would be. It was a great name. Fitting for a great person. Mahatma had a good sound to it. It was respectable. It had three syllables. Anybody who meant to pronounce that name was going to have to stop and think about it. Mahatma Grafton!

"Mahatma," Louise sniffed. "Is that a Negro name?"

"No," Ben was able to answer, "it is not."

Late one September afternoon, Chuck Maxwell asked Mahatma, "By the way, where are you from, anyway?"

Mahatma Grafton hadn't found anything to write about that day. He had been in a dry spell for three weeks and was getting edgy about it. Even the old man had been bugging him about it. "I haven't seen your name in the paper lately. Aren't they giving you enough work to do?" And now Chuck was asking a question Mahatma fielded ten times a week. Mahatma mumbled something silly and went home.

"He says he's from Equatorial Mali," Chuck told Helen. "That's in Africa, right?"

"There's no such place," Helen said. "There's Mali. And there's Ecuatorial Guinea. But there's no Ecuatorial Mali. He's spoofing you."

"Why would he do that?"

"Why'd you ask him where he was from?"

Chuck threw up his arms. "What's wrong with that? We're professionals, right? What's wrong with asking a question?"

"Forget it, Chuck. I'm sure he still likes you."

"How do you think he's doing on probation?" Chuck said.

"They won't hire him unless he puts out more copy," Helen said. "He hasn't been on page one for a while."

"Come on," Chuck said. "The kid's good. Management won't cut him loose."

"How much you want to bet?" Helen said.

Chuck ignored the challenge. "Imagine getting fired. Imagine having to do something else. That's what rots my socks. I mean, outside the newspaper business, what else could I do?"

Helen chuckled. "Chuck Maxwell, Chief of Public Relations, Manitoba Provincial Police."

"Very funny," Chuck said. "My problem is, I hate it here, but what else can I do? You have been to university. But I've been working in this joint since I was sixteen. It's the only job I've had. If Mahatma Grafton fails his probation, he'll just get another job. But what if they axe me? Where do I go?"

Mahatma Grafton was beginning to agree with Chuck Maxwell that newspaper managers behaved "like neanderthals." Mahatma had spent almost two months on the job without any indication of how his work was viewed, or why his own initiatives were usually junked, or why he was receiving little from assignment editors. The only feedback he had was in how his stories were placed. In that sense, his worth was measurable in each day's paper: page one meant good, page forty-nine meant not so good and stories that never ran meant very bad. Nobody told him anything. Except Chuck, who warned Mahatma that his performance would be assessed by numbers. How many stories did he generate? How many ran on page one? Mahatma tried to produce more. But it was hard to dig up news on his own, and his editors weren't assigning him much. He remembered something Ben used to ask him every day after school: "What did you do for humanity today?" As a boy, Mahatma grew to hate the question. He learned to shut out the voice of his father exhorting him to do great things for mankind.

Mahatma was flipping through the paper one day and wondering about the value of his work at *The Herald,* when his horoscope jumped out at him. "Don't be hoodwinked by pedlars of mediocrity. Quality counts. Quantity doesn't. But forget that for now and hustle to save your job."

Mahatma walked up to Helen Savoie. "Something tells me you know my birthday."

"Late January, I believe. You're an Aquarius."

"Do you doctor those horoscopes?"

Helen grinned. "Sometimes I get inspired."

"What does the management think about that?"

"Management?" she laughed. "It doesn't care, dear lad. Management doesn't read the paper."

Don Betts was committed to hard news. Who shot whom, who got charged with electoral fraud, who was advancing the cause of totalitarian communism while working as mayor of Canada's seventh largest city! This was what readers wanted. It was certainly what Don wanted. No entertainment, no comics. No lifestyle puffery. Horoscopes were the only exception—they were Don's one weakness. They seemed written by someone who disliked him. He knew this was impossible—*The Herald* got its horoscopes from a syndicated astrologist in Los Angeles. But it tickled him to imagine some California wacko taking the trouble to insult him every week.

Around 8:30 p.m. on September 20, Don Betts pushed away from his desk and walked to the men's can, taking the horoscope page with him. He settled into a stall and began to read the entry for Taurus: "You will bungle whatever you undertake today. Do the world a favour and call in sick. . . ."

The lights went out. Don swore. He figured there had been a power failure. But someone entered the stall next to his and coughed.

He asked, "That you, Chuck?"

"Oh, you in here too, Don?"

"What the hell are you doing?"

"Can't you hear, Don?" Chuck laughed.

"Why did you turn off the lights?"

"I find it relaxing."

"He finds it relaxing," Don echoed. "He turns off the fucking lights and finds that relaxing!"

"If it really bothers you, you can turn 'em back on."

"I can't even find my way out of here. It's pitch black. Where's the light switch, you nimwit?"

"Hold on. I'll just be a minute. I'll show you out."

For Don Betts, that incident confirmed it. Chuck was around the bend. He wrote useless copy and Don wanted him out. Another person Don hoped to get fired was Mahatma Grafton, whom he despised even more than Maxwell. What infuriated Don was the way Grafton looked up at him blankly, the corners of his lips tugged up in a smirk, whenever Don approached him with a story idea. You could jazz up a quote or be caught drunk on the job, but you could never appear not to give a shit! You could never just stand there and shrug when CBC-TV scooped you. It was unthinkable to say 'so what?' when Edward Slade of *The Winnipeg Star* was the first to catch wind of the sensational murder of a high school cheerleader. Yet this was precisely what Don had heard Grafton say.

Maybe it was racial. Maybe it was cultural. Maybe it came from too much schooling. Don didn't know exactly why, but Mahatma Grafton did not fit in a newsroom. Didn't have the right values. Didn't have *any* values. Don had given the guy a chance. Tried to straighten him out. One time, after Grafton had filed a story so balanced and cautious that it made the reader yawn, Don tried to talk to him. "This story lacks zip. It has no punch. Can't you make the lead stronger?"

"No," Grafton said.

Don tried again. "You have to capture the reader and make him read your story. So pack that story with every punch you have. To do that, you gotta keep one thing in mind. Big or small, local or international, in every story someone is gettin' screwed and someone's doing the screwing. Stick to those basics and you'll never go wrong." Don gaped at Grafton, who was grinning. "What's so funny?"

"So if I understand, our job is to expose fornicators."

Don Betts had no use for smartasses.

Using *The Winnipeg Herald's* computer system, an editor could see what any given reporter was writing at any given moment. Late one afternoon, eight weeks after Mahatma joined *The Herald,* Don found him working on an interesting story:

> American immigration authorities listed John Novak as an "unwelcome alien" from 1952 until he became mayor of Winnipeg ten years later.
>
> After sweeping the 1962 municipal election, the communist politician immediately "took formal steps" to have his name struck from the foreign visitors' "Lookout List" kept at border crossings into the United States.
>
> "I had a life in politics ahead of me and it was entirely unpractical, not to say ludicrous, that the United States should continue to refuse me entry on the basis of my political beliefs," the mayor said in a recent interview.
>
> Section 212(a)28 of the 1952 United States McCarran-Walter Immigration and Naturalization Act bars entry to foreigners who are members of the communist party of any foreign state, who advocate communism or who write, publish, distribute or possess for the purpose of circulation any printed material promoting it.
>
> The same section of the Act, which is still in effect, also states that aliens who are anarchists, mentally retarded, polygamists, illiterate or sexual deviates are unwelcome to visit the superpower.
>
> Producing a file of letters from U.S. immigration officials, Novak said he finally had been given entry for the purposes of his work, although he was placed under certain restrictions, which remain in effect.
>
> "They made me undertake never to participate in any public rallies, or to engage in the propagation of communist theory," Novak said. . . .

Don stopped reading there. "Hat, can you come up here?" When Mahatma walked up, Don said, "Not bad work. But you've got to concentrate on the news aspect of this story."

"The news aspect?"

"That's right," Don said. "Who wants to read about what happened to the mayor in the 1950s, Hat, before he was even mayor? *This* is what you've got to write."

Punching the keyboard with two middle fingers, Don deleted Grafton's first paragraphs and entered his own:

The American government has slapped restrictions on Mayor John Novak's visiting privileges to the United States because of his communist beliefs.

Although he denied a *Herald* report last summer that he was on a U.S. border lookout list barring alien communists, anarchists and other subversives, the mayor admitted yesterday that he had been on the list earlier and that he was still barred from attending public meetings or spreading communism in the United States.

"That looks better, doesn't it?" Don rewrote two more paragraphs. "What other quotes did you get? Anything from the immigration people?" Grafton gaped at the computer screen. "What else did those immigration people have to say?" Don repeated. "Got a quote?"

"Your lead is unacceptable," Grafton said. "And the second paragraph carries a false tone."

"What's the matter with it?" Don raised his voice. Copy editors watched as they worked on the rim. "Do the Americans have restrictions on the mayor? Yes or no?"

"That's not the point," Grafton said. "The point is one of focus, and of the impression that you leave. You make the reader think the restrictions have been imposed recently."

"Did I say that?" Don was growing red in the face.

"You're suggesting it. You can't say that. You should say—"

Don jumped to his feet. "Don't tell me what to write. I'm going to fix this story and you're going to cooperate. Clear enough?" Grafton said nothing. "So just tell me what the immigration people said about—"

Grafton cut him off. "In the second paragraph, you imply that the mayor has not been telling the truth, whereas, in fact, you screwed up the first story and *The Herald* had to admit it. I'm not helping you write nonsense like that." Five copy editors stared at Grafton.

"I'm going to the can," Betts said. "And when I come back, you and I are gonna fix that story!" Don stormed off. Grafton sat in the editor's chair and typed a command that killed all traces of his article in the computer system. Don returned as Grafton was stepping back from the terminal.

"Where's the story?"

"If you want to write about the mayor, you do it. But I'm not helping you."

Don grabbed Grafton by the collar. Chuck rushed up. "Take it easy!"

They pulled Don away. But Don ended Grafton's shift and sent him home. "Talk to the M.E. tomorrow morning."

The door opened and slammed. Ben confronted his son. "You sick?"

"No."

"You didn't quit?"

"NO!"

Ben asked, more gently, "Then how come you're home early?"

"I had a fight with my editor. He sent me home."

"Fired you?"

"No. Sent home. I have to see the managing editor tomorrow."

"Why'd he suspend you? You give him too much lip?"

"He's an asshole."

Ben looked blankly at his son. "Meaning?"

"You'd never understand, Dad. Just take my word for it. He tried to ruin something I've put a lot of work into. I wouldn't let him. I killed the story in the computer system."

"You *what?*" After Mahatma explained what happened, Ben said, "You've always been a tad mulish." Mahatma said nothing. "But you know, son, you have to survive. You have to stay on that job and show them all you're better than they are. You are going to be a great writer, son. You can write circles around all those people. You have it in your blood. Don't be a quitter, son, stick it out and show 'em what you've got."

Mahatma felt a trace of revulsion at the speech. It seemed he'd heard it a million times. Everything you did, someone wanted you to commit your life to it. Mahatma had never felt like committing his life to anything. "Can you imagine," he had said jokingly to university friends, "having some job and sticking with it for twenty years? Or even ten? Five? The same job for five years? It'd be like being in prison!" And as for social causes, he had the feeling that none was worth pursuing. Ben had so sickened him with black history that Mahatma gladly forgot the whole subject, avoided books about race issues and avoided people who talked about them, or any causes. Sure, he had read about the CIA bringing down Allende in Chile, and everybody knew about acid rain and the arms race, but the issues were so distant that it was hard to care about them. Occasionally, in a university class, a professor would be challenged by an angry student. Mahatma and his friends would turn to stare at the student, not to reflect about the complaint, but to wonder about how anyone could care so much. For years, Mahatma moved among peers who would look up, narrow their eyebrows and stare in curiosity if they heard someone wishing he had "done more for society." It never occurred to people in his generation to "do" anything for anybody. That seemed naïve.

Nevertheless, Mahatma had felt a flood of anger earlier that evening, watching Don Betts sabotage a story he had carefully researched and—yes!—begun to care about. The story meant something! It was fascinating that the United States and the U.S. Immigration and Naturalization Service should be brimming with paranoia. The mayor's case intrigued him. Mahatma had dug out the story by talking to the mayor and to Sandra Paquette and to U.S. government officials. He didn't dig it out to see it distorted by Betts.

Mahatma spoke calmly to his father. "I had something to say and my editor tried to warp it. Would you want him to get away with that?"

"Was it a good story?"

"Yes."

"Did you believe in it?"

"Yes."

Ben clasped his son's hand. "Good for you, son! Stick to your guns!"

There had been no television in the Grafton home until Louise bought one, without consulting Ben, a year or two before her death. But Ben advised his son not to watch it. "It will rot your brain," the old man said. "Help me fill out this big book. It's going to be a history of our people."

But Mahatma, eleven by then, had better things to do. Hide and seek. Baseball. Working alone, Ben slowly mounted his "Negro History Appreciation" binder. It contained the odd news clipping of pertinence to blacks. It also contained his thoughts and recollections and interesting tidbits he'd heard in conversation or on the radio.

"Nobody shall think that We have no Reasons for documenting this History," Ben had written years ago in the introduction to his binder, capitalizing nouns that seemed important. "Many times have we been subject to Questions about our History, the Tendency being for citizens of Winnipeg to express Wonder about the presence of Negroes in their city, and to display Incomprehension of certain Facts, namely, our presence."

In this spirit, Ben noted down his own background. "I, Ben Grafton, Jr., was born in Winnipeg in 1908. My father, Ben Grafton, Sr., was born in Nebraska in 1879. He met my mother in Oklahoma and together they moved to Alberta in 1905, where my father worked as a labourer. Two years later, they moved to Winnipeg."

Ben did more than document his roots in his precious "Negro History Appreciation," which attained its peak of thickness during Mahatma's boyhood. Knowing that Winnipeggers were reluctant to acknowledge his place of birth and that they didn't believe that Negroes had accomplished anything of importance, Ben undertook to document Great Negro Achievements, and to insert such information piece by piece in his binder. One such entry read: "Alexander Sergeyevich Pushkin, 1799-1837, a Russian Novelist, had Royal African Blood on his mother's side. His great-grandfather, Abram Hannibal, was an Abyssinian Prince and a Negro, making Alexander Pushkin Also A Person of Colour, no matter how Vaguely! P.S. Abram Hannibal was captured by Moslems, sold in Constantinople, and later adopted by the Russian Czar Peter I."

The bulk of Ben's entries pertained to Canadian blacks such as

Osborne Anderson, who in 1859 had participated in John Brown's raid on Harpers Ferry and escaped back to Canada, and Anderson Ruffin Abbott, the first Canadian-born black doctor. Over the protests of his wife, Ben told these things to his son. "You have been born to do something great for humanity," he told Mahatma in his eleventh year. Mahatma, who was holding a baseball glove at the time, said he had just hit a home run. "Greater than that, son. Name two great Negro writers." Mahatma tonelessly provided the names of Langston Hughes and Richard Wright. "You're going to be like them one day. You're going to stand on their shoulders and reach even higher." Mahatma said his friends were waiting.

Mahatma met the managing editor the next morning. "Do you care to explain what happened last night?" Lyndon Van Wuyss said.

"Betts wanted to change my story!"

"You're going to have to trust your editors. Betts may be abrasive, but that's why he does his job so well." Van Wuyss paused. His eyes narrowed. "How would you like to take on the police beat for the rest of your probation? I'd like to see what you can do."

The crime superintendent was a tall man of the plainclothes type often seen escorting prime ministers and breathing into walkie-talkies. Mahatma reckoned he was about fifty. Leaning out of his office, he peered at reporters seated in the waiting room on the third floor of the Institute of Public Protection. "Mornin' boys, come on in," he said, grinning at a woman who carried a tape recorder slung like a purse over her shoulder.

"Eh-hem," she grunted, punching him on the shoulder as she led the way into his office.

"And lady, of course," said the super. " 'Mornin' boys and lady,' is what I meant to say."

Edward Slade jostled with CFRL Radio reporter Bob Stone for the chair closest to the door. It was the best chair because it allowed for fast exits to cover breaking stories. "Rag writers like you ought to be banned," Stone growled.

"Out of my way, turd head," Slade muttered.

"Knock it off," the super ordered, "or I'll boot you both out!" He gave the coveted chair to Susan Starr. Slade and Bob took the next two seats. Mahatma took the seat furthest from the door. The four plastic chairs were placed side by side, facing the desk of the cop, who sat down. Mahatma surveyed the room. The cop's desk had a stack of reports, several black pens with white letters spelling out Winnipeg's Finest, and a family photo. The crime super had a wife, three kids and a dog. Looking at Mahatma, he asked, "And who are you?"

"Mahatma Grafton. *Winnipeg Herald.*"

"You new?" the super asked. Mahatma nodded. "I'd ask you where you're from, but it's probably against the human rights laws or the Charter of Rights or some damn thing."

"Actually," Mahatma said, "it's against the Criminal Code of Canada. Invasion of privacy."

The cop broke into laughter. "I like a man with humour. Let me assure you that I don't care what colour you are, black, white or yellow, as long as you treat my outfit with respect. Anyhow, pleased to meetcha. I'm Pat McGuirk. Crime superintendent." Mahatma's fingers were sandwiched in the man's grip.

Bob Stone asked, "What do you have for us today?"

"Wee-ell," Pat McGuirk said, flipping through a stack of reports, "I got a couple of 7-Eleven break-ins, I got an aggravated assault, I got a tempt rape, one tempt murder, a few other things."

"How about that tempt murder?" Stone asked. The journalists readied their pens.

McGuirk read, "On October 21st, at 0700 hours, a 28-year-old Nairn Avenue man stabbed his girlfriend in the chest." McGuirk paused. The reporters scribbled frenetically. Mahatma scribbled too. But Susan Starr broke up the dictation.

"Is this man an Indian?"

"You might call it a native domestic."

"Ah, shit," she groaned. "You hear that, guys? It's Indians."

Stone asked, "What else you got, Pat?"

"Well, not much. You fellows want that tempt rape?"

Stone asked, "Any violence involved?"

"Bob!" Susan yelled.

McGuirk began reading. But Bob stopped him. "My pen has run out. Can I borrow one of yours?"

"Cute," Slade said. "McGuirk gives you pens, you give him PR."

"Shut up, Slade."

"You shut up."

McGuirk read the report on the attempted rape. But nobody wanted it. "Anybody want a graffiti story?" he asked.

Slade asked, "What graffiti?"

"Some nut's been painting slogans in St. Boniface."

"Is that all?" Susan said. "You really have nothing for us?"

"What can I say?" McGuirk spread out his arms and grinned. "Why don't you do a story about our low crime rates?"

"Fuck that shit," Slade said, standing to go.

"Hey!" McGuirk said. "There is a lady present."

Susan said, "Fuck that shit," and followed Slade and Stone out.

Mahatma remained behind. He didn't want to return to the office empty-handed. "Do you mind giving me that graffiti business?"

McGuirk flipped through his stack of reports. "On October 21st, the manager of the St. Boniface community centre complained about vandalism to his building during the preceding night."

Mahatma learned it was the fifth consecutive night on which anti-French slogans had been spray-painted on buildings in St. Boniface, a Winnipeg suburb on the east side of the Red River. Mahatma made a few more notes and stood to go. "Say, how do you spell your last name?"

"Any way you want."

Mahatma thought the man was joking. "I'm new around here. Is it M-C-G-U-I-R-K?"

"That'll do." Mahatma frowned. "You're serious, aren't you? You really want to see my name?" The cop displayed his driver's licence.

Mahatma wrote M-C-G-E-A-R-K.

"And here's my birth certificate."

"That's okay," Mahatma said.

"No, look!"

It read: M-C-G-E-A-R-C-Q-U-E. "Which is right?" Mahatma asked.

"Neither. This is the right way." The crime super wrote on Mahatma's notepad: M-a-c-G-R-E-A-R-I-C-Q-U-E. "Pronounced McGuirk. Now, let me ask you a question."

"The answer is Winnipeg."

"You didn't let me ask the question!"

"You want to know where I'm from, right?"

"And you're telling me Winnipeg?"

"I am."

"Where's your dad from?"

"Winnipeg."

"And his dad?"

"Alberta."

"You're telling me your goddamn grandfather was Canadian?"

"Naturalized, yes. So you'd better get used to it, Patrick MacGrearicque. My people have been here as long as yours."

MacGrearicque issued a booming laugh. "I like you. You're funny. Now get out of here. I've got work to do."

Mahatma drove to St. Boniface to see the graffiti, which had been sprayed on a credit union, a public school and on the door of *Le Miroir*, the St. Boniface weekly. Entering *Le Miroir*, Mahatma came upon a man polishing an apple on his sleeve. The man raised his eyebrows in a friendly salute. Five-nine, barrel chest and powerful legs. His nutmeg hair was stringy and unattended. His beard contained more hair than his head, and gave him an expansive air. He looked forty-five or so. Alert and good-humoured, his blue eyes swept over Mahatma. Mahatma introduced himself and learned that Georges Goyette was a columnist with the paper. Goyette bit into his apple. Mahatma asked his opinion about the graffiti.

Goyette ignored the question and said, "Mahatma Grafton. That's quite some name. Where're you from, anyway?"

"I was born and raised in Winnipeg. So were my parents."

Goyette smiled warmly. "Well, I'll be. Fellow I knew on a farm, one time, he was a black guy too, born and raised in Manitoba. He got so tired of people asking where he came from that he finally packed up and left. And you know what? He wrote me a letter that said people were still bugging him about it. Winnipeg, he'd tell them. Ah Winnipeg—that explains it, they'd say."

Mahatma laughed. He liked the man immediately. He asked again about the graffiti. Goyette said it was probably the work of a few kids. They didn't deserve publicity. Nevertheless, the graffiti suggested that anti-French sentiment was growing during the current language talks involving French leaders, Manitoba and Ottawa.

Mahatma asked, "And what do you think of those talks?"

"They should scrap those stupid negotiations and let the courts define the rights of Franco-Manitobans. The Supreme Court of Canada would order Manitoba to translate every statute on the books. You know what the Constitution says? It says English and French are the languages of Manitoba's courts and Legislature! But try looking up a law in French. Try speaking to a judge in French." Mahatma took notes, asked a few more questions and prepared to go. "Business, business," Goyette said, laughing. "You truly are an anglais, aren't you, even if you are one in a different skin." Goyette said this inoffensively, and Mahatma liked him for it. "By the way," Goyette added, "how is Helen Savoie these days?"

"Fine. Although I don't know her very well."

"Ask her about the Franco-Manitoban thing, if you need background."

"Really? I wasn't aware—"

"Helen knows about everything," Goyette said. "And she's particularly informed about la francophonie in Manitoba."

"Funny. I was told she didn't speak French."

"Try her."

"Okay. I've got to get going now."

"Come back sometime. I'll show you around this side of the Red River." They shook hands. Mahatma's fingers were nearly crushed in Goyette's massive paw.

The beginning of Mahatma's story read:

> The Manitoba Provincial Police has doubled patrols in St. Boniface after receiving reports about vandalism there for five consecutive days.
> Crime Supt. Patrick MacGrearicque said police are taking the incidents seriously, although they have been limited so far to spray-painted graffiti and broken windows.
> Area residents such as Mathilde Bernier, a Provencher Boulevard shopkeeper, expressed concern yesterday about the frequency of such incidents.
> "If they're against bilingualism, why don't they mail all their money back to Ottawa? It's printed in both languages, you know!"

Mahatma approached Helen Savoie in the newsroom. Speaking in French, he said, "I met Georges Goyette yesterday. He said he'd known you for years, and asked me to say hello to you."

Continuing to type, she looked at him stonily and said, in English, "Pardon?"

Mahatma shook his head, puzzled. "Sorry to interrupt you. I must have made a mistake."

Two weeks passed. Mahatma Grafton unearthed no major crimes. Every day he wrote something, but often it consisted solely of police briefs and short reports from court. He also wrote a few administrative stories: cops were pushing for a shorter work week; lawyers and criminologists were complaining about overcrowding at the Winnipeg Jail. There wasn't much to write about, in Mahatma's opinion. True, Edward Slade was getting a lot of stuff into *The Winnipeg Star*. But they weren't stories that a self-respecting broadsheet would do. Were they?

Every morning, Mahatma bought *The Star*. He only read stories related to his beat. He aspired, eventually, to read nothing in the paper at all. But for now, he was obliged daily to pick through Crime News, which was often found on page three, near the bikini-clad StarLight Girl. Most days, Slade's nuggets looked like this:

A 68-year-old grandma of ten kayoed a intruder in her home last night.

Armed with a cast-iron frying pan, Lena Bellander of River Avenue connected with a home run hit to the back of the thug's head.

Then Batty Lena, as neighbours call her, whipped up blueberry muffins while waiting for the cops.

Initially, Mahatma chuckled at such articles. They seemed the work of a moralist from outer space. But his amusement soon faded. He worried that readers took the stuff seriously. At first, Mahatma took pains to avoid writing stupid stories. But stories he pursued got little or no play in the paper. He couldn't interest editors in his idea to look into the number of accused criminals who were detained overnight on petty charges. Mahatma began hoping that the cops would announce major crime news at the morning press conferences. He felt uneasy when nothing happened. No crime, no byline. Early morning was always the worst time of day. He rose in a hurry, listening to radio news. If the news contained references to his stories—which were sometimes broadcast verbatim without attribution—Mahatma could tell that his work was displayed prominently in the morning paper. If no mention were made of his stories, they were either buried or not there at all. Most unnerving was to wake to a police report that he knew nothing about. That meant Edward Slade had scooped him.

Chuck Maxwell tried to rescue Mahatma from his slump on the crime beat. "Do more victim stories," Chuck said. "They make the best-read copy in the paper." When Mahatma began to protest, Chuck added, "You didn't commit the crimes. You're just writing about them."

Chuck accompanied Mahatma to court one day. "There's three things you gotta watch for. The first is the big crime. That hardly ever happens, but you gotta be around when it does. The second is famous people. If you're on the cop beat and the attorney general's son gets arrested for pimping and you miss it, you're fucked. The third thing is quirky news. When you hear something offbeat, ask yourself if it's weird enough to get picked up by the wire services and printed all the way over in Australia. Like that vacuum story. If it'll cross an ocean and survive, you're looking at page one for sure."

✧ ✧ ✧

Helen Savoie had lived for ten years above a fur store east of the Red River. Initially, she had used one room to sleep and the other as a study. But after joining *The Herald*, she often slept in her study or wrote in her bedroom, noting ideas for stories late into the night. The landlord had always assumed Helen was a secretary. She never bothered to correct him.

In her earliest days at the paper, an editor had asked her to coach one of the weaker reporters—a fellow named Chuck Maxwell—in the art of writing. Helen took the task to heart. In those days, reporters still used typewriters. Helen would bring home carbon copies of Chuck's articles. In her spare time, she would unite split infinitives, tighten leads and cross out adjectives. Helen eventually realized Chuck would never improve much. But the editing bug had infected her. From time to time, she couldn't resist red-pencilling other reporters' carbon copies and slipping the corrected work into their mailboxes at work. This unsolicited service proved unpopular in the newsroom. Helen let it drop, except for occasional comments to new reporters who appeared receptive to criticism. Although Mahatma Grafton was a capable writer, Helen detected a disturbing tendency in his work. He was too hungry for news. Too willing to write anything. In a recent article, he had happily compared police statistics on the number of rapes this year and last. Helen circled the offensive paragraph and scribbled, "What do you take these for, basketball stats?" before dropping the clipping in his mailbox.

Helen didn't hear back from him. She believed that Mahatma Grafton was rudderless. Capable of producing great work, but equally likely to waste his talent on junk news. Helen pictured

Mahatma lingering on the brink. He could swing one way or the other. Journalists started out honourably, but circumstances—city editors, assignment editors, tabloid competitors—plunged them into trash cans. It took less effort to grab the easy stories—dog bites boy, mayor swears at premier—than to climb out and do something.

Every day, when journalists came to work, they knew how their work had been judged: their stories ran big or small or not at all. Reporters learned how to wring the most gratification from the least work. Helen worried about Grafton. On the cop beat, he exhibited a growing tendency to grab easy news. It disturbed Helen that so many young reporters tossed aside their values to succeed. Perhaps they didn't have any values. Didn't care about anything. "I don't have an opinion, I'm a journalist," they would answer if you asked them anything about anything. Should Canada withdraw from NATO? Bar American cruise missile testing over Canadian airspace? Idiots.

Hassane Moustafa "Yoyo" Ali met Helen Savoie on the bicycle path in Lyndale Park on the east side of the Red River. Helen was out for a stroll, and Yoyo had come to see the Red River, which, he'd been informed, had been a meeting place for Cree and Assiniboine Indians before the Europeans came. "Excuse me," Yoyo said to her. He found her plumpness attractive. Yoyo worried about disturbing her. He knew that Canadians disliked talking to strangers.

"Yes?" she said, eyeing him directly.

He asked, "Is this the historic Red River, travelled once by Louis Riel, father of Manitoba?" He liked her big hips, big bones, big legs. She resembled a good strong African woman.

For her part, Helen noticed his heavy accent. She guessed that he was from Haiti. And so cute: small, like a boy, but in his late twenties, or older. Replying in English, Helen said yes, this was the Red River.

"Should I call you Madame or Mademoiselle?"

"It doesn't make any difference," she said. Oh yes, he emphasized, it made a difference. "Mademoiselle," she said.

Touched by the man's struggle to carry on in English, Helen made up her mind. She began speaking to him in French. Flawless French.

"Alors, vous êtes canadienne-française," he said.

"Mais oui."

"Vraiment?" He studied her with great interest.

"Oui," she said, shyly. She admitted that she was French-Canadian. That she still carried the language with her.

Yoyo told Helen he was spending ten months in Winnipeg as a foreign correspondent while gaining experience as a contributor to the St. Boniface weekly. They spoke of St. Boniface, Canada and Cameroon as they walked through the park. A bitter autumn wind whistled across the river. She could see he was cold, and she, already wearing a heavy sweater, offered him her jacket.

He declined. "That is very kind of you. In my country, never would a white woman lend a black man her jacket."

"There are whites in Cameroon?"

"There are tourists, and there are ex-colonials, and missionaries, and those who wish to rescue us from our misery," he chuckled. "They come over, stinging from vaccinations, suffering diarrhoea from our water, melting under the heat, cursing the roads when it rains, carrying mosquito netting to protect them from malaria, never speaking our native languages, sometimes not even speaking French, yet still, somehow, they remain convinced that they must rescue us from our misery."

"And do they do it?"

"No, they leave, after a few weeks, or months, to rescue themselves from their own misery." Helen laughed again. A long, hearty, simple laugh, mirth that she had barely known in the many years she had worked at *The Herald*. Yoyo was a charming fellow. Handsome, in his way. But thin! His wrists and knuckles seemed particularly frail. Perhaps this was what she found attractive. She allowed herself to dwell for a moment on inconsequential thoughts that could never lead anywhere. Yoyo asked her name. For him, she pronounced it 'Hélène'. "Hélène!" Yoyo said it with urgency, as if he were warning her of a rushing bicycle.

"Oui?"

"Hélène, je t'aime."

They met the next day in the park, on the bicycle path, under a tree with a strange branch that reached straight out and then curved up, like a bent arm. Yoyo told her it resembled the arm of an African woman reaching up to adjust a water pail on her head. Yoyo kissed her cheeks. His lips were thick. Dry. As dry as a twig in the sun. Dry, perhaps, but they exerted pressure. Promising lips! He said, "Hello, my lover!"

"And what makes you think I'm your lover?"

"Come now, Mademoiselle Hélène, if we were not lovers, why would you have met me today?"

He told her she had beautiful eyes. Stunning hair, dark brown, very brown, that hung straight down, grazing her neck. "Tellement foncés, tes cheveux," he told her. As if she had *ancêtres africains.* She was going to tell him she couldn't meet him again. She was going to say she didn't want to get involved. She was going to break it off before it started, but then he told her he was returning to Cameroon in six months. Helen bit her tongue. If he were going soon, why not? He was staying in the home of an old widow; they couldn't go there. So Helen took him home.

Yoyo was a wonderful lover. Less energetic, less thrusting, than her old boyfriend. Yoyo was no bigger than Helen. In fact, laughing, she put him on the bathroom scales and found out he was two pounds lighter. He didn't perform gymnastics and he didn't display Olympian endurance. But he was caring. He made her look into his eyes when they made love; his eyes were so dark that, whenever the lights were dim, she couldn't find the line between his pupils and his irises. Sometimes he spoke in French and sometimes Bamileke, his mother tongue. He said the English language wasn't fit for bedroom conversation.

They made love again. The phone rang. It was out in the hall, on the floor. Before he had undressed her and let her strip him, Yoyo had stared at the beige receiver in the bedroom. "Canadians leave telephones in their bedrooms?" he asked.

"Yes," she said, puzzled at his confusion.

"You leave them right next to a bed?" he asked.

"Yes, why?" she asked.

"And if it rings while you sleep, won't it wake you up if it is so close to the bed?"

"Yes, of course."

"And that doesn't bother you? You would let the phone ruin your rest?" This was the first time the practice had struck Helen as absurd. But Yoyo hadn't finished. "Now, one other thing. If you and I are making love, and this phone rings, what happens then?"

"Well, normally, I would answer it."

Yoyo shook his head. Canadians really had their priorities mixed up. "I have entered you, and we are gasping together, and you are prepared to roll over and answer the phone?"

Helen grinned and said, "You never know. It could be important. Someone could be selling vacuum cleaners." They laughed and kissed, but before going further, Yoyo carried the phone into the hall.

"Do you know what I would like?" They had slept for an hour.

"Anything you want, Yoyo."

"Make me breakfast."

"What?"

"Make me breakfast."

It was 2:00 in the afternoon. "Why breakfast?"

"In my country, when a man and a woman make love, if the man does a good job, the woman makes him breakfast. A huge, whopping breakfast. She treats him like a king. It is thought that he deserves it, if he has satisfied her."

"Well, how about eggs and orange juice and toast?"

"I'll take the toast and the eggs," he said. "Many eggs and much toast. But no juice! By no means juice! Just give me tea with honey."

"You don't like orange juice?"

"I don't like what Canadians call orange juice! In those frozen cans? How can one freeze the juice of an orange? I nearly choked, the first time I tasted it. We have beautiful oranges in Cameroon and we know how to make orange juice. The richer a nation becomes, the less capable it is of producing respectable orange juice." Helen laughed hard, hearing that. It sounded particularly funny when pronounced with Yoyo's West African accent. She made him breakfast.

✦ ✦ ✦

Nobody threw a party like Georges Goyette. He threw one in November in his second residence, a renovated farmhouse thirty miles south of Winnipeg. He had a fridge stocked with beer, friends who were fiddlers, and a knack, himself, for clacking spoons. He invited a roomful of people who didn't believe in letting a party die before dawn. He brought Yoyo along, telling him that it would do him good to get out of the city. "Ca va te déconcrisser," Goyette laughed, slapping his friend on the back.

"Ca va me quoi?" asked Yoyo, who was unfamiliar with Goyette's personal slang.

"You know, it will loosen your bones, let your blood pump, show you a good time."

Yoyo nodded, unsure of what to expect. Georges Goyette, a man of many interests, was not one to invite only francophones to his parties. If certain language purists couldn't cut their parties with anglos, then those purists, as far as Georges was concerned, could go roll hoops. Georges liked a party with two languages, loud music and wild jokes. His fridge never ran out. It seemed to get fuller as the night wore on. Asked about it, he would stroke his beard and refer to the Bible: "You have heard of the story of the multiplication of the bread? Well, this is the multiplication of the beer. Why not? Both have yeast, right?"

Georges invited Mahatma Grafton to the party. Grafton had originally struck him as a bright young journalist, but he was now giving Georges reason to pause. Grafton had been producing silly crime stories lately. Georges would have liked to talk about it, but Grafton couldn't come to the party. Other journalists did come, however. Chuck Maxwell, a long-time drinking buddy of Georges', came. And so did Norman Hailey. And Helen Savoie. So did Sandra Paquette and the mayor, John Novak, who had known Georges for a long time.

Sandra met Yoyo, whom she found fascinating and whom she introduced to the mayor. The two men hit it off. They spoke passionately about world politics. Yoyo spoke at length about Cameroon. He equated the tensions between the English and the French there with those in Canada. The mayor said he would love to see Cameroon. Goyette jumped into the conversation until fiddles sounded from the barn. The farmhouse emptied. Everyone flocked to the music except Helen, who hesitated, knowing that Yoyo would want to dance with her and not wanting to make such a public declaration about their affair. To avoid meeting Yoyo, she slipped out of the farmhouse and walked down a country road. A man appeared beside her suddenly, giving her a start. "Take it easy," said Chuck Maxwell, "it's only me." After a moment he added, "It's sure getting a little heavy in there."

"Heavy?"

"Everywhere you turn, people are speaking French. It's rude, if you ask me."

"Nobody's asking you," Helen said.

"Don't you think they could speak English when other people are around?"

"It's a party. The host is French-Canadian. So are half the guests. So what's your problem? You want rules for party talk?"

"They all *can* speak English, you know."

Helen sighed. "What do you say we just enjoy the nature?"

"French extremists want the moon," Chuck complained. "If they keep it up, Manitobans are gonna say, 'Whoa! enough's enough, if you want to speak French everywhere, just move to Quebec!' "

"Chuck!" Helen said softly.

"What?"

"You're a good guy and you're my friend. But you still haven't figured out that this province, and this country, were founded by the French and the English. So spare me your bullshit, okay?"

PART THREE

THE TEMPERATURE IN WINNIPEG DROPPED TO -40° CELSIUS, WHICH was the same as -40° Fahrenheit, on November 22, 1983. This was a record for the month of November. It was colder in rural Manitoba. Automobile gas lines froze. Block heaters had to be plugged in, but even then, many cars wouldn't start. Yoyo was horrified. He feared the sub-zero merging of Celsius and Fahrenheit. Imagine! So cold that it didn't even matter whether you were referring to one or the other! For a while, Yoyo refused to go outside. Inside, he wore a hat. He wondered what would happen if the heating system broke down in his house. He had stepped out two days before it hit -40. At that point, it was -20 and dropping. The cold had bitten his forehead. Yoyo had never suffered from headaches, but the stinging cold gave him one. He longed for the summer and for his country.

Midway through this cold snap, and shortly after Mahatma Grafton passed his probation at *The Winnipeg Herald,* Manitobans woke up to news of the most bizarre crime story in years.

It happened in the St. Albert-Princeton hockey arena, thirty miles south of Winnipeg, on a Thursday night. St. Albert, a predominantly French-speaking town, was bordered by Princeton, which was mostly English. Each town had its own mayor and city hall and bylaws, but they shared a library and recreation centre. Each town had its own hockey team, but they shared the St. Albert-Princeton arena.

The fight started around 8:30 p.m., peaked five minutes later and faded abruptly when the police arrived. Georges Goyette, who was watching his son's St. Albert team play Princeton, witnessed the brawl. It started when a sixteen-year-old St. Albert player punched a Princeton player in the face. He hit him again and the Princeton boy fell to the ice. The players on both teams cleared the bench. The results: two broken noses, one concussion, a fractured wrist, a broken ankle, many cuts and much bruising. Nothing serious happened to the original two combatants. But a St. Albert player who had broken one nose and blackened four eyes in the brawl ran into fatal luck as police stormed the arena. When he turned to look at the cops, someone—nobody seemed to know who—clubbed his head. The boy died before he was carried off the ice. His name was Gilles Baril, the son of the town baker.

Some parents joined the fighting, but Goyette hopped over the boards and towed his son off the ice before the brawl had reached that point.

Edward Slade dived into the story. A good one. At last. He called the cops in St. Albert. A constable gave him the basics: one kid killed and six hospitalized. But the constable wouldn't name the dead boy.

"Can't you tell me anything about him?"

"He's dead."

Slade eased off. He started chatting about violence in hockey. Fighting was getting out of hand these days, wasn't it?

"Yeah, but you haven't seen the likes of this before," the cop said. "You wouldn't have believed it. Those kids went wild."

Slade, who was unmarried and childless, said such incidents made him worry about the safety of his own kids.

"You got kids too, eh?" the cop said. "I got three little terrors."

"I've got two," Slade said. "And we've got another on the way. Try living on my salary with kids."

"Don't I know it," the cop said.

"My boys will be hitting the hockey age pretty soon. I worry about what's going to happen to them in those leagues. I mean, today's violence, you think we'll see more of it in the future?"

"Between you and me," the cop said, "I think we can expect to see more of this. Things could get worse."

"Even for kids that age?"

"You bet. They're the worst. They're animals."

"How old did you say that boy was? The one who got killed?"

"Well, I'll tell you, but you didn't get it from me. Sixteen."

"Thanks, buddy."

"Sure. See you."

"Bye." Slade scribbled out a possible lead: " 'Bloody brawls in boys' hockey will skyrocket after yesterday's brutal slaying of a 16-year-old player in the St. Albert-Princeton arena,' police predicted yesterday. . . ."

Slade consulted a rural phone book and made several random calls to St. Albert residents. The third person he reached was able to tell him the name and number of the hockey coach. After dialling it, Slade got the coach's twelve-year-old son. His father was talking to police at the arena. The boy answered all Slade's questions: the name of the deceased, his address, his parents' names. But he wasn't able to provide directions to the victim's home. Slade asked for the phone number of someone who could direct him there. "Who is calling anyway?" the boy asked.

"This is *The Winnipeg Star,*" Slade barked. "And it's urgent. We need someone else's phone number. Someone who can give us directions."

"I don't think I'd better," the boy said. Slade pushed the boy but it didn't work. The boy simply hung up. Slade drove to the town. Someone there would direct him.

Ben was flipping through a magazine and chewing a toothpick. Mahatma, who lay on a couch, watched his father. Neither moved when the phone rang at 8:50 p.m. It reminded Mahatma of work. It made him think of hanging around court, taking notes, interviewing crime victims, squeezing information from cops. He wondered, as he let the phone ring, if he would dream of work that night, which he had been doing with increasing frequency. Mahatma hated dreaming of work. The phone finally stopped.

"What kind of foolishness is that, calling at this hour!" Ben said. "Anybody who phones at this time of night has been raised upside down!"

It started ringing again. Mahatma took it.

"It's Don Betts. I need you to do some overtime. Got a car?"

"No."

"Then take a cab over here, on the double."

Mahatma hung up and turned to his father. "Don't wait up for me."

Only a few minutes ago, Ben had been planning to go to bed. But now he no longer felt like it. The house didn't seem right with his son gone. Since Mahatma's arrival four months ago, Ben hadn't slept well until the boy got home from work. Ben would stay up and leave the porch light on and be watching by the curtains when Mahatma came home. He would greet his son, lock the doors and then sleep deeply.

Mahatma knew that Slade was onto the story. It was inconceivable that Slade would not be working on this. Slade would expect to clobber him. But Mahatma had no intention of letting himself get scooped. Not this time. This time he was giving it everything. He drove a *Herald* car straight to the town, knowing that his job would be impossible if Slade got there first. Slade had a reputation for erecting roadblocks for his competitors. When he could, he would cart off a family's entire photo album so no one else could get it.

Mahatma arrived at the arena seventy-five minutes after the riot ended. Pushing into the crowd, he got the name of the boy who was killed. Then he found a boy with a Princeton Hawks jacket. Peter Griffiths had been in the penalty box when fighting broke out. "Why were you in the penalty box?"

"I was doing two minutes for frog bustin'."

"I see," Mahatma said. "A penalty."

"I speared a frog. Big deal. Everybody does it. You're not putting that in the paper, are you?"

"I'm just doing research right now," Mahatma said. "I don't know what will go into the paper."

"If you're just researching, I guess I can talk to you."

Griffiths said he had been waiting for his penalty to end when a St. Albert player—Emile Moreau—clobbered an English opponent—Jack Hunter—right in the face. Hunter was so stunned that Moreau was able to hit him again. This took place by the boards, after a whistle, and so close to the penalty box that Griffiths could almost touch the blood on Hunter's face. Griffiths hopped over the boards and cross-checked Moreau, knocking his helmet off. Moreau fell to his knees. Hunter recovered in time to break Moreau's nose. He cut him over the right eye with a second punch. And a third.

"Why didn't you pull Hunter back?" Mahatma asked.

"Because Gilles Gendron from St. Albert hit me when I wasn't looking," Griffiths replied. "Then Ernie Cohen took Gendron out. Then a frog knocked down Ernie. I took on that frog. Then everybody got into it."

The more Mahatma heard, the faster he wrote. Griffiths said the tensions were nothing new. "We've always hated them and, I guess, they've never been exactly crazy about us."

"Why do you hate them? Why was that kid killed?"

"Hey, I didn't do it, I didn't kill him, you're not going to put in there that I killed him, are you?"

"No."

Friends led Peter Griffiths away. "Hey man," one said, "don't talk to that guy. He's a fucking reporter."

Mahatma interviewed another player and three parents. The teams apparently fought a lot, but nobody could say why the

French and English hated each other. "Why don't you get along?" Mahatma asked a player.

"We just don't."

"And where are all the French people now?"

"They hang out at the community centre. You're not going to talk to them, are you?"

"Maybe. Where's the community centre?"

Slade spent half the time Mahatma had spent in the hockey arena, and interviewed half the people Grafton had seen, but still managed to extract vivid quotes. "People say you guys are getting rowdy and that local hockey should be banned for kids your age," Slade told a few English hockey players. They replied that the fight was the fault of the French, that Gilles Baril deserved what he got, and that English hockey players were banding together in the streets. "What if they came after you in dark alleys?" Slade asked. "Have you thought about that? How will you protect yourselves then?"

"We'll break their skulls with hockey sticks!"

From this, Slade wrote the lead for one of his many stories: "Teen-aged Anglo goons have vowed to prowl St. Albert-Princeton at night, carrying hockey sticks to fight the French. . . ."

Slade asked boys in the arena where the victim's family lived.

"You wanna go there?" someone answered. "That's not where the other reporter was going. He was going to the French community centre."

"What reporter?" Slade asked.

"Black guy."

"Mahatma Grafton? Shit! Where'd he go?"

"To the community centre. What kind of name is 'Mahatma Grafton'?"

"Not sure," Slade said, "but it could be French."

"You telling me that black guy's a frog?"

"Could be," Slade said.

"Get off it! Black guys aren't French! They're English!"

"Well, this one's a bit of everything. See ya."

"What explains the violence?" Mahatma asked a woman at the French community centre.

"We'll have to look into that," she shot back at him. "What do you want from us?"

"Something to help people understand what happened tonight."

"You're not interested in our pain," the woman told Mahatma. "You can't know our pain if you're an outsider." She was accusing him, excluding him, but it was a good quote. He wrote it down. It wasn't until he had lived in Quebec six years ago that he had been forced to see himself as an anglo. People there were keen to categorize him. He was a man, Canadian, a student, black, but there, in the eyes of those living around him, Mahatma Grafton was an *anglais*.

"Why can't anglophones understand your pain?" he asked. "Aren't English parents suffering today too?"

"When people see an English boy in the streets tomorrow, are they going to say: 'There's the one who killed Gilles Baril'? Of course not. But when they see a French boy five minutes later, they will say: 'There's the one who started the riot.'" Mahatma wrote that down. "I don't want that in the paper," she said. He kept writing. As far as he was concerned, it was too late: she had already spoken. And anyway, what harm could it do her? Now, he simply needed her name. How would he get it? She would refuse, of course, to give it. At that instant, two men swept up to her.

"Louise," one man said, "I'd like you to meet Pierre Gagnon. Pierre, this is Louise Robitaille, one of our town councillors."

There. He had her name. Then he had another stroke of luck: he spotted Georges Goyette! "Georges! What are you doing here?"

"My son plays for St. Albert. I came to watch the game."

"You saw it, then?"

"Yes."

"Is your son okay?"

"He's fine. I dragged him off the ice when the fighting began."

While Mahatma scribbled, Goyette described the fight. "It was tragic. I saw two fathers going at it in the stands. Part of the age-old hatreds around here."

"By the way, do you know where Gilles Baril's family lives?"

"You're not going to bother them?"

"I have to."

"You have to? Just tell your editors the family was out."

"This is my job."

"That's how you see your job? To invade families in times of shock?" Goyette, for once, wasn't smiling. The comment didn't affect Mahatma. He had no time to think about it. He spent half an hour finding the modest bungalow on an icy rural route fifteen miles out of town.

"Qui est là?" The woman didn't want to open the door.

Mahatma knew that getting her to open it would be the hardest part. He held up a card with his photo. She unhinged the chain and opened the door. "Police, encore?" She urged him in so she could close the door.

"No, Madame, I'm with *The Winnipeg Herald*," he replied in French. "I'm awfully sorry to trouble you."

"With *The Winnipeg Herald* and you speak French like that! My Lord, you speak well. You speak better than we do. We're simple folks out here, but we never hurt anybody, either." She was a thin woman, about five-two. She had grey hair and clear blue, baggy eyes, and she wore a pink nightgown and knit slippers.

"I'm terribly sorry about your son, Madame."

She hung her head to the side, then looked at him again. "What can you do? The Good Lord needed him." Mahatma slipped the pad out of his pocket and noted that down. He could picture the quote on the front page.

"I won't bother you for long. It's just that . . ."

"Sit down. My husband and my other son have gone out to take care of everything. It's hard, staying alone at home when your son has died." Mahatma got that down too. She asked, "Would you like some tea?"

"Please."

"You speak a very nice French. Are you from Haiti?"

"No, I was born in Winnipeg."

"Vraiment? Such good French."

She walked into the kitchen. Mahatma studied the room. Pictures of the boys playing hockey, playing baseball, at communion, at Christmas. Family pictures. A simple living-room. A rocking chair, a blanket-covered couch, a TV. An ashtray, five times bigger than necessary, and a statue of Christ and, in the corner, a photo album. In his notepad he described these objects, as well as the dim lighting, the simple wallpaper and the thin rug. She brought him tea, milk and sugar. And a slice of pie. "You're young. I bet you love sugar pie. It was Gilles' favourite." Mahatma jotted that down. "So this is for the paper?" she asked. The idea pleased her. "When will it be out?"

"Tomorrow, Madame."

"Please, call me Gisèle."

"All right, Gisèle. May I see a picture of Gilles?"

"That is him on the wall."

Mahatma looked at the sixteen-year-old with a peach fuzz moustache. "Do you have any other photographs of him? We would like to put his picture in the newspaper. Perhaps one with the whole family."

She reached for the photo album. "You can borrow this album. Just bring it back next week."

Mahatma placed the album in his briefcase. He asked for Gilles' full name and the other son's name, and their ages, and her husband's name, and her husband's work. She offered surprising details. "I burnt a pecan pie yesterday; Gilles was furious. He told me if I didn't watch so much television it wouldn't have happened. I don't think he really meant it. Do you? I think he really did love me. I do watch television, that's true, but I'm not lazy. It's a lot of work taking care of a husband and two boys. And I drive the school bus in the morning and the afternoon too."

"Why do you think this happened?" Mahatma asked. "Do you think there's tension between the English and the French?"

"I don't know about things like that. Ask my husband."

"But you, personally? Do you sense the tension?"

"Sometimes. The other day I was shopping in Princeton with a friend, talking to her, you know, in French, and this man passed us and said, 'In Manitoba we speak English!' Why would that man tell us that? What would he care what language I was using?"

"Did Gilles have English friends?"

"His best friend was English. And he had an English girlfriend."

"Had Gilles been in any fights recently?"

"My boy almost never fought. But last week he had some problems with an English boy. It wasn't about language, though. The English boy was after Gilles' girl." Mahatma took that down. The doorbell rang. "You're a nice man, would you please send them away?" Gisèle asked. "I'm very tired now."

"Certainly." Mahatma walked to the door. "Who is it?" he called.

The Winnipeg Star!"

"Mrs. Baril doesn't want to be disturbed," Mahatma said. Two eyes stared through the glass at him.

"Mahatma! Lemme in!"

"Sorry," Mahatma said cheerfully.

"How'd you get in there?"

"Tell you later."

Turning back to Gisèle Baril, Mahatma suppressed a grin at the shouts from outside. "Let me in, Grafton!"

"Who was that?" Gisèle asked.

"A reporter."

"His language is not very Catholic." The doorbell rang three times. "Who are you?" Gisèle called through the door.

"I'm with *The Star,*" Edward Slade shouted. "Please let me in, Ma'am, I'm freezing."

She opened the door. "You're a reporter too?"

"That's right, Ma'am," Slade said.

"Can't Mr. Grafton tell you about all this later? I feel tired now."

"I'm afraid that won't do, Ma'am. If you let him in, you have to let me in too. It's only fair."

"Oh dear."

"I'm awfully chilled, Ma'am. Do you mind if I close the door? You wouldn't have a sip of something hot, by any chance?"

"Well, if you're cold, do come in. We have tea and sugar pie."

She went into the kitchen again. Slade elbowed Mahatma. "Nice try, jerkoff."

Gisèle returned with tea and pie. Slade got to the point. "If you don't mind me asking directly, Ma'am, who killed your son, and what do you think should be done about it?"

"I'm not sure."

"Well, would you say the anglos are a bad lot?"

"Some of them, sure. I mean, as I was telling Mr. Grafton here, my son Gilles was fighting one of them a few days ago, but it had nothing—"

"So they *are* a bad lot, are they?" Slade scribbled. "And your son was fighting one of 'em, was he? When was that? Last week?"

"Yes, I think it—"

"Fighting an anglo last week," he said, flipping a page of his notepad. "He get roughed up badly, ma'am?"

"He came home with a black eye, but he said—"

"They gave him a shiner, did they? I see, I see! Can you spare me a photo, Ma'am?"

Gisèle turned to Mahatma. "Could you give him one from the album?"

"Certainly," Mahatma said. The door opened. Gisèle's husband and second son came in.

"Dehors!" the husband shouted.

"What's he saying?" Slade asked.

"He wants us to leave," Mahatma said, tugging on his boots. Gisèle began to sob.

Slade approached the father. "Sir, the two of us should have a chat. Man to man. People want to help you through this tragedy, but, to do so, they need to hear from you. *The Star* can help them hear from you."

"Sacrez-moi ce tabarnac dehors," the father shouted to his second son, who, although only fifteen, was bigger than Slade. He pushed the journalist toward the door as Slade continued to protest, "Sir, I have a job to do, and the public is very upset about this and is demanding to know why this happened to your son, and how to prevent it in the—"

Slade found himself flung outside, where Mahatma was buttoning his coat. "My boots," Slade shouted, pounding on the door. It opened. Two boots sailed out into the snow. Slade ran after them in his socks.

Mahatma had locked his doors and put his key in the ignition when Slade rapped on the window. "The photos," Slade said, "give me some photos!"

"Can't hear you!" Mahatma revved his engine.

"You heard me! Turn over those photos. She said we were to split them!"

"Call me later."

"Bastard!" Puffs of vapour formed and vanished outside Slade's mouth. "You sneaky bastard!"

Mahatma drove off, leaving Slade gesticulating from behind.

The next day, Mahatma's story provided pictures of the family, quotes from the mother and a detailed description of the riot. Slade had quotes from the mother, a photo he'd dug out of a school yearbook borrowed from the victim's school principal, and quotes from English and French hockey players. *Murder at Anglo-Franco Battle,* read *The Winnipeg Star* headline. *One Killed, Six Wounded in Hockey Riot,* read *The Herald.* The news flashed across the country.

Mahatma didn't get to bed until five that morning, and had to be up early to attend a press conference given by the Manitoba Amateur Hockey Association. He arrived with bags under his eyes. He felt shame when he saw the headlines and his byline. He hadn't misquoted anybody, and there were no errors of fact in his story, but the incident seemed repugnant now. His intrusion on Gisèle Baril seemed ugly.

St. Albert—One boy died and another six were hospitalized here last night in a hockey brawl which pitted English players against French opponents and raged for ten minutes until police burst onto the ice.

Gilles Albert Baril, 16, of St. Albert, died immediately when struck by a hockey stick in the back of the head. Manitoba Provincial Police homicide detectives have questioned Baril's teammates on the St. Albert Lions and players on the opposing Princeton Hawks, but no charges have been laid.

Held in the Manitoba Legislature, the news conference was packed. *The Toronto Times,* CBC-TV, every local TV and radio station, and newspaper reporters from across the country had crammed into the room. Out-of-town reporters kept stopping Mahatma for questions. The press conference did not go well. Jean-Guy Robert, the hockey association president, condemned the riot. He vowed to do everything possible to prevent such a thing from happening again. He said the league had cancelled the hockey season for boys in the sixteen- to seventeen-year-old division. Journalists demanded to know why English and French players were fighting. "I don't know. We'll look into it."

"Who do you blame for the altercation?"

"I don't have enough information to say."

"Did a French player begin the fight by punching an English opponent?"

"We haven't had a chance to look into that yet."

"Do you think this fight reflects language tensions in the province?"

"No," said Robert, biting the hairs under his lower lip into his mouth.

"You deny there are tensions?"

"Boys started fighting. It got out of control. Several were hurt. One was killed. I knew his parents. They—" Robert bit his beard again, then, suddenly, his face collapsed into his hands. This made national TV.

Meanwhile, word spread that an opposition member of the Manitoba Legislature was available for comment. The reporters rushed into an adjacent room.

Facing the scrum of journalists, the politician accused the government of ignoring violence in amateur sport and fomenting language tensions by planning in secret to extend French language

85

services. "This may have been avoided if the government had listened to the people instead of plotting to ram French down our throats."

Slade continued to chase the story. One day, he cited police sources claiming the killer was one of the few anglos on Baril's team. The next day, he wrote that a source revealed the killer was an anglo from the other team. On a third day, he penned an article under the headline *Mystery Killer Eludes Cops*. Slade was interviewed on national television and quoted by reporters across the country. But his wave of popularity subsided. His predictions about retributive violence didn't materialize. And the people of St. Albert and Princeton began to dislike him.

They grew tired of his interviewing every hockey player in town. They found it offensive that he attended all subsequent games in the arena, hoping to witness fresh violence. Mostly, they resented his depiction of the townspeople as hockey fanatics steeped in language hatred.

And Slade, for his part, grew bored with the story. Nothing was happening. Nobody was arrested, nobody charged. After four days, the story had fallen off the front page. Slade felt he was wasting his time hanging around St. Albert-Princeton, living out of a motel room. Moreover, his stay was growing unpleasant. Somebody slashed two of his tires. Someone else jostled him as he entered the hockey arena. Even the waitress in the café where he took his breakfast grew sullen after he asked her a question, wrote down the answer and asked her name. His editor made him stay put a little longer—"just in case, Slade, you understand, just in case."

Seven days after the brawl, on the night Edward Slade intended to return to Winnipeg, something did happen in St. Albert. It was what Slade had been waiting for. It happened around midnight, on an icy road eight miles out of town. Slade heard about it on his police radio scanner, which he had been monitoring in his hotel room. He heard the name of the victim: Peter Griffiths. Slade raced to the scene, arriving minutes after ambulance workers had carted away the body.

Peter Griffiths, the sixteen-year-old Princeton Hawks player, had lost control of his car on the highway leading out of town. His vehicle shot over a guard rail and down a ravine. The boy's body was found in the front seat. His head and chest were crushed. Slade had a way with cops. He had learned, long ago, how to talk like them. Edging down the slope toward the officers, he said, "Hey Sarge, what's it look like?" He sounded casual. Vaguely interested. Slade had met this cop. They had spoken after the hockey riot.

Standing on the hill in the darkness, with his back to Slade, Sergeant James Hetler grunted, "Some prick forced the kid off the road."

"Oh yeah," Slade said.

"The rear left bumper and rear left side of his car are smashed. Paint from another vehicle on them."

Slade asked, "Homicide?"

"Damn right."

"You giving this to the press?" the other officer asked Sgt. Hetler.

"No way. Not yet. We'll just report a highway fatality and release no names until we reach the Griffiths family."

"Who do we go after?" asked the officer.

"The frogs. The kid knocked the shit out of a few of them in that fight last week."

Slade memorized every word. He climbed back up the hill. "Gotta make a call."

Sgt. Hetler grunted. He was still looking over the car.

Slade drove into town. There was only one Griffiths listed in the Princeton telephone directory. Slade drove to the house, saw a police cruiser in the driveway and parked down the street. He waited and watched. The door opened. An officer stepped out and drove away. Slade rang the doorbell three minutes later. "Mr. Griffiths? I'm Slade, from Winnipeg. I was just speaking with Sergeant Hetler." Bill Griffiths invited Slade in without any questions. Slade asked a few general questions, noting the boy's age, his hockey background and details on the family. Continuing to write and glancing occasionally at Griffiths' face, Slade noted the man's appearance from close up: "His eyes, wrinkled and sleepy, light blue, struggling to grasp the fate of his son," Slade scribbled. Colour was what he needed, more colour: "Six feet, easily 180, Bill Griffiths says his son was already bigger. 'Just this evening, he took me in an arm wrestle,' the man said."

"Where was he going?" Slade asked.

"He had a girlfriend."

"Who do you suspect?"

"Some French kid."

"You sure of that?"

"Who else? Peter hammered half a dozen of 'em in that fight last week. But my son did his fighting on the rink. Off the ice, he was a gentleman."

Slade took that down, word for word. He rose from his chair, mumbled something about how he might be in touch again, wished the father good luck, expressed his condolences, and opened the front door. "Oh, can you lend me a photo of your son?" Slade said. Bill Griffiths gave him one. Slade thanked the man and left.

A girl in pyjamas ran to her father. "How come you talked to that reporter, Daddy?" said the girl, who had seen Slade all over town. "Everybody hates him." Walking down the street with friends three days ago, she had been stopped by Slade, who wanted information about the hockey fight. Did they know who had killed Gilles Baril? he asked. He tried to interview her and every one of her friends. They jeered at him and ran off.

Edward Slade incinerated his competition. *The Star* splashed Peter Griffiths' picture all over page one. No other paper had a word of the story. Slade outraged police, the Griffiths family and the Princeton community so thoroughly that it was impossible for other journalists to match the story. Nobody would speak to the media.

Mahatma Grafton was taking two extra days off when Slade got his scoop. Mahatma immediately unplugged his phone. He wasn't getting roped into anything by any editor! He couldn't stop thinking that he had taken advantage of a woman in shock to get his hockey brawl story. He couldn't stop thinking of Gisèle Baril offering tea and pie and the photo album. Mahatma had vowed never to interview the family of a dead victim again unless there was a compelling reason to do so.

Nobody was arrested for the murder of Peter Griffiths, or for the slaying of Gilles Baril.

Edward Slade flew to the Caribbean for a vacation.

On a Saturday in late November, the Francophone Association of Manitoba held a demonstration outside the Donald Street office of the Department of Francophone Affairs, a government agency responsible for the rights of French-speaking citizens. Mahatma attended. Reporters from every news outlet in town attended. But only a few hundred demonstrators turned up. They listened to some speeches urging the provincial government to proceed with its plan to recognize the constitutional rights of Franco-Manitobans. Nothing of interest happened and no reporter found anything new to write about.

Then in early December, FAM announced it would stage another demonstration on the following Sunday, again outside the Department of Francophone Affairs. FAM promoted the event vigorously, plastering posters all over the city. It struck out with reporters, who remembered the last demonstration and declined, for the most part, to attend. But FAM pushed ahead anyway. Media or no media, FAM organizers believed they would attract a good crowd this time. Maybe four hundred people. Maybe more.

Mahatma decided to attend. His editors had refused to agree to pay him to work on Sunday, but Mahatma planned to do it anyway. He wanted to hear the people speak, see how they felt, see how many came out. He had a feeling that something was going to happen.

They met in the Renaissance Café on Portage Avenue. Yoyo came to eat and to talk. In that order. He had accepted Helen Savoie's offer to purchase lunch for two, and he ate unreservedly. He ate minestrone soup, bagels with cream cheese, quiche Lorraine and a side dish of perogies. He drank tea before the soup and coffee after the salad, loading both drinks with cream and sugar. He ate carrot cake for dessert. Throughout it all, he kept up a conversation. "People here in Canada love democracy," he noted. "They ask the name of my country's leader, then they look sad when I explain that our leaders are not elected by popular vote. But I have read that not all people vote in elections here, Helen. Is that true?"

Helen leaned back in her chair. "In federal elections, we get a seventy-five percent turnout. In local elections, a lot less."

"Exactly," Yoyo said. "So if so many people don't vote, why do they care about democracy? It's like religion: you don't go to church, but you believe in God." Helen laughed long and loud. "May I ask you a personal question?" Yoyo said. "Why do you have no children?"

"I've never really wanted them. Anyway, I wouldn't want to do it on my own, and there's no man I'm serious about."

"Very interesting! I suppose you want no babies because you work? In Africa, we have heard much of North American women who like work more than babies."

"Plenty of women still like to have babies," Helen said. "The world won't fall apart without my contribution."

"The world needs babies! It needs your babies too! Helen! Marry me! Marry me and and have my child!"

"Nice try," Helen scoffed. She thought he was kidding. When she realized he wasn't, she told him, "No man tells me how to run my life." He stared at her, perplexed. "I have to go now," Helen said. "But do you want to meet next Sunday?"

"Sure."

"Do you know Polonia Park?"

"Sure." They agreed to meet there at 9:00 a.m.

It had seemed a perfect day to eat a potato outside. He had the potato carefully wrapped in his pocket, a leftover from a reception for the Ukrainian community. Jake Corbett sometimes went to such receptions, looking for free snacks. Last night he had eaten three sausages on the spot and pocketed the potato for later. Jake didn't mind eating cold potatoes. They were filling and, he had heard, healthful. He thought it might be nice to eat his potato in a park. His room was damp and smelly, but outside, it was a stunning December day: on this first Sunday of the month warmth was calling out to every Winnipeg resident. Even the papers were talking about it. On Friday, when Winnipeggers were prepared for Arctic winds and snowstorms, the temperature had risen to 12° Celsius. On Saturday, it went to 15°—an all-time record. Today it was sunny and going up to 18°. All the snow had melted. Everyone was out in the streets.

Jake took the Main Street bus south to River Avenue. There he got out and, with his right hand balled around the potato in his pocket, walked west to Polonia Park. A young woman wearing a T-shirt and track shorts rode by on a bicycle. Jake smiled, watching her round a corner. The girl on the bike made Jake think of Eva, his barber. Eva was the only woman who had ever touched him. She touched him every month. She worked at a Greek barbershop and she cut Jake's hair, and she didn't seem to mind that his face looked like the potato in his pocket. Jake often went to see Eva. Once he had his hair cut twice within seven days. Eva didn't mind. She didn't grimace and stay at arm's length and treat his head roughly, as if it were rotten. Eva was eighteen. She wore safety pins for earrings. Jake was happy about that. He didn't feel so ugly, going to a young lady who had pins for earrings and her hair up in spikes. So Jake closed his eyes when she cut his hair. He liked it when she shaved the back of his neck. He smiled when she shampooed his hair and rubbed it with a towel. Sometimes, alone at night, he imagined her shampooing his hair and it made him long to see her again. She gave him little shivers when she whisked the hairs off his cheeks and forehead. Eva was a wonderful barber.

Jake entered Polonia Park on the south bank of the Assiniboine River and found a bench free of bird shit. He sat down. It was like a spring day. He barely even needed his jacket, which held his potato, but he kept it on, feeling the sun against his face and thinking it would be sad to die and never feel the sun again, or have a potato in his pocket, or watch a girl in shorts ride her bicycle in December, or feel Eva's hands on his scalp.

Walking along Provencher Boulevard with two bananas in his hand, Yoyo wondered if white storekeepers in Canada raised prices for black customers. Whites paid more than blacks in Cameroonian markets; Yoyo wondered if the opposite were true in this country. He was hungry, having eaten little the night before. Heading toward Polonia Park, he could have devoured the bananas in seconds. But in Cameroon, it is uncivil to eat in the street. Though Yoyo had frequently seen Canadians snacking in public, he had his dignity to uphold. He ignored his stomach cramps, walking upright so that no one could detect his pain. Canadians liked to put benches in their parks; there would surely be a bench in Polonia Park. There he would sit and eat his fruit in peace.

Yoyo had never experienced such hunger. Before coming to Canada, he had been told that his billet in St. Boniface would provide him daily with breakfast, lunch and dinner, and that he would require only a small sum of pocket money to meet expenses. Twenty Canadian dollars a week, amounting to $840 for his ten-month stay in the country, had seemed, while he was still in Cameroon, a generous stipend.

Yoyo found himself on Portage Avenue on his first full day in Canada with $840 in his pocket, face to face with signs outside a department store announcing Super Sale, Prices Never Lower and Bargain of the Century. Remembering his expectant relatives, and concerned that he might never encounter such sales again, Yoyo purchased several pairs of shoes and slacks, as well as three sports bags, two soccer balls, two pairs of ladies' slippers, four transistor radios, two ghetto blasters, six cartons of radio batteries, one Sony

Walkman, twelve blank cassettes and three wristwatches, thus spending three-quarters of his cash.

That same afternoon, entering the St. Boniface home where he'd been given a room, he asked about the supper hour.

"Jeune homme," said his landlady, "I fed you last night from the goodness of my heart, but don't expect more such favours from me!" Yoyo was baffled. "That's correct, jeune homme! You will receive a continental breakfast here between the hours of 7:00 and 7:30; and lunch at half-past noon, but you are *not* to have supper here. I have been paid only to provide you with breakfast and lunch, and I shall not be taken advantage of!"

Yoyo nodded and went upstairs. He entered his room in a state of shock, not at the prospect of eating only two meals a day—which was standard fare for many of his countrymen—but at how the woman had spoken to him. He, a guest in her home, subjected to such verbal abuse! The shame! Had he offended her by his dress, or his manners? Why did she dislike him so? Yoyo was too upset to join the woman for breakfast the next morning. He met her for lunch and received one cold cheese sandwich with a pickle, a glass of milk and a cupcake, which he liked very much. He skipped the next day's breakfast as well, and began eating one light lunch a day at the home of his host. Sometimes he would buy bananas and Joe Louis chocolate discs. They went well together.

On this first Sunday in December, Yoyo felt hungrier and weaker than usual. Arriving in Polonia Park, he sat exhausted on a bench, oblivious to the man beside him. Yoyo felt a brittleness in his chest. There, with his feet on the ground, he felt rooted to the universe and distinctly mortal. Listening to a bird peep, he looked up at a branch.

"A chickadee!" muttered Yoyo, who had read two books about Canadian wildlife before leaving Cameroon. "I believe that's a black-capped chickadee!"

Jake Corbett said, "Goddamn nice day, isn't it?"

"Very nice," Yoyo agreed. Someone would have to explain this English word to him. Yoyo heard it everywhere. 'God' meant *Dieu*, and 'dam' meant *réservoir*. Could this mean *un réservoir de Dieu*?

God's reservoir? By calling warm winter temperatures 'Goddam' weather, were Canadians suggesting that it was issued from God's love for the universe?

Corbett said, "Nice to see birds out, isn't it?"

"Yes. Very nice Goddam birds," Yoyo said.

Corbett began laughing. "You say that real funny."

Yoyo turned to look again at the man on the bench. "I know you! You are the famous Jake Corbett. We met in your room! I was researching an article for my newspaper in Cameroon."

"Right," Corbett said. "I knew you but I forgot your name."

"It's Yoyo. Would you like a banana? I have two."

Corbett accepted and ate his banana in three bites. "Do you got people on pogey in Africa?" Yoyo didn't understand the question. He smiled uncomfortably and nodded. "They treat them better over there?"

"Yes."

"Goddamn!"

"Goddam," Yoyo repeated, shyly. Looking up, he saw Helen approaching. "I must go now."

"That your lady friend?" Corbett asked, admiringly.

"Yes."

"Goddamn," Corbett said.

"Yes, Goddam and goodbye."

Helen Savoie made up her mind as she walked to Polonia Park. Her relationship with Yoyo had to end. He was taking this fling the wrong way. Talking about babies and marriage. Helen put off her decision when she saw her lover in the northwest quadrant of the park. He was so beautiful! He sat on a bench, back straight, feet properly planted on damp grass, posture fine enough to balance a book on his head. Dressed immaculately, he was eating a banana. So was the man slouched next to him, who tossed his peel behind the bench. Yoyo followed suit. Then he saw her. He jumped up to greet her! When was the last time someone had done that for her? She threw her arms around him. "Kiss me!" Yoyo hesitated. Helen cupped his head in her hands and devoured his lips.

"I needed that," she said.

"I was going to give you a banana," Yoyo said, "but the gentleman beside me wished to eat it. Say, what's that noise?"

"I don't hear any noise."

"Listen!"

Helen turned to see a dozen people sprinting down a slope into the park. They were yelling and pursued by others, including a cop who ran with a club in his hand.

"A fight?" Yoyo asked.

"There's a demonstration outside Francophone Affairs," Helen said. "Must be that."

"A demonstration? I can cover it for my newspaper."

Jake Corbett stretched his sore legs out on the park bench. He closed his eyes. He thought he heard rumbling in the distance. Voices, shouting. Many voices, many shouts, indistinguishable but growing louder. He opened his eyes. People by the dozens were running down a slope into the park toward him. Police pursued some. Others pursued police.

Screams of pain and anger fused. One policeman fell down and someone kicked him in the head. Police swung sticks. People threw rocks. Jake saw a police officer club Yoyo. Men and women swarmed around. Someone hurled an unopened Coke can at a young police officer, striking him on the temple. The officer fell on Jake's outstretched legs. Jake screamed in agony and began shoving the officer, pounding on his back, trying to get the weight off his legs. This was the last thing he remembered when he regained consciousness in a paddywagon. His head was pounding. The potato was still in his pocket. He had no idea what had happened. He wasn't sure if he could move his legs. He lost consciousness again.

At 8:30 a.m. the same Sunday, Judge Melvyn Hill was listening to Handel's *Water Music*. He opened his back door to test the temperature. He felt lonely but free. Lonely for company, for somebody to admire all he had made of his life, or, at least, for somebody to like him. And free of the second Mrs. Judge Melvyn Hill, Doris, who had decamped five months ago, leaving not a word, a letter, or any furniture. Doris had hated him. In their last years together, she didn't sleep with him. Didn't even sleep in the same room. Didn't allow him to touch her and, if he happened to, she would turn and level the coldest of stares, ask what exactly he wanted, and remind him that he was a pompous jackass held in contempt by every citizen of Winnipeg and by the souls of most of the dead.

But today he was lonely. So, on that gloriously sunny and springlike December morning, he set out for a lengthy walk. He had no wife and few friends, but Melvyn Hill had perfect health. He was a short, slender man with a full head of hair, normal blood pressure and a good heart. He kept in shape by walking. In all but the worst weather, Melvyn Hill walked to work, to do his shopping and to go to the cinema. He was probably the only judge in Canada who owned no car.

Today, the sun blazed. The sky took on the hue of a sub-zero prairie day. A couple rode by on bicycles, with a hockey-helmetted tot perched behind each parent. A woman jogged past. "Good morning," she sang out. Melvyn Hill felt happy to be alive. He walked parallel to the curving Assiniboine River, which rose high on its banks. Someone ahead of him threw a stick. A springer spaniel tore after it, its ears flapping like wings. The dog dropped the stick and chased a squirrel. The cold, grey river ran on, its current flexing around rocks and bends.

Melvyn came to River Avenue, proceeded east and crossed Osborne Street. He decided he would turn back at Polonia Park, now half a mile away. Polonia Park was shaped like a cereal bowl, its low, flat surface about the size of two football fields. Old, sprawling elm trees were posted like sentries around the park's upper perimeter. Through them passed a walking path.

Melvyn planned to rest there before returning home. He had some thinking to do. Particularly urgent was his age problem. He would be sixty-five soon. Normally, when Provincial Court judges hit sixty-five, they could choose to retire. To continue, they needed a contract renewal from the provincial attorney general's office. This was Melvyn's preference. He pictured retirement as sad and useless—no family, no woman and not even a job. Melvyn had written the attorney general three months ago, requesting permission to carry on past age sixty-five. But he had received no response. And his sixty-fifth birthday was less than a year away. What was the hold-up?

Shouts and cries pulled Melvyn from his thoughts. Looking down into Polonia Park, he saw a scene of madness: demonstrators screamed in anger and in agony. Melvyn Hill edged down the slope and into the hub of activity. Placards were waving in the air, falling to the ground, being swung as weapons. One slammed into the face of a man in blue who was swinging a club. Several men in blue rushed into the crowd. Policemen! Ten, twenty of them, rushing down the hill. Two young boys, no older than twelve, ran into the park, stopping near the judge. Melvyn told the boys to leave the park immediately.

One boy said, "Up yours, you old fart." The boys ran into the fray. Melvyn sighed. He would have to talk some sense to the hotheads who had let this thing get out of control. He edged into the melée, which involved several hundred demonstrators and a growing body of cops. Melvyn found himself sandwiched between demonstrators and cops. "Let me through," he shouted, pushing desperately. "Let me through this instant! I am a judge! Son, let me through. Young lady, let me pass. Officer. Officer! Let me go! I'll have you know, I am a judge! I am a—" Melvyn Hill was knocked down.

It was a pleasant walk from Lipton Street to the Department of Francophone Affairs, and, at 8:00 on a Sunday morning, no slower than waiting for a bus. It was a fantastic, springlike day. Mahatma Grafton was happy to be outside—even though he was working.

With the lean build of an ex-swimmer, Mahatma swayed as he walked, shoulders ho-humming from left to right, flat feet slapping the ground. He passed Mrs. Lipton's restaurant, stopped at a bakery for a hot cinnamon bun and munched on it as he walked east along Westminster Avenue past treed lawns and modest homes.

During his twenty-minute stroll, Mahatma reviewed all the kinds of people he had been mistaken for, in his life. Moroccans had spoken to him in Arabic, Jamaicans had assumed he was Syrian, Peruvians thought he was Andalusian and Spaniards had taken him for a Mexican, but nobody, not even in Winnipeg, believed he was Canadian. Oh well, Mahatma thought. You can't win 'em all.

Arriving early, Mahatma sat on a curb across the street from the office and waited. He wished he had brought a camera. Georges Goyette, who was setting up a table with flyers denouncing the English-French violence, spotted Mahatma across the street. "Hey, Mahatma, come on over here!" They chatted while FAM volunteers unfurled banners and erected effigies of bilingualism opponents.

A rented bus pulled up along Donald Street, dropping off sixty demonstrators. By 8:45, a throng of people had arrived on foot, some bearing their own signs, others chanting slogans, others watching and waiting. The demonstrators attracted a growing crowd of spectators.

Mahatma climbed up the fire escape to one side of the office. To estimate the number of people, he divided the crowd into ten equal sections and counted every head in a section. He came up with thirty people, so he multiplied by ten. "8:50 a.m.," he wrote in his notepad, "about 300 people outside." He descended to conduct interviews, but few people would speak to him. Many didn't believe he was a reporter. Others were hostile: "I don't talk to the press. You'll fuck it up anyway. . . . You slant everything. . . . I don't want my name in the paper." The hostility troubled Mahatma. He didn't mind antagonizing businessmen known to pollute rivers; he didn't object to harassing politicians about lies the week before. But ordinary people sensed, perhaps rightly, that most journalists would rather highlight the crowd's idiosyncrasies than discuss its message.

Mahatma finally found a middle-aged woman who would talk. Her name was Hanna Masson. "My teen-aged daughters think I'm crazy to come here."

"So why'd you come?" Mahatma asked.

"Because you should stand up and be counted when you believe in something."

Georges Goyette addressed the crowd with a megaphone. Mahatma wrote down most of what was said. Then he climbed the fire escape again, ascending three storeys. He sat on a metal platform and let his feet dangle in the air. Leaning against a horizontal bar, he counted heads again and made notes. He spotted an unmarked police cruiser with two officers fifty yards north on Donald Street. Swivelling around to look west, he saw three marked police cars in a lane parallel to Donald Street. Then he heard the shouting.

Georges Goyette, who had been winding up his speech and urging the crowd to follow him north to Polonia Park for skits and more speeches, was rushed by three young men dressed in combat fatigues. They looked like teenagers. American flags were stitched onto their shirts, swastikas etched on their sleeves. "French scum," one spat into the megaphone, "go back to Quebec!" Two of the young men knocked Goyette off the platform; the megaphone fell down with him. The boys pushed aside a woman who had been standing with Goyette. They hurled eggs at the crowd, jumped off and escaped down a side street. Shouts erupted in the crowd. Several people—the same people Mahatma had seen earlier setting up the demonstration—supplied protestors with eggs. Mahatma made notes of that, and of the barrage of eggs and stones thrown at the office. Glass smashed. Cries grew into mayhem. Police cruisers appeared on Donald Street. Demonstrators pelted them with eggs, cheering each time a white shell exploded into yellow guts on a police car. Sirens wailed. Goyette hollered to the crowd to go to Polonia Park.

In the confusion that followed, Mahatma saw many people run the wrong way and come up against a line of police cruisers. Some took advantage of the mayhem to kick the cruisers. Police warded them off with billyclubs. They pinned two demonstrators against a cruiser and frisked them, handcuffed them and shoved them into the car. Mahatma scrambled down the fire escape, through a back lane and over to the west end of Polonia Park. Hundreds of people ran into the park, spilling like dice down its slopes.

"Vivent les Franco-manitobains!" cried Goyette.

"Aaiieee," screamed a woman, "you bastard! Let me *go,* tabarnac!"

The voice seemed familiar. It came from down a slope, near a bench. Mahatma located the voice; a cop was dragging a hollering woman by the arm. It was Helen! Mahatma pocketed his notebook and ran down the hill. Two young demonstrators ploughed into the cop, who released Helen and swung at the men, felling one of them with a blow to the head. The officer pursued the other, taking three furious strides after the man, who fled in the direction of a bench where Jake Corbett sat. The cop collared the man. But someone hurled a Coke can through the air; it struck the cop on the temple, thudding audibly. The cop fell on Corbett's outstretched legs. Corbett began to scream. He screamed like a man being tortured but the big cop remained inert.

Helen tried to roll the cop off Corbett. She couldn't budge him. She grunted, tried again, grunted. Mahatma stepped in to help, pulling the weight off Corbett and easing the officer to the ground. Another cop charged toward them, shoving through the crowd. Helen and Mahatma eluded him by pushing deep into the crowd. Helen only noticed him when they were safe.

"Mahatma! What are you doing here?"

He grinned. "Reporting."

"Not any more you're not," she said. "You're involved now. I have a friend over there who is hurt." She led him in another direction. The crowd was scattering as more cops and cop cars raced onto the scene. A paddywagon had driven onto the field. Mahatma reached for his back pocket, but his notepad was gone. Shit! It must have been knocked out down below, near Corbett. What was that crazy bastard doing at the demo, anyway?

Helen knelt by a black man. His eyes bulged. He made no

noise. Spittle clung to his lips. He lay on his side, head bleeding on the grass. "Ca va Yoyo, ça va?" Helen patted his shoulder desperately. She clasped his hand and spoke rapidly. Seconds passed before Mahatma grasped the fact that Helen was speaking French. Perfectly. "N'aies pas peur, Yoyo," she said, "on t'amène à l'hôpital." Mahatma knelt to help. He pressed a handkerchief against the man's bleeding scalp.

"Courage, frère," Mahatma told the man, who moved his lips but made no sound. Mahatma bent closer.

"Enchanté de te connaître," Yoyo whispered before he lost consciousness. With Helen's help, Mahatma carried the African up the hill. They stopped at the first house. Mahatma called an ambulance. After it took Yoyo and Helen away, he returned to the field to search for his notepad. By this time a television crew had arrived, but the demonstrators had fled and all that was left to film was debris on the ground. Mahatma couldn't find his notepad. He used a spare one and tried to interview a cop, who told him to screw off. Mahatma asked where his superior was. The cop wouldn't talk to him; he merely pointed across the field. There was a clutch of police cars on the far side. Mahatma found MacGrearicque in a cruiser and asked whether the police had used unreasonable force.

"Unreasonable force? We did what was necessary to stop that violence. Try being a cop in a mob of thugs. It's no tea party. There were people throwing rocks, swinging sticks, ganging up on officers; now let me ask you, what do *you* do, tuck in your tail or defend yourself?"

"How many people have you arrested?"

"Don't know."

"Fifty? A hundred?"

"You think we had an army down here? Thirty—maybe."

"I saw one officer . . ."

"I don't care! You fucking reporters just see what you want to." MacGrearicque rolled up his car window and drove off. There was nobody left to interview. Goyette had disappeared. So had Corbett. A police officer inspected a few sheets of paper in the mud. He found a megaphone at the base of a tumbled stepladder and carried them both to his vehicle. Mahatma climbed the northwest bank of the park, passing a muddied figure on a bench.

"Stop! Call me a taxi! Please! I need help!" Mahatma whirled around and stared into the bloodied face of Provincial Court Judge Melvyn Hill. The judge was filthy. Swollen lips slurred his speech. Blood dribbled from his cheek.

Mahatma asked, "Should I take you to the hospital?"

"No. Call me a cab."

When the driver came, he looked at Melvyn Hill and shook his head. "Uhn-uh," the cabbie told Mahatma. "I don't take drunks."

"He's not a drunk. He's injured."

"This ain't the Good Samaritan service."

"He can pay," Mahatma said.

"Someone stole my wallet," the judge said.

The driver started rolling up his window. Mahatma said, "I'm your fare and I'm bringing him along. Where do you live, Judge?" Mahatma helped Melvyn Hill into the back seat of the cab, then got in beside him and sighed, recalling everything he had seen: the cop falling on Jake Corbett, the whiteness of bone breaking Yoyo's skin, Hanna Masson saying her daughters thought she was crazy, demonstrators egging the building, cops flailing at demonstrators, people swinging placards at cops, cops swinging billysticks, protestors kicking free. He felt tired of it all. To date, reporting had involved mirroring events and repeating what others had said. This time he had to be analytic and draw conclusions. And without his notepad.

"What's the matter, son? Aren't you going to ask me anything?"

The voice startled Mahatma. "I didn't think you recognized me."

"What do you take me for, Mahatma Grafton? A fool? What are you going to write this time? That a taxi driver mistook me for a drunk?"

"I won't write anything about you."

"Well, you can quote me on this: the police really lost their cool, and there is no excuse for that." Mahatma wrote down the quote, drew a line across the page and set down his pen. He wouldn't push the judge into an interview. But the judge said, "Quote me on this too—" Under the line he had just drawn, Mahatma wrote "Melvyn Hill" in his notepad and began scribbling as the judge spoke. "My Sunday stroll was interrupted by gross mayhem at Polonia Park. The demonstrators were ruffians and fools, but I have never seen police behave so badly in all my life."

The judge fingered the cut on his cheek. "You know who gave me this? A police officer. I saw the police chase adults into the park. I saw police club people without provocation. I was knocked down by one and nearly trampled by demonstrators. I don't agree with the French activists, but the police used too much force." The taxi stopped by a house on Craig Street. Judge Hill had one leg out the door when he handed Mahatma a muddied notepad.

"I found this. You might need it."

Mahatma entered the newsroom with blood on his jacket, a twig in his hair and mud streaking his face.

Betts asked, "You were there?" Mahatma nodded. "Good. What's your lead going to be?"

"Give me some time, will you?"

"Never mind. I was there. With Van Wuyss. A clutch of loonies threw eggs at us. Did you see those crazy demonstrators?"

"Some."

"Good. Make that your lead."

Mahatma didn't argue. But he didn't agree, either.

Within two hours, the temperature dropped ten degrees. Mahatma noticed the stiff north wind as he left the newsroom to conduct some interviews. He drove a company car to the Accidental Dog and Grill. Frank, the owner, was suspicious of Mahatma at first, but then fell all over him when he learned Mahatma was a reporter. Mahatma took the wobbly steps upstairs. Jake Corbett lay supine on his bed, feet raised on a rolled blanket, sweating. He lifted a hand a few inches off his bed.

"How're you doing, Jake?"

"Not so good, Mr. Grafton."

There was no place for Mahatma to sit. Books, documents, legal statutes, tracts, newspaper clippings and encyclopaediae were strewn on the window ledge, the dresser, the chair, the bed and even on the floor. Leaning against a wall, Mahatma took notes about what had happened to Corbett. The potato in his pocket. The African with two bananas. Everything. Mahatma wondered how much to believe. Corbett was clearly inventing parts of it. For example, he claimed that the African had written about him for a foreign newspaper. Corbett also said a bearded man had taken pictures of police beating him.

"I'll look into it," Mahatma said. "Did the cops arrest you?"

"They took me in. But they didn't do anything. Some guy said 'not you again' and let me go." Mahatma prepared to leave. "And Mr. Grafton?"

"Yes."

"I want my money back!"

"What money?"

"My $602.38 overpayment deduction money. You want my lawyer's phone number? We're gonna take those welfare people to court!"

There were few reporting tasks Mahatma hated more than sneaking into hospitals. He was sure that nurses saw reporters as vultures and, to a degree, he agreed. Today, however, the task seemed justifiable. Yoyo was not critically injured. And Mahatma needed a separate account of police brutality at the park.

Yoyo was propped up in bed, his head bandaged. His eyes latched onto Mahatma. "You're a good man," Yoyo said. "I want to thank you."

"Don't mention it," Mahatma said. "How's the pain?"

"They have given me pills. The white man has pills for everything. The thing that has always confused me is, how does that pill know where you need it? How does it know your head is hurt? Could it not go where it isn't needed? The wrong leg, for example?"

Mahatma laughed. "What did they do to you?"

"They operated on the arm. Now they're watching my concussion. But let's not worry about that. For a long time, I have wanted to meet you. You are responsible for Cameroon's interest in the famous Jake Corbett."

"Corbett? Famous?"

"I have written of him several times since you reported his arrest outside City Hall."

"You've written?"

"For *La Voix de Yaoundé,* in Cameroon."

Mahatma laughed. Jake Corbett, famous in Cameroon? It seemed an absurdity. "Could you answer a few questions about Corbett?"

"Most certainly."

Aside from confirming that he and Corbett had shared a banana in the park, Yoyo said he had seen the cop fall on Corbett's legs, and he had seen Goyette snapping pictures at the demonstration. Finally, Yoyo described how his bone was broken. Mahatma wished the little man well and hurried out.

Georges Goyette had a black eye and a fat lip. He ushered Mahatma in with a swat on the back. "Anglos, anglos! You don't come to parties. You never drop by to say hello. You just come for business."

Mahatma smiled. "Describe what you saw at the demonstration."

"I would have had the pictures to prove it, if a cop hadn't belted me and snatched my camera."

"I'm surprised you let that happen."

"He got a hand from his partner."

"You were taking pictures?"

"Yes. I got them hitting Corbett on the head. I got them clubbing Yoyo's arm. Pauvre gars. He has had it rough in Canada. Did you know that he hasn't been eating?"

"No. I just met him, actually. What do you mean, not eating?"

"He has no money. I learned today his landlady won't feed him. But he came here believing she would provide all his meals."

Mahatma couldn't afford to get off track. "What happened between him and the cops?" Goyette confirmed what Yoyo had said. "And then?"

"Then two cops laid into me." Goyette fingered his puffy face. "They knocked me about, then stole my camera."

"Did they charge you?"

"Participating in a riot. I go to court next week."

"They hurt you?"

"Naw. Torn clothes. Sore cheek. Sore chin. Black eye."

"How many were charged?"

"Hey man," Goyette said, "they didn't give me a press kit. But there were a lot of us in the paddywagon."

"You regret staging the demonstration?"

"No! We've got a right to protest. And the cops have no business beating up on us."

Mahatma asked about the young men in army fatigues who had disrupted the demonstration. Goyette said, "Nobody knows who they were." When Mahatma had to leave, Georges said, "I guess I'll see you next time there's an airplane crash or something."

Mahatma stopped next at Helen Savoie's home in St. Boniface. "I'm writing about the demo for tomorrow's paper. Can you tell me what happened to Yoyo?" She complied, concisely. When she was done, Mahatma asked, "By the way, what were you doing there with him?"

"He's a friend. We met in the park. I had no idea that the demonstration would end up there."

"Alors," Mahatma said, "tu parles français après tout?"

"Et oui," she said. "One day, I'll tell you about that."

Mahatma worked alone in the newsroom. He felt good. He felt he was doing something worthwhile, something that wouldn't be reported if not for him. He wrote the main story about the demo, and two sidebars.

The Manitoba Provincial Police acted with savagery and brutality yesterday in quashing a riot outside the Department of Francophone Affairs, according to Provincial Court Judge Melvyn Hill.

"The police had no business clubbing people," the judge told *The Herald* yesterday.

Fourteen demonstrators were charged with participating in a riot after counter-demonstrators and police broke up the Franco-Manitoban rally.

Seven police officers and a number of protestors were injured, including a foreign journalist hospitalized after a police officer clubbed him with a billystick.

In an interview, Crime Supt. Patrick MacGrearicque conceded that "the officers really lost their cool and there is no excuse for that." Still, MacGrearicque insisted that his men had no choice but to crack down on violent demonstrators. . . .

Ben made Mahatma a potato omelette, spiced with Tabasco sauce he claimed to have discovered in Spain. "Come off it, abuelo," Mahatma said, "Spaniards wouldn't touch Tabasco sauce if you paid 'em. They wimp out on spices."

Ben pulled a long face. "Why is a boy of your education using a term like 'wimp out'?"

"I said it for your benefit, abuelo."

"Hush up and eat your eggs." Mahatma did that. But Ben objected to his shovelling food into his mouth, with his back hunched and his elbows on the table. "I hope you don't eat like that in public, son. People will think you were raised in the street."

"The son of a communist is raised in a chateau?"

"I'll chateau you. And I'm not a communist."

"You're not?"

"Old men like me have no time for -ists and -ites. Socialists, communists, Trotskyites, Troglodites—humphh! They could save us all a lot of earaches by dropping their hot air and saying what they mean!" Ben stole a spoonful of his son's omelette, then asked, "So, how was the demonstration?"

"Pretty rough."

"Was your friend Goyette arrested?"

Mahatma looked up, surprised. "Yeah. And charged with participating in a riot."

Ben whistled. "And your favourite judge? I hear he was knocked around a bit."

"You heard?"

"I still get around."

"You were going to tell me about him someday."

"Soon, son. Soon."

Mahatma Grafton was awakened by the morning radio news: "Police Crime Superintendent Patrick MacGrearicque has reacted angrily to suggestions that his officers used violence to quell a demonstration yesterday. He dismissed *The Winnipeg Herald*'s claim that police clubbed protestors outside the Department of Francophone Affairs. And he was outraged by a quote that had him criticizing his own officers for losing control at the riot."

Mahatma groaned. Had he misquoted MacGrearicque? He couldn't have. What, exactly, had he written? He rolled out of bed, dressed, threw on his coat and hurried out to a newspaper stand. There, he saw MacGrearicque quoted, saying his officers "had really lost their cool and there's no excuse for that." Mahatma remembered having written it, but now he knew it was wrong. Or was it possible that MacGrearicque had said it? He rushed home to consult his notebook.

While Mahatma was flipping through it at the kitchen table, Ben joined him. He asked, "You haven't eaten yet?"

"I'm in deep shit."

"Meaning?"

"I misquoted a cop in a big story in today's paper. Melvyn Hill blasted them for losing their cool at the riot, and I attributed his comments to this big-shot cop who's gonna want my head."

"You misquoted a cop?"

"Yes."

"Without malice?"

"Yes."

"Well, he may want to burn your hide, but he can't kill you."

"My story is discredited now."

"Just stand up and say 'folks, it was my fault and I'm sorry.' That'll take the sting out of the harshest critic."

"But what about the rest of the story?"

"Is it important to you?"

"Yes!" Mahatma surprised himself by the vehemence of his answer.

"Then check all your facts, be sure the rest of the story is watertight, and stand by it."

"I'd better get to work, Dad."

"Keep your chin up, son. You didn't beat anybody up, you know. The cops did."

When Mahatma checked his stories in the paper, there were no other errors. He noted with relief that *The Herald* had downplayed his work. Only the first six inches of his main story made it onto page one, in one short column under the fold. Inside, the story and sidebars ran on page eleven. They had reservations about the story. Ordinarily, such news would have been the line story on page one. Mahatma showered and dressed, choosing to wear a jacket and tie—items he normally left in the closet. Ben touched his shoulder as he was running a pick through his hair.

"Son, I've made waffles. They're on the table. Eat them. African warriors never set out on an empty stomach."

Winter had returned to Winnipeg. Wind bit Mahatma's face as he trudged north on Lipton Street to catch the Portage bus.

In the newsroom, people avoided him. Everybody seemed to know something he didn't. Finally, Chuck Maxwell slid into place next to him.

"I screwed up, Chuck. I misquoted MacGrearicque."

"Was it your only mistake?"

"Yeah."

"Then hang tough. You oughta see some of the doozies I've fallen into, over the years."

"So what's going to happen?"

"Don't you know about the second run?"

The second and final edition of the newspaper rolled off the presses around 9:00 a.m. It had the broadest circulation of all editions and was delivered to Winnipeg homes in the afternoon. Running fresh news out of eastern Canada, Europe and the Middle East, it also carried the stamp of Lyndon Van Wuyss, who arrived at work each morning to order some article replaced or rewritten.

Mahatma asked, "What about it?"

"Betts pulled your stories."

"Pulled?"

"The works. He wrote a three-paragraph blurb on the front page, saying there had been a row between police and demonstrators near the consulate, saying how many people had been arrested and what the charges were."

"Jesus."

"He came in here swearing like a trooper. Saying he was going to can your ass. Saying he had *told* you how to write that story."

"So where is Betts?"

"He's out right now."

Mahatma checked his mailbox: no pink slip awaited him. He flicked on a computer and opened his electronic mailbox: no nasty note there. He wrote one to Betts, explaining the misquote. Having no instructions to the contrary, Mahatma went to the daily press conference at the cop shop.

Officers in the building scowled at him. A magistrate who had provided him with court information shook a finger "tsk tsk" from a distance. Mahatma went into the detective division and waited. He was five minutes early. Randa, the secretary, raised her made-up eyes at Mahatma. "MacGrearique is pissed at you, Hat. If I were you I'd boot it."

"Thanks for the advice. But I'll stick around." Mahatma flipped through *The Winnipeg Star.* No mention of the demonstration. He scanned the crime pages, where Edward Slade usually had a column. "Edward Slade returns from holidays tomorrow," said a boxed message near the bottom of the page. A crowd burst through the doors. MacGrearicque, who glared at Mahatma, was followed by Bob Stone, Susan Starr, Edward Slade and three other reporters. All but Slade jabbed microphones in Mahatma's face.

"Do you stand by your articles today?"

"I unintentionally misquoted Superintendent MacGrearicque, and I apologize for that honest mistake. But I stand by the rest of the story."

"Why were the stories pulled from your second edition?"

"Ask my editors."

"And the rumours about you being pulled from the crime beat?"

"I don't know anything about it. Now if you don't mind," he said, pushing the mikes away, "I want to attend the news conference."

Mahatma entered MacGrearicque's office with Edward Slade following behind. "Fuck 'em, Mahatma. They're amateurs."

MacGrearicque excused himself for a few minutes.

"So you missed the demo?" Mahatma whispered to Slade. He wished he had squared off against Slade yesterday. Then at least one other paper would have corroborated his story.

"I was off yesterday. Last day of holidays. Too bad about your error. Cops love misquotes. Gives 'em a chance to dump all over us. Don't worry, though. These things happen. You'll be back after your suspension."

"Suspension?"

"Didn't you know?"

"No. Or that I'm to be pulled from the cop beat."

"Well, you are."

"Where are the rumours coming from?"

"You know Superintendent Butters? Vice squad? Short, fat little guy? He's your boss' brother-in-law."

"Van Wuyss'?"

"You've got it. He called some journalists into his office this morning. Not me, mind you. They hate *The Star.*" He laughed a coarse, but likeable, laugh. "Almost as much as they hate *The Herald*. But I don't care that he didn't call me. I wouldn't print that bullshit. I'm no goddamn flak."

Behind him, Bob said, "Ah, shut up, Slade!"

"So Butters told them I'm getting yanked off cops?"

"And suspended."

"How long?"

"Two weeks."

Just then, MacGrearicque came back. He made an oblique remark about Mahatma as if he weren't there. So this is the game, Mahatma thought. They've decided not to recognize my presence. He tested his theory at the end of the news conference. "Do you have something to say to me?" he asked.

MacGrearicque nodded at a buddy at the door. "Hey, Tom, do you see anybody here?"

"No, I don't see anybody there."

"Neither do I. Coffee?"

Heeding the summons to the managing editor's office, Mahatma considered his situation. He didn't have the best job in the country. But as long as he was doing it, he may as well do it properly. He wouldn't back down. He had made an error. But that was no reason to throw up his arms.

Lyndon Van Wuyss laid it out for him. "Look, Mahatma, you've been a good reporter. And that's why we're not canning you over this error—only suspending you."

"Okay. But why did you pull the stories?"

"You have admitted to a major error. The police say the story is biased and inaccurate. We have your word against theirs, but your word has been tainted. It's been an embarrassment to *The Herald* and it would embarrass us further to play up a story that we may have already blown out of proportion."

Mahatma, going into the office, had planned to remain silent and dignified. But, as the M.E. spoke, Mahatma felt his skin prickle. He was angry. "I saw people beaten. I have to write that."

"It's your word against theirs. Unless you have proof, we're dropping the story. Also, I have no choice but to suspend you for two weeks. And when you come back, you're off the crime beat. You're going to ethnic affairs."

Mahatma stormed out of the office. People stared at him as he left. They had never seen him angry before. He wondered if he had ever *been* angry before. He felt good. Clean.

Ben Grafton stood at the window of his Lipton Street bungalow, watching his son walk up the steps. "What will you cover when you go back?"

"Ethnic relations!" Mahatma said. "Can you believe it?"

"That's not so bad," Ben said. "Don't think of it as a demotion. Think of it as a chance to write about something new. They're not telling you what to write, are they?"

"They will."

"Cross that bridge when you reach it. Worry if you're still stuck on the beat in two years. But you won't even be at *The Herald* in two years. Cheer up, son. I'll treat you to a meal at Mrs. Lipton's."

"Okay," Mahatma said. "And while we're at it, why don't you tell me that story of yours about Melvyn Hill?"

"All right."

Mrs. Lipton's was a health-food restaurant with four small rooms and a billboard covered with flyers pushing acupuncture, holistic medicine, yoga, feminist theory and a male awareness encounter group. Ben guided Mahatma to a table. "Here we can talk in peace."

"Abuelo, have you ever looked at the junk on the walls here?"

"Doesn't bother me. What's wrong with health nuts preaching to each other? At least they don't promote racism or warfare."

"It's still propaganda!"

"No more than those Block Parents signs on street lamps and in house windows."

"Block Parents?"

"Yes. If two of these Block Parents saw a black stranger talking to their kid in the street, they'd panic. But if it were some white

113

stranger, they'd think he was some fellow needing directions. There's a kernel of racism in that Block Parents business. If they want to call themselves Black Parents, that's another thing!"

Mahatma laughed. "You're crazy!" They ordered and their soup came soon after.

"Do you have everything you need?" Ben asked.

"Yes."

"Good. Because this is going to take a while. I'm about to take you way back in time."

"Right, right," Mahatma said. "You were born here in 1908 and your parents came from Alberta one year earlier."

"Who's telling this story?"

Ben began, "In 1937, there were so few coloured people in Winnipeg that most knew each other. Many roomed off Main Street, near the Canadian Transcontinental Railway station, and everyone noticed a new man when he showed up looking for work.

"One Friday afternoon in June, Harry Carson, another railway porter, showed up at my room and asked, 'You hear about that Grenadian kid?'

"He was talking about an island boy who'd had the audacity to ask for the manager of a bank that morning, seeking employment as a clerk. Harry and I shook our heads.

"All through the next week, Harry kept bringing me news. The upstart, whose name was Melvyn Hill, tried two more banks, the City Hall, two mining companies and *The Winnipeg Herald*, spreading word of his high school diploma.

"Finally, Harry asked me, 'Who does this boy think he is, Ben?'

"I said I didn't know, but I wished him luck.

" 'Ain't no luck gonna get that boy a white man's job.'

"I left town on a run down east and back. Two nights on the

train plus one in Toronto, shining shoes, carrying luggage, making beds, mopping floors, dusting windows, keeping out of trouble, you know. Trouble, in those days, meant instant dismissal. There was an old porter used to say, 'Trouble's like air coming tru the winda. You can't shut the winda and you can't stop the draught; you just step aside so you don't catch cold.'

"In Toronto, I spent the night with a cousin to avoid the bunk-bed flophouse the company ran on Huron Street. When I got back I learned from the inspector that the company had just trained Melvyn Hill.

" 'We'll put him in your car on the next trip to Toronto,' the inspector told me. 'Show him the ropes. Let me know how he does.'

"Melvyn Hill had piano fingers. That was the first thing I noticed: no blisters, no calluses. He was short and had little meat on him and was neither photo handsome nor fighting ugly. Small eyes that hardly blinked. Chin that stuck out. And dark skin. Not high yellow. Not brown, like mine. This baby was black.

"Though I didn't speak to Hill except when necessary, I was glad when the trip ended. He hardly spoke during the entire trip, made a fuss about cleaning toilets, refused to eat with other porters and went out alone on his night off in Toronto."

Ben had eaten his soup and he was fussing with a glass of water.

"Hill was made a full-time porter at a salary of $87 a month, plus tips. They put him on the spare board, meaning that he didn't work a regular train run, but filled in for others here and there. Weeks passed before I saw him again. But I heard Harry muttering about him from time to time. 'He acts like he knows it all. He thinks he's better than us.'

"Almost a year passed. One day while Harry and I were sitting on a window ledge upstairs in the Porters' Club, I saw a middle-aged coloured man with a serious, dignified face walking our way. Pressed grey suit. Polished shoes. With him, a woman who was also well dressed. A white woman, one hundred percent white. And that wasn't all. Two boys toddled behind them. They had straight, dark hair. The younger one's skin was very light.

Almost white. The boys wore yarmulkes, which I saw as the family crossed Main at Sutherland, walking north.

"Harry and I thought they were quite a sight. Neither of us heard the footsteps on the stairs, and suddenly I found myself face to face with the coloured man in the suit. For a moment I didn't know what to say. The man stood tall and with perfect posture. His eyes were light brown and his greying hair, curled and cropped close to his head, was clipped above his large ears. He was in his mid-forties. Behind us, the room had fallen silent. The man said he was looking for me. Said he had recently been to porters' training school, and was supposed to start Monday in my car. He introduced himself as Alvin James."

Mahatma tapped his fork on the table. "Alvin James? Aren't we getting off track here, abuelo?"

"Patience. Alvin James was the first black man to graduate from the University of Manitoba with a Master's degree in sciences. Also, he had converted to Judaism because his wife was a Ukrainian Jew. That's why we called him 'the Rabbi'. It wasn't meant to be derogatory. Quite the contrary. Even though he was educated and had tried to get other jobs, all he could find was porter.

"Of course, the other porters held him in awe. Some went to him with questions. One asked him to help fill out an income tax form. Alvin James complied. Another two porters had him settle a dispute. All this time, Melvyn Hill was running to Toronto and back. So for more than a year, Melvyn, Harry, Alvin and I worked the same train down east and back.

"Melvyn pestered Alvin James all the time with questions about books and university. He even started dressing like the man, always in a jacket and tie.

"Hill was so enamoured that he told us a story about Alvin James. Apparently, the Rabbi had found twenty dollars in the bedding of a passenger and had jumped off the train at White River, Ontario, to give it back. Harry Carson said the Rabbi was a plain fool, giving up good money. But Melvyn said it showed that Alvin James had class. And that Negroes would never get ahead by dishonest means.

"A couple of weeks later, the passenger wrote a letter to the superintendent, praising James and enclosing a hundred-dollar bill. Here's the stinger. Alvin James refused that too. Though he did suggest the hundred be used to buy new mattresses for the company's flophouse on Huron Street in Toronto. The superintendent lost his temper when he heard that. Alvin didn't get the hundred, and the flophouse stayed the way it was."

Ben Grafton was starting on his meal now, an omelette with mushrooms and tomatoes. "Now we jump to 1940 when everyone was talking about enlisting. Well, just about everyone. Alvin was too old to go to war. And Harry wanted nothing to do with it. He said, 'White people wanna kill each other, they don't need my help. Anyway, I got myself a good job.'

"Melvyn applied to the Air Force, did not hear back, tried again three months later, and was told the Air Force was filled up. He applied once more and was contacted shortly thereafter for testing. Melvyn became an Air Force man. They wouldn't let him fly a plane, navigate, operate guns or aim bombs, but they let him do tarmac duty for two years. Then they taught him how to service aircraft. He stayed on ground crews in Canada until 1944 and finally made it overseas.

"I became an Army private, went overseas in '44. You know all this. When we got back in '46, we found that job doors didn't swing any wider than before the war. We got our old jobs back. Before we had a chance to see any of our old buddies, the Rabbi died. You should understand that I had just come back from a war that I was sure would kill me. Melvyn, ten years younger than me, was exhausted from the war. Neither of us could accept the news of the Rabbi's death. We'd seen all kinds survive in Europe. Why that man, of all people? He was a good man.

"Harry Carson was too upset to work the trip back to Winnipeg. In Sudbury, a doctor had to shoot tranks into his butt. He was a mess all the way home. When the train carrying the Rabbi's body got back to Winnipeg, we learned that he'd died in a fire at that flophouse. The worst part was that the company blamed him for the fire."

Ben stopped and fingered the napkin beside his plate. His omelette was only half eaten. When Mahatma coughed into his hand, Ben roused himself and went on.

"We went to a shiva, a Jewish wake that lasts seven days, in the Rabbi's home. I had my only suit pressed. We passed a hat and in two hours collected one hundred dollars. That was a lot of money in those days. Later, we heard the Canadian Transcontinental had offered the Rabbi's widow only fifty. At her house on Bannerman, we met John Novak and the Rabbi's widow, Deanna, and her two boys, now about ten and twelve years old. I was fascinated by their pigmentation. Peter, the older one, was brown-skinned, but I might not have guessed that Alvin, the ten-year-old, was born of a Negro father. Alvin Jr. seemed almost as light as his mother.

"I gave John Novak the envelope from the porters. He was impressed. He steered me toward two chairs in a corner and told me, 'The company says the porters had been drinking and partying and that Alvin had been smoking in bed.'

"He knew, like I did, that Alvin didn't smoke. He wanted to know why, if there was a party going on, only Alvin got killed. How come he was the only person in the house?

"I told him what I could. That the flophouse had two rooms upstairs, each with six bunk-beds, but that the company never filled the place. Porters resented staying in bunk-beds while white train crews slept in hotels. I hated the place and usually stayed with my cousin. Most porters avoided the place. Slept with relatives, girlfriends, whatever.

"The Rabbi stayed there out of principle. He said nobody would end segregation if porters avoided the place. He said black people had to fill that place up and keep filling it until someone took notice. But the porters wouldn't listen. It's true that the men partied there, sometimes. About a year before, some of the boys had a real shindig there. They brought girls in and tomcatted and drank until neighbours called the police.

"After that, the doors were locked every night at 9:30. They came early in the morning to let you out. It was stupid but the company wouldn't do a thing about it. But Alvin kept staying there. He wouldn't give up. And that flophouse, that dignity cost him his life.

"He was the only man in that house. And even though firemen axed down the door, they were too late. They found him right there, dead on the floor."

Ben looked up at Mahatma. "I told all this to Novak in so many words. It was at the funeral, remember, and I didn't know that he was a lawyer, or that he would soon earn a seat on City Council and later become Winnipeg's first communist mayor. I didn't know that Novak had contacts with reporters and civil rights groups across the country. Or that he would come after all us porters to testify about that flophouse and get even with the company. All of us except Melvyn Hill, that is. He wanted to get ahead and he knew that testifying against the company could hurt his chances. He told us, 'I'm going to climb the ladder, make something of myself. You should do the same.'

" 'Nobody gave me no ladder,' Harry said.

" 'Then make your own,' Melvyn said.

"We argued with him and told him he was being a fool and an insult to his race. He said he was going to law school and would become a judge and one day we'd see who was the fool.

"I've never seen Harry get so mad. His voice sunk down as low as a gravel pit, and he said, 'You could live like Methuselah for a thousand years, but *still* you'd never be no judge!'

" 'There's no point talking to you!'

"Harry snared Melvyn's collar. 'You know something, boy? Your shit smell just like mine.'

"Melvyn wriggled free. 'You're disgusting.'

"Soon after that Hill quit the railroad and went back to school."

Mahatma sank back in his chair. He let out a long sigh. His work, the long hours put into the Polonia Park story, the tension stemming from his suspension and now Ben's description of his railway life had exhausted him. He thought again of Melvyn Hill bloodied in Polonia Park.

"So he finally went to school?"

"And made judge," Ben said. "I never thought he'd do it."

"Do you see him much now?"

"From time to time."

"And where's Harry?"

"Still hanging around the Porters' Club. It has changed names and it has a café upstairs, now. He runs it."

"When did he retire?"

"Years ago, son, just like me."

PART FOUR

FORTY-EIGHT HOURS INTO HIS TWO-WEEK SUSPENSION, MAHATMA Grafton invited Chuck Maxwell to dinner. "Let's not talk about work," Chuck said.

"Bad day, eh?"

"Don't even mention it. I don't want to say a word about it. Do you know what Betts . . ." Ben entered the room, bringing tea for Chuck. "Aren't you people having any?" Chuck asked.

"Black people can't drink tea," Ben said. "It affects our livers."

Chuck laughed. "You know something? I've never thought of Mahatma as *black*. If you know what I mean." Chuck saw Ben's eyebrows arch. "I mean, I hardly notice his colour!" The eyebrows lifted higher. "What I'm saying is, when I see a black person, I don't notice his colour. As far as I'm concerned, he's white, just like me."

"Isn't that the most amazing thing?" Ben said. "And until you brought it up, I never thought of you as white, either. I thought you were black." Ben cleared his throat and went off to make dinner.

Chuck laughed. "What a guy. Your old man comes across so deadpan, I'd hate to play poker against him. Say, you know what they did to me at work today? They gave me a memo saying my writing is sloppy. They're building a case against me. When they've got enough memos on record, they'll sack me. All this is giving me an ulcer!"

"How did you ever end up in journalism, Chuck?"

"I didn't start as a reporter. I started as a copy boy. You're talking way back. You're talking 1962. You're talking high school drop-out down on his luck and flat broke. You're talking copy boy at *The Herald* for twenty bucks a week—message boy, actually, the guy who got everybody's coffee and scanned the copy from Reuter and Associated Press. You're talking two years of joe-jobs until they finally gave me some work on the city beat. So I'm no Shakespeare, I'm no Hemingway. But I was a good journalist in my day. I broke my share of scoops. I was a man of the people and still am. I know what it means to make fifty bucks a week. I did it for years. And what do I get for giving the paper the best twenty years of my life? Harassment! What happens if they sack me? What else can I do? News is the only thing I know."

"Let's go out for a walk," Mahatma said. "It's snowing. It's nice out there. When we come back, we'll have dinner. My dad is making cornbread."

Chuck brightened. "Cornbread! Sounds great!"

Mahatma slept in on the third day of his suspension. He woke up at 10:00, made coffee and lay on the living-room couch, listening to Vivaldi and thinking how much more pleasant the music was than the sound of radio news first thing in the morning. Ben came in with a bag of groceries. He asked, "Hey, son, ready for lunch?" Ben normally ate breakfast at 6:00, lunch at 11:00 and dinner at 5:00.

"Are you crazy? I just woke up."

For Mahatma's breakfast and Ben's lunch, they ate grilled cheese sandwiches, for which Ben used three-year-old cheddar. "Man-o-man, I love that cheese," Ben mumbled as he ate. "Stuff's so good, it would make you fight your relatives."

Mahatma picked up the next line, which he had learned as a

boy. "It's so good, it'd make you beat back your grandmother—
and dare your grandfather to stick up for her."

"You know, son," Ben said after eating, "you ought to do some
fighting back of your own right now. About that suspension they
handed you." Mahatma felt his chest tighten. He, too, believed he
shouldn't take the suspension without a fight. "Now take it easy,"
Ben said, "I'm not telling you what to do. I'm just saying what I
would do, if I were you."

"Okay, go ahead."

"I would reclaim my honour. You're a Grafton, and—."

Mahatma finished it off, "And Graftons aren't ordinary people."

"You're not really just going to sit back and do nothing but eat
meals on Spanish time until your suspension ends?"

"No. I've already been thinking about something. Didn't you
tell me once that an old friend of yours works for the Manitoba
Provincial Police?"

Mahatma met Sgt. Reynolds Wilson in the Princess Street doughnut shop. He had no trouble spotting the man. "He eats orange
crullers," Ben had told Mahatma. "He eats about ten a day. He also
happens to be black. He's so black he's almost blue."

"Reynolds Wilson?" Mahatma asked, offering his hand.
"I'm—"

Reynolds Wilson kept his arms on the table. "You're five
minutes late."

Mahatma sat down. "Sorry. Doughnuts any good?"

"I stick to crullers. You want a bite?" Wilson let out a snorting
laugh that sounded like a car backfiring. Mahatma took off his
coat and pulled out a notepad. "Put that away," Wilson said.
"Whatever I say is off the record. As a matter of fact, we never
even met. Okay?"

"Okay."

"I want to hear you say it."

"We never met and this is off the record."

"Good." Wilson smiled now. "Any son of Ben Grafton must
have a few decent genes. I'm gonna count on your honesty, but

I'm going to enforce it too. Last guy who double-crossed me had the lifespan of a cruller." Wilson let out another snort.

Mahatma frowned. "Can we stop pissing around now and talk some details? A friend of mine named Georges Goyette was taking photos at the Polonia Park riot. Two cops grabbed his camera. I want the photos."

"I've gotta go now," Wilson said. "Nice meeting ya." They stepped outside. A gust of cold air bit Mahatma's face. "Suppose an unmarked envelope comes your way," Wilson said.

"If it does, I won't know who sent it."

"Why do you think I agreed to see you today?" Wilson said.

"Tell me."

"I used to work the trains with Ben. He saved my son's life in 1964. Kid was about three. We were standing on the sidewalk by the Porters' Club, chewing the fat. My son got loose of my hand and ran right into Main Street with a truck coming on strong. I froze. Couldn't move. Couldn't even yell. Ben nabbed the kid like a shortstop nabbing a line drive. Fished him off that road just in time and whoosh, the truck went by."

"That's quite a story," Mahatma said.

"Don't tell me things I already know."

Mahatma sighed. "Goodbye, Mr. Wilson."

Reynolds Wilson walked into the wind.

Ben Grafton heard the mailbox open at 5:00 in the morning. He heard a car drive off while he put on his bathrobe. By the time he got to the door, nobody was there. Just an unmarked envelope inside the mailbox.

The photos showed scenes of mayhem. Mouths torn wide with shouts and agony, arms swinging, people stumbling, hair and backs cluttering the photos. In one, a police officer swung a billyclub at Jake Corbett's head. In another, an officer grabbed a woman by the hair. In a third, an officer punched a man in the throat. Mahatma studied the photos over and over, revolted but delighted.

They kept Yoyo three days in the hospital. He gained a few pounds; he hadn't eaten so well since leaving Cameroon. He wasn't bored or depressed in the hospital. He considered writing about the experience for *La Voix de Yaoundé*. Several things had surprised him and would surely interest readers in Yaoundé: no patients brought their own food, no relatives came to sleep by their ailing family members, and no nurses worked with babies slung on their backs.

The day that Mahatma received the photos, Edward Slade slipped, uninvited, into the the chair by Yoyo's hospital bed. His manner displeased Yoyo. He was unshaven. His clothes were unkempt. He started interrogating Yoyo without displaying the common decency to enquire into the state of his health and that of his family. In fact, he barely introduced himself. "I'm with *The Star*," Slade said, pulling a notepad from his coat. "I'm doing a story on how the police handled the Polonia Park riot." Yoyo nodded weakly. "How do you feel about how the police acted?"

"I can't really blame the police," Yoyo mumbled. "Things got out of control. If this demonstration had happened in my country, people would have been killed."

"But what about your arm?"

"It will heal."

"But they broke it?"

"Yes, they did."

Slade scribbled, "They broke my arm." Then he asked, "Weren't the police brutal?" Yoyo gulped at the memory of his arm cracking in the riot. He felt food rising in his stomach and fought off the urge to vomit. "Hmm, Yoyo, what do you say to that?" Yoyo grunted and nodded his head slightly. "You agree? You agree with that description?" Yoyo nodded. He had to vomit. He had to get Slade out of there. "I need a picture," Slade said.

Yoyo weakly lifted his arm. "No pictures."

"C'mon," Slade said, "don't worry about it. It's just a photo. C'mon, put your arm down. That's it."

Slade shot half a roll of film in ten seconds. "Thanks for your help. Get well now. I've got to run." He took off. Yoyo rushed to the toilet to vomit. When he was finished, he wept in humiliation. To be invaded in such a way—to be displayed at one's weakest in a photo. *Quelle honte!* Yoyo didn't know how, or when, or where, but he vowed to get even with Edward Slade.

Pat MacGrearicque said, "I'm in a hurry."

"This is important," Mahatma said.

"I thought you were suspended."

"I'm back."

"Jesus Christ. You've got one minute to tell me what you want and to get out of here."

Mahatma stared into MacGrearicque's blue eyes. Then he set the photos on MacGrearicque's desk. The cop flipped through them and tossed them back at Mahatma. "So, what do you want?"

"C'mon, Superintendent. These are photos of police brutality."

"I don't know who took those photos, or when or where they were taken."

Mahatma knew he had him. He knew MacGrearicque was panicking. He had to be desperate to argue the time or place of the photos. "For the record, let me ask you again if you believed your officers behaved well at the riot."

"I have already commented on that. And as for these photos, I don't know a thing about them."

"Are you not concerned to see photographs of your men clubbing one man, punching another in the throat and grabbing a woman by the hair?"

"Get out of here before I throw you out."

"What about the fact that your officers stole the camera that took these photos, developed the prints and then sat on them?"

"I said get out of here."

"If you change your mind and decide to comment on these photos, you'll be able to reach me at the newsroom today. If I'm not there, try the managing editor's office."

Fifteen heads turned when Mahatma walked into the newsroom. Helen Savoie waved. Chuck Maxwell shouted a greeting. Mahatma smiled at his friends but kept walking. "I've got something to do, but I'll see you a bit later."

Lyndon Van Wuyss and Don Betts were meeting in Van Wuyss' office. Mahatma tapped on the managing editor's door, then opened it.

Betts saw him and swore. "Jesus Christ," he began.

Van Wuyss placed his hand on Betts' arm. "If it can't wait, Mahatma, please get to the point."

"These are photos from the riot. The cops stole the camera that took them, developed the photos and sat on them. I managed to find them."

The managing editor's mouth dropped.

Betts grabbed the photos. "Well, sonofabitch. Sonofabitch, would you look at those cops. Hey, who gave you these photos?"

"A source," Mahatma said. "I want you to run these photos and I want you to run my story. In that story, I'm going to lead off with Georges Goyette accusing the police of stealing his camera after he took those shots. I'm going to quote the police if they care to comment. I'm going to quote Jake Corbett about getting roughed up. And I'm going to describe the riot. If you don't run the photos—"

"Fucking right we'll run it," Betts said. "We've got the photos, we can back up the story. We have to run the stuff. It's news. Good hard news. I still think you're a smartassed bastard, Hat, but if you've got a good story I'm not getting in the way."

"Great photos," Van Wuyss said. "But what about the way we've already handled this story?"

"Who gives a shit?" Betts said. "People will call us idiots for changing our tune. It gives 'em something to do. But the point here is that we have a story. We have to run it."

Van Wuyss seemed to agree. "Well done, Mahatma."

"Take good care of those photos," Mahatma said. "Now if you'll excuse me, I have to knock out that story."

"Hold it, Hat, and listen for a sec," Betts said. "I'm gonna tell you how to handle this story, and I don't want you getting all high

127

and mighty. What you've gotta do is play up the cops covering up the photos. That's what's new. Then you can rehash some of the Polonia Park stuff at the bottom of your story."

"I was thinking the same thing."

Mahatma rolled over in bed and turned on the 7:30 a.m. radio news.

> Crime Superintendent Patrick MacGrearicque refused to speak to CFRL Radio this morning about photographs of police brutality and allegations that his officers had stolen the film to cover up the incident.
>
> The pictures appeared today in *The Winnipeg Herald.* They show police officers beating one man on the head, punching another man in the throat and yanking a woman's hair during the Polonia Park riot last Sunday.
>
> Another embarrassing photo appeared in *The Winnipeg Star* this morning, which showed an African journalist in his hospital room after being allegedly beaten by police at the same riot. . . .

Mahatma Grafton was bombarded with attention after the morning news. It started with his father, who wandered into Mahatma's bedroom. "Good work, son. I knew you didn't mess up."

Then the phone rang. CBC wanted to interview him. Had he been surprised to find the photos? What did he think would happen now? Mahatma said he wasn't surprised because he knew the pictures existed and that they would be uncovered in time. He called for an inquiry into police behaviour at the riot. Mahatma hung up. The phone rang again. It was CRFL Radio, with similar questions. He answered them. Six other radio stations called, and two TV stations, and *The Toronto Times,* and *The Brandon Advance.* After that, Ben unplugged the telephone.

Jake Corbett hung up the phone in Frank's Accidental Dog and Grill. "They're gonna put me on TV."

"Right," Frank said. "And they're gonna put me on the moon."

"CBC is gonna innerview me about welfare and my constitution rights and about me being subject to cruel and unusual treatment at that demonstration on Sunday."

"Somebody take this man's tempitcher," Frank called out.

"When the TV people come, send 'em up."

Before the CBC arrived, a young woman from *The Brandon Sun* came to interview Corbett. She was a student.

Jake began, "I was born with epilepsy but they took it for psychological problems and put me in Selkirk Mental and gave me electric shock treatments and kept me there seven years! It's 'cause of all that that I'm having all those there problems with the welfare people. But my troubles began in public school, before they sent me away to the mental, when one day I . . ."

The student reporter scribbled wildly while Corbett skipped back and forth over time. He confused her totally. When the CBC crew arrived, Corbett tried to retell his tale.

"No no no no no," said the CBC reporter. "I ask the questions. You answer them. First, how did it feel when the police clubbed you at Polonia Park?"

"I didn't feel much. It knocked me out. But when I woke up, I wasn't one bit happy."

"Had you started the trouble? Did you hit any officer?"

"I was minding my own business, thinking about my potato—"

"What potato?"

"The baked potato I got at the Yooker-Anian reception. I was gonna eat it in the park."

"But you initiated no trouble of any sort?"

"No. Is this going on the 6:00 news?"

"Maybe. Why were you in Polonia Park?"

"It was a nice day. I was having a banana with an African and then all these people came running in and I got hit in the head."

"Do me a favour," the reporter said. "Forget the Ukrainian potato and the African banana, would you? You're just going to confuse our viewers. When we get you on camera, stick to how you were minding your own business, relaxing on a park bench, and the next thing you knew the cops had knocked you over the head and loaded you into a paddywagon. Okay?"

The 6:00 news showed Jake Corbett talking about being knocked out by a billyclub. Jake was keenly disappointed. The TV people didn't mention his overpayment deductions. They didn't even talk about the welfare people not giving him enough to live decently. Reporters never told it straight. They didn't know how.

Georges Goyette's St. Boniface bungalow had been vandalized the night before. Walking up the porch steps, Mahatma Grafton saw spray-painted on the door, "Frogs Go Home!" Goyette swept the door open. "Come in, jeune homme." Newspapers from around the world cluttered a coffee-table. *Le Monde, El Pais, The Washington Post, The Toronto Times.* Goyette excused himself, retreating to the kitchen. One of Goyette's columns in *Le Miroir* had been framed and hung on a wall. Mahatma studied the column, in which Goyette attacked the provincial government for trying to water down minority language rights.

Mahatma stopped reading. To date, he had seen no details about the government's position on French language rights. *The Herald* had only reported that the Francophone Association and the government were negotiating a language deal whose details remained secret.

Mahatma checked the date of the column: September 20, 1983—that was three months ago. He read on, seeing Goyette's description of Manitoba's "first negotiating position" on the language question. How did *Le Miroir* have this information? Why didn't *The Herald* have it?

Goyette returned with a platter of cheese and pâté. Mahatma protested. "Don't say a thing. You're hungry. I'm hungry. So let's eat." They sat by a window, looking out at children playing hockey in the street. "Ever played hockey?" Goyette asked.

"No. Never had skates. You?"

"You're asking a French-Canadian if he's played hockey? Sure I did. Try that Brie!" Mahatma spread the soft cheese on rye bread. It struck him as incredible that in the six months he'd been in Winnipeg, this was the first time he had slowed down enough to enjoy Goyette's company. "Beer?" Goyette asked.

"Sure."

Goyette came back with two bottles and more food.

"To friendship," Mahatma said.

"And to your restored honour."

They clinked beer bottles. Mahatma tried some chicken liver pâté. And some Camembert. Then he asked Goyette about the framed column.

"You are probably the first anglo to read it."

"You broke that story and no English media picked it up?"

"Exactly." Goyette had acquired the provincial negotiating document, written the story and watched it remain ignored by the English press.

"How could that happen?" Mahatma asked.

"Les Anglais don't read our newspaper."

"But we've spent months trying to find out the government's position." Goyette nodded. Mahatma asked, "How come you never told me about this?"

"Do you run to me with scoops that I can read in your paper?" For a moment, they ate in silence. "What do you think of the language negotiations?" Goyette asked.

"I'm no expert," Mahatma said. "I don't really have an opinion on it. I'm just an ordinary person. Just a reporter."

"Just a reporter! What does that mean?"

"It means my job is to report facts, not to editorialize."

"Editorialize? I'm asking you to *think!* And don't tell me you're not an expert. You are. You are a news expert. You are paid to stay abreast of the news. You attend demonstrations, you watch people get beaten up and you grill police superintendents. Don't bullshit me about being an ordinary person. If you can't think for yourself, who the hell can?"

Mahatma made a sad, inward smile. He had nothing to say.

Spewing out daily news had deadened his thinking. If he had to write an editorial on any subject, he wouldn't know where to start or what to say.

✧ ✧ ✧

The day after his suspension was revoked, Mahatma was handed a scrap of paper that said 205 Killarney Avenue, Apt. 4. "A murder just came over the radio," Betts said. "Our new crime reporter is doing another story. Better get down there fast."

A cop opened the victim's door. He wouldn't speak to Mahatma. Wouldn't tell him anything. Mahatma didn't fight it, didn't argue.

Standing alone in the green-painted corridor of an apartment where a young woman had lived until a few hours ago, Mahatma felt weary. He didn't remember murder stories bothering him so much before. He remembered the thrill of beating Slade to the home of the French hockey player killed in St. Albert. He remembered how keenly he took quotes from the mother. It seemed like another era. Another life.

Mahatma rang a neighbour's buzzer. The lady who answered the door named the victim—Katie Bonner—and said she was in her early twenties and had lived alone. "She had men coming in every night! Different ones!"

Mahatma started, mindlessly, to jot that quote down, then stopped himself. He was fighting the story. But that wouldn't get the job done.

Another neighbour said he had heard the shot and called the police and seen the ambulance attendants carry the body from the apartment. Mahatma forced himself through uninspired questions: What time had the shot rung out? How many police officers had come? Mahatma did not want to pursue the story. Nor did he want to lose his job. He concluded that the minimum effort required to avoid another suspension would be to try to talk to

Katie Bonner's family. He looked up the name in the phone book and found a P. Bonner on McAdam Avenue. Mahatma drove there. A woman opened the door. "Are you Katie's mother?"

"Do we have to do this again?" she said. "That other man made us talk. He was from *The Star.* He said they would fire him if we didn't talk about Katie."

"You don't have to talk if you don't want to," Mahatma told her.

She didn't want to. Mahatma checked the woman's name and her husband's name, and then he left her. He collected his thoughts in the car. What was he doing? Searching for people to speculate publicly about the murder of someone they loved. He tracked down another Bonner in the phone book. Katie's aunt. This woman gave a few details of the victim's life. Mahatma didn't push her. What purpose would it serve? At most, entertainment. Mahatma asked the police a few questions and let his investigation end there.

"What'd you get?" Betts asked before Mahatma had his coat off.

"Neighbours didn't know much. Family wouldn't talk. I've just got a few inches." Betts scowled. Mahatma ignored it and wrote what he had. Two hours later, the phone rang on his desk. It was Helen Savoie and she was speaking rapid French. Mahatma listened, astonished.

"I can't explain now, but you're in trouble and I'm going to help. Tell me who you interviewed on the murder story and what they said. Talk to me in French." Mahatma complied. "Don't tell anyone we were talking," she said. "I'll be fired if you do." She hung up. Mahatma shrugged and wrote a five-inch story on the murder. The next morning, Helen called him at home. She told him to meet her after work at the bar Pantages, but not to approach her in the newsroom.

Helen Savoie's first contact with *The Winnipeg Herald* came in 1964. She was thirteen. As a grade seven student, she had won a prize for her history essay. She and eight other top students—all boys—were escorted through *The Herald* newsroom, which Helen concluded was a secretarial pool. A strange one. With men, instead of women. Talking on the phone, listening to radios, shouting, typing very fast with two fingers, walking around with their shoes off. Helen studied the clattering machines and decomposing telephone books and ringing telephones and paper clicking out of wire machines, but could make no sense of the chaos. She and the other students were hurried into the office of the managing editor where they were awarded plaques and doughnuts and fruit juice. Their names and pictures were to run in the Saturday paper. The managing editor gave a short, boring speech. He spoke like a military officer. "Society has its hopes pinned on young men like you." A ruddy hand clasped Helen's shoulder as if it were a doorknob. "Your name?"

Helen gave her first name only.

"Helen," thundered the managing editor, "is a fine British cognomen."

"No it's not, sir," she said.

"I beg your pardon?"

"Helen is not a cognomen. A cognomen is a surname, sir. And Helen is my Christian name."

"Very good, Miss. Very good. Have a doughnut!" The managing editor disappeared.

A young man about eighteen years old came up with a fresh tray of doughnuts. "Take one," he said. "Take two." He winked at Helen. "So you're pretty smart, eh? That's good. Don't drop out of school like I did."

Helen was scandalized. "You dropped out of school?"

"Had to. I needed a job."

"My dad had to do that too, but I didn't know it was still going on."

"It sure is. But you stay in school, okay?"

"Don't patronize me," Helen said.

The doughnut man's brow furrowed. He obviously didn't know the word 'patronize'.

"What do you do?" she asked.

"I'm the copy boy."

"Coffee boy?"

"*Copy* boy! I handle news copy from all over the world. I sort it out, take it to editors. I get to read it too."

"So you know the news before the rest of us?" Helen asked.

"You bet."

"So what happened in Europe today?"

The copy boy's mouth fell open.

Helen decided the young man wasn't too bright. But out of politeness, she asked his name.

"Chuck Maxwell. Look for my byline. I'm gonna be a reporter soon."

"A reporter?" Helen said. "Don't you have to be real old for that?"

"Nope. Reporting takes energy. Lots of it. It's a young man's game."

That, as far as Helen was concerned, was the only credible thing Chuck Maxwell had said.

Helen Savoie became a news addict. She read *The Herald* daily. She read *The Toronto Times*. She read American papers and, studying languages at university, began reading Spanish and French newspapers. She read magazines in all three languages. She developed an extraordinary knowledge of world affairs. She wanted to become a journalist. She felt that writing for a newspaper would allow her to speak her thoughts, to participate in public life and to exercise influence. She would have liked to have started at a top newspaper such as *The Washington Post*, or at least at a prestigious Canadian paper such as *The Toronto Times,* but they never responded to her letters and résumés. So, in 1975, at age twenty-four, after finishing an undergraduate degree in modern languages and travelling for two years in Europe, Helen Savoie lowered her professional sights to take a job at a starting salary of $170 a week at *The Winnipeg Herald.*

"Oh yeah, hi kid," Chuck Maxwell said when Helen identified herself. But she could see that Chuck didn't remember meeting her years earlier. Helen quickly learned that Chuck couldn't spell or write. He also knew very little about the news.

The Pantages bar was underground on the north side of Portage Avenue. Arriving before Helen Savoie, Mahatma Grafton ordered a tonic water and crushed the lime slice between his fingers, stirring the pulpy citrus bits into the drink. He hadn't spoken to Helen today. He'd been busy and Helen had been out of the office. But he was curious about Helen's secretive phone call. This morning, Mahatma had looked at the murder story he'd written the day before. It carried everything he wrote and one other small detail. He wondered where the extra detail had come from. No byline. That meant something was wrong. Somebody was unhappy with him.

"Hi!" Helen Savoie slid into a seat opposite Mahatma. "Did you see the extra detail in your murder story? The age of the victim's mother?" When Mahatma nodded, she added, "I put that in. I got the whole story, more or less what you got, with the age being about the only detail you didn't have."

Mahatma put down his drink. "They sent you out to do the story?"

"That's right."

"After I did it?"

"That's right. It's called double coverage. If I had come back with stuff you missed, then they could have said you weren't doing your job."

"So you saved my job," Mahatma said.

"You would have done the same thing, in my place."

Mahatma paused to take that in. "Why're they after me?"

"You embarrassed them on that Polonia Park stuff."

"I thought I straightened it all out with them."

"Fat chance. Betts really holds a grudge."

"I don't know how to thank you," Mahatma said.

"Don't bother," she said. "We work together, right?"

Sandra Paquette had a head full of knowledge. Mahatma went to see her in the mayor's office to ask about the Franco-Manitoban situation. He wanted to break a scoop about language negotiations and he thought Sandra might know a few things. As it turned out, she wasn't able to tell Mahatma much. Sitting in her office, they talked about Mahatma's suspension and about the troubles he had had when trying to write about the mayor's U.S. border troubles. They talked about Jake Corbett and joked about the time Melvyn Hill had him arrested. Sandra laughed, remembering the event; Mahatma found her mood uplifting. On a whim, he invited her home for dinner.

"My old man's a good cook," Mahatma said.

"Great," Sandra said. "I'd love to meet him."

When they were seated at dinner, Ben asked Sandra, "So you work for the mayor, do you?"

"I'm his executive assistant."

"The mayor's an old friend of mine," Ben said. "I dropped by his office a few years ago; we were going to go say hello to a friend."

"I remember," Sandra said. "You were going to look up a retired railway porter. A man named Carson, I believe, on Annabella Street. I remember you and the mayor joking about him being somewhat corpulent."

"Fat," Ben said. "We called him Fat Harry and we were going to a porters' reunion with him. But the reunion was a disaster."

"Why?"

"Because of Judge Melvyn Hill."

"Judge Hill? *He* used to be a porter?"

"That was the only job he could get," Ben said.

"So what happened at that reunion?" Sandra said.

"Melvyn handed out his business card and told everybody to call him Judge Hill. Harry got drunk and started picking on him. 'Hey, boy, shine mah shoes,' Harry told him. Then they got into pushing at each other. Melvyn was furious. He left early. Harry got so drunk I had to help him home. He started going on about his parents and head taxes and so on."

Sandra said, "You mean they were part of that migration before World War One?"

Ben looked surprised. "Yes. From Oklahoma. They settled on the prairie with a lot of other blacks. But the whites were so afraid they demanded a head tax on Negroes."

"Right," Sandra said. "So blacks stopped coming here."

Mahatma was astonished that Sandra knew what he had forgotten years ago. He thought of the many times Ben had tried to cram details into his head.

Yoyo, who had been to visit Mahatma's home, had commented one night, walking south on Lipton Street, that the homes seemed vulnerable under the cold, unending sky. Winnipeg's winters were so cold and miserable that Yoyo felt vulnerable himself. What if the furnace broke down? In subhuman cold that turned water into ice, nature couldn't be trusted. Yoyo missed Cameroon. In the warm villages to the north, no citizen could freeze. You could lie on a mat outside the door and stay there all night; blankets and coal and gas and oil were superfluous.

"I will return to my country soon; you must come and see me there," Yoyo spoke in the night air, under a lamplight, struck to see his own breath wafting out of his mouth. Even when he kept his lips sealed, he could see columns of vapour leaving his nostrils.

"But not in the hot season," Mahatma said.

"No," Yoyo said, "not in the hot season. Don't come in March. Come with the rains. Come in July. Or August. Venez quand vous voulez. Mais venez à tout prix nous voir."

Looking out his bedroom window at midnight, Mahatma reflected on Yoyo's invitation and on the evening he'd just spent talking with Ben and Sandra. He couldn't sleep. With his lights out and curtains open, he saw the stars. He saw far more than he could usually see in the city. "Star," his dictionary read, "a self-luminous gaseous celestial body of great mass whose shape is usually spheroidal and whose size may be as small as the earth or larger than the earth's orbit." Larger than the earth's orbit. Burnt out and gone, possibly, thousands of years ago. Gone before his father was born, gone before slavery died, before the Moors took Spain, before Christ lived, before Homer wrote, before Peking man found fire.

"Go do some great thing," Ben had told Mahatma, seeing his son onto the train to Toronto seven years ago. "Do something great for humanity."

Mahatma hadn't done anything for anybody. He hadn't even tried. He had gotten a Master's degree and learned two languages and returned to Winnipeg to chase the families of murder victims.

He couldn't sleep, so he switched on the light. In the closet were boxes, heavy with papers. Junk. Ben's souvenirs. Mahatma pulled one from a shelf and began thumbing through brochures, handwritten notes and newspaper clippings. A headline caught his eye: *Group Demands Explanation over Porter's Death*. "The Canadian Jewish Congress has demanded an explanation from the Canadian Transcontinental Railway about the death of one of its porters in a Toronto rooming house. Alvin James, 55, a Negro Jew who had worked eight years for the company, died in the Huron Street fire last month." A clipping from the same paper, a day or two later: "Canadian Transcontinental Railway porters were frequently locked inside the Huron Street rooming house in which an employee was killed by fire last month. 'They were always locking us in at night,' said one porter who asked not to be identified. 'We didn't like it. Most of us slept elsewhere when we came to Toronto.' "

Another headline: *Company Denies Door Was Locked*. Subsequent clipping: *Company Says Door Locked to Protect Employees*. And finally: *Fire Commissioner Says Huron Street Home Had Faulty Wiring*.

Mahatma recalled Ben saying years ago that the Rabbi's death had become a news scandal. When Ben had pushed Mahatma too far—made one too many sermons about black achievers—Mahatma tuned out altogether. At school, he grew interested in chess, math, computer science. By the age of fifteen, he wouldn't read a newspaper. He didn't watch TV news, didn't care about Vietnam or civil rights. At university, he lost interest in science and moved over to the humanities, but ignored courses about human rights or blacks.

Mahatma saw a clipping from 1952: *Porter Runs for City Council*. "Ben Grafton, 43, is the first Negro to seek civic office in Winnipeg. Running in Ward Three under the CCF banner, the railway porter pledges to fight for better housing for the poor, better job opportunities for minorities, better schooling in the north end. . . ."

Populist Porter May Become Winnipeg's First Negro Alderman.

Negro Candidate Loses to Communist John Novak and . . .

Mahatma scanned the story: "Railway porter Ben Grafton came within fifty votes of winning one of the three spots for Ward Three Alderman on City Council last night. He was beaten by communist John Novak and by incumbent Liberals John Alexander and Peter Hlady in yesterday's civic elections."

Mahatma scanned other articles, looking for more details on his father. He found nothing. He remembered nothing more. His father had run as a socialist, lost narrowly and not run again. But how had he campaigned while working the trains? Why did he run at all? If Ben were to die tomorrow, who could answer Mahatma's questions? If he were to die tomorrow, how could Mahatma tell his future children who their grandfather had been? After all Ben's speeches, tracts and tirades, if the old man were to die tomorrow, Mahatma would go to his own grave ignorant about the life of his father.

The Huckleberry Finn story took less than an hour to research and write, but it generated fifty letters to the editor. It came to Mahatma while he was talking on the phone. The receptionist tapped him on the shoulder. "A Charlene Thompson wishes to see you." Mahatma swallowed. Charlene Thompson. He hadn't heard from her since high school. They had dated a few times, but the more she showed an interest in him, the more wary he became. Charlene Thompson was a black activist and her strident behaviour made Mahatma uncomfortable. He didn't disagree with her ideas—he just didn't want to be associated with them. Her soapbox arguments reminded him of his father. Still, Ben had made a good point when he'd heard they'd stopped dating. "She made you feel ashamed, didn't she?" Ben said. "You didn't like going out with a black girl, having your white friends see you together? Remember that you're black too, and as long as you reject black people, deep down, you won't like yourself, either."

Mahatma recalled his horror at his father's perceptiveness. Until high school graduation, he avoided Charlene Thompson. Now he saw her again, walking across the newsroom toward him. She said, "I've got a story for you."

"Good," Mahatma said, "shoot."

Initially, Mahatma left his pen lying on his notepad. But soon he began writing. The story ran the next day.

> A Winnipeg high school has banned the study of *Huckleberry Finn* and education officials may strike the American classic from all Manitoba classrooms because of complaints about racist stereotyping.
>
> Mark Twain's 1884 novel was removed from Franklin High School when Principal John Butler learned last week that one of his pupils—a 15-year-old girl of Jamaican origin—had cried in class after being made to read aloud a section about the runaway slave character 'Nigger Jim'.
>
> The girl's mother complained to Minorities of Manitoba President Charlene Thompson, who in turn contacted the principal and the provincial Department of Education.
>
> "It was hurtful to the girl," Butler said. "It shouldn't have happened and won't happen again."
>
> Officials are preparing a report on the matter for Education Minister Renate Midland, who is to announce the fate of *Huckleberry Finn* next month.
>
> " 'Nigger Jim' is simple-minded and superstitious," Thompson fumed yesterday. "Imagine making a black kid read to her peers about those stereotypes! That book's no classic. It's a classic insult to people of colour!"

The book paints an absurdly optimistic picture of the slave-owning 'Miss Watson' by having her set free 'Nigger Jim'—who escaped because she planned to sell him for $800—in her will, Thompson complained.

"They could chain their field niggers and trade them for cattle, but deep in their hearts slave-owners were good people," she said sarcastically.

Education Department spokesman Peter Fowler said the province may strike the novel from school reading lists. "It's great literature but it may be too sensitive for high school."

Fowler pointed out that the novel—about the Mississippi River raft adventures of a rebellious white adolescent and the runaway slave—paints Jim as one of the only good people in the book. "But how do you get that across in the classroom?"

'Nigger Jim' uses a hairball from an ox's stomach to predict the future, and claims to know all about devils and witches. In a typical scene early in the novel, 'Nigger Jim' is terrified to see Huck, who is thought to have been murdered and dumped in the Mississippi.

"Doan' hurt me, don't!" 'Nigger Jim' cries out. "I haint never done no harm to a ghos'. I awluz liked dead people, en done all I could for 'em. You go en git in the river agin, whah you b'longs, en doan' do nuffn to Ole Jim, 'at 'uz awluz yo' fren'."

The next day, callers swamped *The Herald*'s switchboard. Don Betts took ten calls in half an hour. He didn't understand what the fuss was about. So Nigger Jim was big and dumb and superstitious and kind-hearted. What was wrong with that? Wasn't that true half the time? Weren't a lot of blacks like that? The phone rang incessantly. It was Grafton's day off, so Betts sent Chuck Maxwell out to do a man-in-the-street opinion survey about *Huckleberry Finn*.

Charlene Thompson wouldn't tell Edward Slade the name of the girl. Nor would the school principal. But he wasn't discouraged. Franklin High was in a wealthy suburb south of the University of Manitoba. How many fifteen-year-old black girls could possibly be in grade nine there?

Slade got to the school at lunch hour. He spotted a girl walking alone and asked her. Firmly. With authority in his voice. "Excuse me. I need to reach the girl mentioned in the paper today about the *Huckleberry Finn* incident. I forgot her name. What was it again?" She was an easy find in an all-white crowd. "Susan? I'm Edward Slade. Can I talk to you for a moment?"

She put down her sandwich. "Sure."

"How about at another table?"

"Here's okay," she said. Pleasant, mature voice. Cute kid. Soft brown skin. Braces. Long braids.

He had a tape recorder running inside his vest pocket. "I need to know about the Huck Finn incident. What happened, exactly?"

"I'd rather not talk about it," she said. "Who are you, anyway?"

"I'm with *The Winnipeg Star.*"

Susan's friends stared at him. One boy tapped Slade's shoulder. "Why don't you give her a break, eh?"

Slade persisted. "All I need to know—"

"I won't talk about it," Susan said. She turned to one of the boys. "Tell him to leave."

"You heard her," a second boy said, pushing Slade. "Stop it."

Slade stood up. Someone tripped him and he was knocked to the floor. A man and a woman rushed up. Both were gym teachers. Both were bigger than Slade.

"He's a reporter," one girl announced. "He was bothering Susan."

"We told him to leave her alone but he wouldn't go," one boy said.

"You'd better leave," the woman told Slade.

When Slade reached the door, the students broke out in a chorus of jeers and laughter.

It took Chuck an hour to get twenty people to stop and talk on Portage Avenue. It was cold outside. His pencil had broken and his pen kept freezing. Of the twenty, four had never heard of the book, six had no opinion, and ten said it was nonsense to ban the book. The twenty-first was a good-looking black woman in her late thirties. When he asked his question, she laughed nervously. "Do you know who I am?"

"No."

"You really don't know who I am? Is this some joke?"

"Lady, I don't have a whole lot of initials after my name. And I don't own a fancy house. But I'm an honest person and I do an honest job."

"I didn't mean to offend you. But I have no comment." The woman looked him up and down. "I do, though, have time for a coffee."

They found a table in the Eaton's cafeteria.

An hour later, Chuck charged into the newsroom.

"I found her," he shouted to the people clustered around the city desk. "I got hold of the girl's mom. The girl in the Huck Finn story."

"Well, don't talk about it," Don Betts said. "Write it."

Chuck hadn't had a scoop like this in months. He thought again of Elizabeth Manning: her strong, soft tones; her beauty, which he had found intoxicating. Chin raised, unflinching hazel eyes, slender brown cheeks raised in dimension by high bones. She had two children, Susan and a younger boy. She was a physiotherapist. She hadn't mentioned a husband. Chuck hadn't asked. They had had coffee, then refills; she had even let him buy her a croissant. He had felt a pang, with his notepad full, seeing her walk away. Maybe he should have found a woman and settled down and raised a family. He was thirty-seven and had been working twenty years and what did he have to show for it? Nothing. She was thirty-eight and, by all accounts, she had two kids who loved her. What more could one want? She had written down her address and phone number. She had reminded him that she didn't want to be named, or to have her daughter named. Elizabeth didn't want to have to make explanations at work, and she didn't want "half the world" singling out her daughter. Chuck had said he understood. Then she asked him a few questions. She wanted to know where he lived, if he had a family, how he liked his job, what other interests he had. Answering made him sad. "I don't have other interests, Madam, newspaper work is all I know. But I like people. I like people a lot. I consider myself a person." She laughed. He blushed. "What I mean is, I'm a person first, and a reporter after." She had to go. "I'll call sometime," he said. She smiled and offered her hand. He would call her. For sure. As soon as this article was out of the way. He'd just like to be her friend. Meet her kids. Chuck liked kids a lot.

A Jamaican-Canadian teen-aged girl likes *Huckleberry Finn* but resents having been picked from a Franklin High School class of 30 students to read aloud parts containing stereotyped references to blacks.

So says the girl's mother, who sparked a controversy over the teaching of the classic American novel after learning that her daughter had cried in class while reading the dialogue of 'Nigger Jim'.

In an exclusive interview with *The Herald,* the mother—who asked to remain anonymous—said it had been emotionally harmful for a grade nine teacher to assign the reading part based on the girl's skin colour.

"My daughter was singled out unfairly. It was implied that she could naturally read the part of 'Nigger Jim'. And that is wrong. She resembles a Missouri slave no more than anybody else in her school."

Chuck Maxwell knew his work wasn't great literature, or even great reporting. But the main thing was to get the facts right, make it interesting for people, and to remain fair. Okay, he could admit it: he wasn't a great reporter, never would be. Mahatma had potential, Chuck didn't. That was life. He could live with that. The thing to do was to change his priorities. Broaden them. He needed more in his life. He needed a woman.

"Chuck!" Don Betts was calling to him.

It was 5:00. Chuck donned his coat first, to signal to Betts that he was finished for the day. He put his notepad in his open coat pocket. Then he approached the city desk. His Huck Finn story was on Betts' computer screen.

"What's the lady's name?" Betts asked.

Chuck swallowed. "That's private."

"The names, Chuck. Don't give me a hard time."

"I have an agreement. . . ."

Betts jumped out of his seat. "You're an inch away from another suspension," Betts hissed. "This is a daily newspaper, not a cover-up society." Grabbing Chuck's lapel, Betts shot his free hand into Chuck's coat pocket and snatched out his notepad. He released Chuck and stepped back.

"Give me that back!" Chuck shouted.

Betts slipped behind a big desk. Chuck stepped after him. Betts danced around to the other side.

"Don!" Chuck warned.

"Ho ho," Betts said. He flipped open the notebook, dashed around the desk again to stay clear of Chuck, consulted it, ran again, turned two more pages, and found what he needed. "Elizabeth Manning, 245 Silverstone Avenue. Daughter: Susan Manning. Here you go, Chuck. Jolly good. You can go home now." Don Betts tossed him the notepad.

"You can't use that, Don."

"Oh?" Betts, smiling, typed something into Chuck's story.

"We had an agreement."

"What? Was this off the record?"

"No, she . . ."

"Did she speak to you on condition that you not use her name?"

"She asked me not to identify the family."

"Tell her your editor refused the request."

"But she made it clear she didn't want to be named."

"Chuck," Betts said, sighing, "you've been around a long time. You know the rules. If she didn't explicitly say she wouldn't talk unless you promised not to name her, we're clear. You can go home with a good conscience. If she gets angry, tell her it's my fault. Tell her to call me."

"But she understood that I wouldn't be using her name. She didn't have to put it in such words."

"That's her problem, isn't it? What are you so worried about?"

"It could hurt her," Chuck said.

"How?"

"At her work. She doesn't want people to know. It would embarrass her. And she's worried about her daughter. It's embarrassing for a teenager, having a newspaper say that you cried in school."

"She'll survive. It won't hurt her a bit. People like publicity. Makes 'em feel important. Don't worry about it, old buddy. It's in my hands now."

Chuck Maxwell's face contorted. He felt sick to his stomach. He had betrayed Elizabeth Manning.

"This is hardball, Chuck." Betts spoke softly. He stood up and patted the taller man's shoulder. "You make news, you ride the waves. Don't worry about the girl. She'll be fine. Now go home and celebrate! You're gonna be on page one."

Susan Manning answered the door. It was 8:00 on a pitch black January night. Outside, it was -4. The streetlights were out. Chuck noticed that all the porch and apartment lights on the street were out too. Power shortage. The girl at the door held a burning candle. Cute kid. Strangely, the braces made her cuter.

"Chuck!" Elizabeth welcomed him, but her eyes showed wariness.

Chuck told her what had happened. He apologized. He told her he was tempted to resign.

"You gave him your notebook?" Elizabeth said.

"He grabbed it. The man's crazy. He *grabbed* it from me." He told her he would try to strike their names from the story before the paper went to press.

She showed him out. "I never want to see you again "

Mahatma Grafton opened the door. A long time had passed since he had seen a man cry. "Chuck? What's the matter?"

Chuck blew his nose. "Do you have five minutes?" He told Ben and Mahatma every detail.

"I'll talk to Betts," Mahatma offered. "But don't hold your breath."

Mahatma found Don Betts in the Winnipeg Press Club. Betts clapped him on the shoulder and ordered two whiskies.

"I'll stick to beer," Mahatma said.

"You do that. I'll take the whiskies." Betts signalled again to the bartender. Then he looked back at Mahatma. "Put that money away! I'm paying!"

The drinks came. They sat for a moment, sizing each other up.

"How's your beer?" Betts asked. Pool balls kissed. A love song wailed from the jukebox. Mahatma sipped from his glass. "I know you can't stand my guts," Betts said, "and think I'm a heartless asshole. But you want something from me. Otherwise, you wouldn't be here."

"It's about Chuck's follow-up on the Huck Finn story."

"He's pissed off that I'm naming the kid and her mother."

"You made him betray a confidence. Chuck wants you to protect the woman's anonymity. That's what he had promised to do."

"This is a newspaper! Every day we name people against their wishes."

"Nothing would be served by publishing the kid's name."

"How about the public's right to know? How about the competitive advantage of *The Winnipeg Herald?*"

"What 'competitive advantage'?"

"You know and I know that Edward Slade is onto this story. And even if we hold the names, he won't. It'll be right there, out in the public, printed by *The Winnipeg Star.* Why let them scoop us? Tell Chuck to forget it. We're naming the Huck Finn lady and her kid, and that's it."

Yoyo was researching one of his last major articles on Canada. Since education was of utmost importance to his countrymen in Cameroon, he focussed on that subject. And since prominent newspaper articles for two consecutive days had referred to a school crisis involving the study of an American classic, Yoyo tackled that issue. He had heard of Mark Twain, but had never read his works. He borrowed *Huckleberry Finn* from the library, but found it hard going. Yoyo read newspapers and magazines without difficulty; he had read books on botany in Canada, he had read about politics, and he had even tried stories by Ernest Hemingway and Alice Munro: all this he had understood. But *Huckleberry Finn* baffled him. The author struck him as close to illiterate, using colloquialisms such as 'ain't'. It eventually became evident to Yoyo that the author was speaking through the voice of a boy. This struck Yoyo as unreasonable. Why use a boy who can't speak properly? And if he can't even speak properly, how could he write a 220-page book? Worse still, large chunks of dialogue muddled Yoyo beyond measure. "Dog my cats ef I didn' hear sumf'n." What could that mean? Yoyo consulted a dictionary frequently. But neither Webster's nor the reputable Oxford defined 'sumf'n'. And 'dog' as a verb?

Mahatma Grafton was working at a furious pace. So far that day, he had placed ten phone calls and filled a notepad with scribbling. He had talked to two lawyers, three leaders of the Franco-Manitoban community, four politicians and a mandarin in Ottawa. He had managed not only to confirm Goyette's scoop about constitutional negotiations between Franco-Manitoban leaders and government officials, but to push the story further! He would have it sewn up within two days. He dialled another number. Busy. He massaged his right hand. It was stiff from writing. He had a sore spot on the inside first joint of his middle finger.

A hand landed on his shoulder. Mahatma bolted up in his seat.

"Hey, Hat," boomed Chuck Maxwell's friendly voice, "I've seen you dial the same number four times in two minutes. The guy's on the phone, man, give him a second. Relax. You'll get an ulcer working like that. You should consider that, you know. Does *The Herald* pay your life insurance? Are they gonna support you if you burn out and stop producing?"

Mahatma sat back and exhaled.

"That's better," Chuck said. "Why kill yourself for a newspaper that couldn't give a shit about you? Sometimes you gotta get existential about these things. You know, like, 'What am I doing this for?' "

Mahatma dialled the number again. Chuck opened a *Playboy* magazine. He tried to direct Mahatma's eyes toward a pair of breasts. Mahatma ignored him, got someone on the phone and bent his neck to scribble.

Don Betts signalled to Chuck, who walked up to the city editor's desk and was handed a letter to the editor. "This guy calls himself the president of the League Against the French Takeover of Manitoba. Find out what he has to say. Here's his address. Don't phone him. Drive out to his place. Better go right now." Betts walked him to the coat rack and watched him leave the newsroom. Mahatma hung up the phone and began dialling again. Betts interrupted him. "Hat! There's a health convention at the Holiday Inn. Cover what's left of it, would you? Hurry up—the federal health minister is to give a major speech there in a few minutes." It was 4:00. "Cover the whole conference. File two stories if you can. We'll pay the overtime."

The president of the League Against the French Takeover of Manitoba wasn't home. His wife directed Chuck to the school where he worked. Chuck got stuck in traffic and didn't make it there until 4:30. The man was out and didn't return until 5:00. They spoke for ten minutes. Chuck didn't understand a word of what the man said. He took notes as best he could, raced back to the office, got there at 5:30 and filed his story just before 6:00, which was when his shift ended. His short, confusing article was woefully inadequate.

"Perfect," Don Betts mumbled after bidding Chuck good night. Just as he expected. Chuck had fucked up, again.

Mahatma returned to the office at 6:30 and filed two stories. Betts asked, "Can you do some more overtime?"

"I've already done an hour and a half," Mahatma said.

"We need this for tomorrow. And it's up your alley. This guy says he's president of the League Against the French Takeover of Manitoba."

Mahatma identified himself to the woman who answered the door.

"Media?" she said. "Someone was here earlier looking for Wilbur. And you're from *The Herald?* I thought he was too. But I guess not. He must have been from *The Star.*"

A tall, gentle-looking man appeared. He had a dark beard. "Good evening! I'm Wilbur Lawson." He spoke with a resonant confidence; his little eyes shone. He extended a fleshy palm. Mahatma introduced himself. "Will you join us for coffee and dessert?" Lawson asked. "My wife just baked a pie."

"If you don't mind," Mahatma said, "I'll pass on the offer. I'm facing a deadline and would like to start right in with a few questions."

Lawson said that would be fine. Mahatma began with the basics: Wilbur Lawson was forty-six, taught at John Bell Elementary School, formed the league two months ago and had no official members yet. He planned to hold an introductory meeting in two weeks to explain his beliefs and take memberships. Dozens of people had responded to his ads in community newspapers. Lawson showed him one such ad: "Do YOU want YOUR CHILDREN to HAVE to speak French? To face UNEMPLOYMENT and DISCRIMINATION if they don't?"

"Do you honestly believe that?" Mahatma asked.

"I wouldn't write it if I didn't believe it," Lawson said. "I don't expect you media folks to agree with me, but you owe it to the public to take dissenters seriously." Lawson went on for a few minutes about the Franco-Manitoban issue. Suddenly, three phrases jarred Mahatma: "I don't say ban the language. That would be premature. I won't complain if they speak it in the privacy of their homes."

Mahatma scribbled the sentences in his notepad. Then he asked, "Why do you refer to a takeover of Manitoba? What takeover?"

"Throughout this century, English has been the increasingly dominant language of Manitoba. Ukrainians, Poles, Germans, Icelanders and others have accepted English as the language of our legislature, our courts, our government, our businesses.

Speaking it didn't diminish your ethnic roots; it just meant you were Manitoban. Canadian. But all of a sudden, the French want to jump the queue. They want the same status as the English. But what about the rest of us? Why recognize only the French? What makes them so special? Population-wise, they are smaller than the British, the Germans and the Ukrainians in Manitoba. Why should they impose their language on us?"

"You believe you won't be able to function in Manitoba without speaking French?"

"My children won't. If they want a good job but they can't speak French, forget it." Mahatma took a few more notes. The inaugural meeting in two weeks would be followed by a protest rally. "When the government comes clean and announces its French plans, Manitobans are going to kick up a fuss the likes of which people haven't seen in decades."

Mahatma hurried back to the newsroom. After calling the Francophone Association of Manitoba and the premier's office for reaction, he wrote the story.

> A Winnipeg school teacher has founded a league to battle what he claims is the pending "takeover" of the province by Franco-Manitobans.
> "I have nothing against French," said Wilbur Lawson, 46, "as long as it is spoken in the privacy of one's home. . . ."

As he passed the Manitoba Legislature on his walk home, something struck Mahatma as bizarre. Why was Don Betts so good-humoured that night? Why did he happily authorize Mahatma's overtime pay sheet?

Don Betts got precisely what he expected. Grafton's story was well written. It included comments from critics of the league. It was good reporting. Which made it one hundred times better than the story filed on the same subject by Chuck Maxwell. Which set Chuck up for a suspension due to incompetence. Betts dropped the note on Chuck's lap at work the next morning.

Chuck emerged from the city editor's office in tears. He ran up to Mahatma, who was staring at disbelief at *The Herald*. His health seminar stories hadn't run at all, but the blurb on Lawson had hit page one.

"They suspended me for two weeks," Chuck howled.

Everyone in the newsroom was watching. "Why, Chuck?"

"'Because you scooped me."

"I *what?*"

"You double-covered me on that Lawson story. But how could you know? I fucked up and you scooped me!"

Mahatma walked with Chuck to the coat rack, walked with him to the elevator, rode down to the first floor with him, and then took four flights of stairs, very slowly, back up to the editorial room. He walked past the city editor's desk, ignoring Betts. He walked past Lyndon Van Wuyss' secretary, who was talking on the telephone, and opened the managing editor's door. "Revoke Chuck's suspension," Mahatma said.

Van Wuyss stared blankly at him. Betts ran into the office.

"It's totally unfair," Mahatma said. "Chuck assumed he had to finish that story before his shift ended. He had ten minutes to talk to the man. I had an hour. He didn't have time to call other people. I did. He isn't familiar with the issue. I am. You used me to hurt him and that is insulting to both of us. Revoke the suspension."

"Don told me Chuck had all afternoon to get that story," Van Wuyss said.

"That's a lie," Mahatma said. "I was talking to him at 4:00 when Betts assigned him the story."

"Don?" Van Wuyss asked.

"What's it matter?" Betts said. "He fucked up. He always fucks up."

"He had ten minutes to talk to the guy and ten minutes to write the story," Mahatma said. "He lost the rest of the time in rush-hour traffic."

"Is that true, Don?" Van Wuyss said.

"His copy was a mess. He's useless, Lyndon."

"You could have had another reporter fill in the gaps," Mahatma said. "I resent being manipulated, especially to hurt another reporter. Revoke the suspension or I'm quitting." Mahatma felt a surge of freedom. Of power.

"You don't have to get dramatic about it," Van Wuyss said. "I'll revoke the suspension because Don misled me about the situation. I am, however, giving Chuck three weeks off. With pay. He needs a rest. You can get back to work now."

As he left the managing editor's office, Mahatma heard Betts grumbling, then raising his voice. Mahatma passed the secretary and entered the newsroom and could still hear Betts shouting. So could several other reporters. They crowded around Mahatma, demanding details, slapping him on the back.

"What's Betts doing in there?" someone asked.

"His wild man routine," someone else answered.

"We should phone Chuck."

"Yeah, let's call Chuck. Let's tell him about it."

But Chuck wasn't home. His phone went unanswered all day.

Mahatma broke his big story two days later. It ran across four columns over the fold on page one. It was moved by Canadian Press and picked up by *The Toronto Times, The Toronto Star,* the French and English dailies in Montreal, and other major newspapers across the country. It sent reporters from *The Times, The Star* and all the Manitoba media scrambling to match the story.

> Premier Gilford has agreed to amend the Canadian Constitution by making French an official language of Manitoba.
>
> In a tentative accord with the Francophone Association of Manitoba and federal officials, Gilford has agreed to translate 450 public statutes, double the number of bilingual civil servants and entrench a constitutional obligation to provide more government services in French, *The Herald* has learned.
>
> In exchange, FAM has agreed to drop plans to ask the Supreme Court of Canada to invalidate thousands of Manitoba laws that have been enacted in English only. . . .

Television, radio and newspapers zoomed in on the language accord. Radio talk shows were deluged with calls accusing the provincial government of "ramming French down our throats." Anti-French graffiti reappeared in St. Boniface. *The Herald* was swamped with angry letters. Media coverage raged for three days and was beginning to die down when Edward Slade broke a scoop in *The Star* about the Princeton-St. Albert hockey riot.

> Manitoba Provincial Police have quietly charged a 17-year-old English-speaking boy with killing Gilles Baril, the Francophone youth slain here last November in a bench-clearing hockey brawl.
>
> Police arrested the accused youth in his Princeton home late Tuesday afternoon. He was driven to the Winnipeg Detention Centre and held overnight.
>
> On Wednesday, instead of appearing in the Winnipeg Youth and Family Court—which is closely watched by reporters—the boy was returned to a smaller court in Raleigh, a town 20 kilometres southeast of Princeton.
>
> The case was remanded for two weeks. The accused, who by law cannot be named by the media, was granted bail on condition that he remain in Princeton in his parents' custody.
>
> The hockey brawl made national headlines when . . .

Every media outlet in Manitoba scrambled to match the story.

Wilbur Lawson pushed ahead the date for the first public meeting of the League Against the French Takeover of Manitoba. He also changed the place of the meeting, calling on Manitobans to converge in Princeton in support of the town's English community. Lawson advertised the time, place and purpose in *The Herald* and *The Star.* People showed up at his door ahead of time and volunteered to help. He had to disconnect his phone to sleep at night. In a rented church basement in Princeton, the first meeting of the League Against the French Takeover of Manitoba attracted eight hundred people.

"Fellow citizens," began the bearded orator. "I have a question to ask. You, undoubtedly, have a question to ask. Will anybody answer us?" He was greeted by thunderous applause. "I'm not worried for myself. I can survive. You, surely, are not worried for yourselves; you are industrious people. My question is, what is the future for my children? Where are they going to work? Why do they have to learn French? Who has the right to change the rules in the middle of their lives?" The audience roared. Media coverage was guaranteed. Mahatma had attended the meeting.

So had reporters from *The Winnipeg Star, The Toronto Times,* CBC-TV, six radio stations and Montreal's *La Presse.* To the rolling cameras and ready pens, the crowd jumped to its feet and picked up a cry from the back: "No More French. No More French." Wilbur Lawson waved his arms in protest. After five minutes, he got the crowd to settle down. He called out for tolerance. He said that he had nothing against the French and that they had every right to live in Manitoba. He just didn't want them taking over the province.

"But who started the hockey riot?" shouted a voice from the crowd.

"And who murdered the English kid, on the highway?" someone else cried out. "Why haven't the cops nabbed *his* killer?"

Applause burst out again. Lawson waited it out, told the crowd to leave criminal matters to the police, and outlined a strategy to end the French takeover. He urged LAFTOM members to write to public officials and to prepare to attend the next meeting, which would be a rally in front of the Manitoba Legislature.

A marriage proposal by Yoyo—the second within two weeks—prompted Helen to break off their affair. The first proposal made Helen chuckle. But the second frightened her. The man was serious. "But you are my woman," he argued. "You will have my children. You will come to Cameroon and become my mother's daughter."

"No. Is that clear? No. I don't want to see you again. And I will certainly not marry you. Ever."

Yoyo kept his dignity. He didn't argue any more. And he didn't call her again.

One of Mahatma Grafton's articles left Helen spellbound. It was the story about Wilbur Lawson. "I can't believe it," she muttered.

Lawson was still at it. After all these years. She thought back to public school, to her sudden refusal to speak French as a child, to all the years she had detested all that was French in her. Helen recalled everything about Lawson. For years she had tried to forget the incident; now she lingered over it.

She had been six years old. In grade one. Betty Perry, sitting behind her, had yanked her pigtails; Hélène, as she was known then, swivelled in her chair. "Stop it Betty." "I don't want to." "Stop it!" "You're just a little brat!" Betty told her. "Et toi," Hélène hissed back, slipping into the language in which she knew insults, "tu es la plus stupide de toute la classe!"

Betty raised her hand. Her words rang out in the class, terrifying Hélène. "Mr. Lawson!" Betty cried out. "Mr. Lawson, Helen is saying bad things in French!"

"Is that true, Helen?" Mr. Lawson said. She said nothing. "Come to the front of the class and repeat what you said." Hélène shook her head from side to side. "To the front of the class!" Walking up between two columns of desks, Hélène thought she was going to die. "Tell us what you told Betty," Mr. Lawson said.

"I said . . ."

"Tell us in French."

"J'ai dit qu'elle était la plus stupide de toute la classe."

"Say that again, Helen."

Hélène said it again.

"Does anybody understand what Helen is saying?" Three other girls in the class were francophones. Hélène spoke with them in French in the school yard, in the school corridors and when they played at home. But Cécile, Linda and Sophie remained mute when Mr. Lawson asked the question. "Nobody understands what you said, Helen." The teacher's hand gripped her shoulder. "Do you think that's fair? Would you like it if somebody talked to you in a language you couldn't understand?"

"No."

"Are you going to speak in French again to Betty?"

"No."

"Then tell Betty you're sorry."

"I'm sorry, Betty."

"You may sit down now."

The next day, Mr. Lawson again called Hélène before the class.

"Tell everybody how to say 'hello, how are you?' in French."
Hélène said nothing. "Go ahead."

"Bonjour, comment ça va?" she whimpered.

"Say it again."

"Bonjour, comment ça va?"

"Did everybody hear that? 'Bonjour, comment ça va?' means
'hello, how are you?' in French. Would some of you like to try
saying it? You don't have to if you don't want to." The class
mumbled the new sounds. "That's it. Now you know how to say
'hello, how are you?' in French. That's one language. It's okay to
speak in French if everybody knows what you're saying. But
English is the language we speak in class. Isn't it, Helen?"

"Yes, Mr. Lawson."

"You may be seated."

Around that point, Hélène started calling herself Helen.

Helen thought about it for a week. But after Mahatma broke the
scoop about the language accord, and after he continued writing
about the Franco-Manitoban controversy, she decided to speak to
him. She came to him in the newsroom, where he was writing a
feature about French history in Manitoba. "Hat, when we were at
Polonia Park, I promised to tell you about myself one day. Speaking
French, and all that." He looked at her now, with interest. "How
about tonight, at seven, at the Lox and Bagel?" Helen said.

"Great."

That evening, they sat in a café serving hefty soups and
muffins. Mahatma heard the espresso machine produce a
rushing gurgle of steam; he watched the man pour frothy milk
over coffee and dot it with cinnamon. A waitress brought them
two mugs of café au lait. "So you speak French after all, but you
don't like to admit it," Mahatma said.

"Oh, I don't mind admitting it any more. You'll see. This all
has to do with Wilbur Lawson."

"Really?" Mahatma studied her face. Her brow was pinched into intense little ridges of flesh; her eyes were brown and large. "He was my grade one teacher at the John Bell Elementary School. He made me ashamed of my language. I suspect he is still doing it to other students. And now he is getting favourable press. Even your article legitimized him." She described the incident.

"Did you tell your parents?" Mahatma asked.

"Are you kidding? I hated them because they were French. I wanted to be like the English kids."

"Did Lawson ever harass you again?"

"No. But he did drone on about how French people had to live in English in Manitoba. The French had lost on the Plains of Abraham so they might as well accept the fact that Canada ran on English. That was how he said it. Canada runs on English."

Mahatma got a phone call from Wilbur Lawson the next day. "I have a story for you," he began. "I have a letter here from the superintendent of the Winnipeg School Division. He has suspended me for 'activities incompatible with my role as a teacher.' "

"What does that mean?"

"It means they didn't like me talking about English rights."

"Does the letter actually say so?"

"Yes."

"Why do you think this happened so quickly?" Mahatma asked.

"The French activists did it. I have information that they leaned on the minister of education, who leaned on my superintendent. This is a gag. It's frightening and it shows how right I was about a French takeover."

Mahatma scribbled down the quote. He was sceptical about the French activists angle, but curious enough to look into it. In the meantime, the suspension was news in itself. Mahatma arranged for Lawson to send him the suspension letter by courier.

The story fell into place easily. The superintendent confirmed the suspension, and the head of the Francophone Association of Manitoba admitted to telling the premier that Lawson should be fired. "He shouldn't be teaching children—some of whom are French—if he publicly promotes anti-French attitudes."

Mahatma took a company car to the Legislature, hoping to catch somebody in the premier's office for comment. This had the makings of a good story.

Nobody had time to see him. Mahatma Grafton was too busy. So was No Quotes Hailey. Nobody had time to see Chuck Maxwell during his three-week suspension. *The Herald* was calling it a paid vacation, but Chuck considered it a suspension. You were a nobody if you didn't work. You felt different, walking down Portage Avenue. You wondered if people looked at you and asked themselves: Doesn't this bum work?

They called on the last day of his suspension to say that he would now be working the 4:00 to midnight shift. He didn't complain. He was glad to have any shift at all. He would show them. He would chase down some great stories and scoop the competition. Arriving in the newsroom, Chuck looked for Mahatma and heard he was out researching a story. Chuck shook out a newspaper and scanned it. He sat close to the police radio in case something exciting broke. He had a feeling about himself. He was going to make it. If he kept his ears and eyes open, he would prove to *The Herald* that he still had a few tricks left.

Don Betts came in at 4:15 but assigned nothing to Chuck. Two hours passed. Chuck phoned the police and fire departments; that earned him a few news bullets. He wrote them carefully, double-checking for spelling and accuracy.

Betts stepped out for coffee at 8:00 p.m. Ten minutes later, a voice blared on the police radio. Chuck turned it up. "Provencher Boulevard," the voice crackled. "Francophone Association of Manitoba, 348 Provencher Boulevard; there has been an explosion at the Francophone Association of Manitoba, major fire has broken out, onlookers must be kept back."

Chuck grabbed his coat and ran to the elevator. He passed Don Betts on the way. "There's been a big explosion at the FAM."

Chuck started his car. While it warmed up, he pulled his rubber boots and workpants and raincoat from the trunk. He carried them in his car for situations like this. You didn't cover a fire wearing a $400 suit. Chuck wriggled into his clothes and sped north on Smith Street. He ran two red lights.

Chuck knew fires. You didn't park too close. If it spread, cops and fire-fighters would need room. He parked on a side street and jogged toward the blaze, which was red and orange and grey against the bluish-black sky. He noted six police cruisers. Three fire-trucks. Now was the time to pick up information. Once the cops got organized, they would rope off the street. One cop was trying to keep people back. He was having a hell of a time. Chuck smiled. He knew the cop. He knew half the cops in Winnipeg. "Hey Bill," he cried out. "How's it hanging?"

"Bad, Chuck. Better keep back."

"Ah, don't try that on me, old buddy, you know I've got a job to do."

"You're going in there at your own risk, Chuck."

Chuck advanced. The heat toasted his face. Firemen were shooting water at the flames. The jets seemed useless against the fury of red and orange and yellow, and the crackling hiss of three storeys of burning wood. Sloshing through water, Chuck approached a fireman aiming his hose at the east side of the building. Somebody shouted a warning at him. He kept on, using an arm to shield his forehead from the heat. He coughed but didn't even hear the sound, which was swallowed up by the roar of flames devouring wood. He got beside the fireman. Chuck looked into the man's face. Hell, he knew that guy! It was Keith Tysoe. They had played hockey together years ago. "Keith. What's happening? How did it start?"

"You!" Keith Tysoe shouted. "The fuck you doing here? Get back!"

"How did it start?"

The ground erupted. Chuck landed on his back. Tysoe had also been blown off his feet. The fire hose twisted in the air, smashing Tysoe between the eyes, drawing a river of blood and snaking away.

"*Keith!*" Chuck crawled through the mud and the water. He heard screams. Light flashed high above him. A blinding swirl of heat curved outward and swooned down through the air. Something smashed his leg. Weight bore down on him mercilessly. His clothes were burning. Chuck screamed. He pulled. He scraped and clawed and squirmed but he couldn't move, couldn't free himself, couldn't help Keith Tysoe, couldn't do anything. I'm going to die, he thought. He twisted again, gasping and choking. Even his hands were on fire. I thought I was wearing gloves. I *was*. I *was* wearing gloves. Something pulled him, lifted him, took him away. He lost consciousness.

It was a cloudless winter night. Mahatma drove away from the Manitoba Legislature. All he had to do was write the story of Lawson's suspension. He had found out that the premier's office had, indeed, contacted the school superintendent to complain about Lawson.

Mahatma looked forward to talking to Chuck, who was returning to work today from his suspension. Mahatma would slap Chuck on the shoulder in welcome. He felt guilty about not having had time to see Chuck recently. Mahatma stopped at a red light and flicked on the car radio. "Here is a flash news bulletin. An explosion rocked the offices of the Francophone Association of Manitoba minutes ago. Police and firemen are at the scene. The building is ablaze. The group has been the object of intense criticism recently. . . ."

Mahatma accelerated, ran several yellow lights, motored over the Provencher Bridge and into St. Boniface. He heard sirens. An ambulance overtook him and another came behind. A fire-truck charged around a corner. Mahatma saw flames and the black, belching clouds of smoke against the moonlit sky. He parked and ran to the scene. He pushed through the crowd until he came to a rope drawn across the sidewalk. Patrick MacGrearicque barred his way. "Superintendent! Superintendent! Let me through."

"No way. One of your buddies has just about killed himself."

Mahatma shouted, "I can't hear you."

"Chuck Maxwell just got himself fried. Got too close. Beam ripped loose, came down on him."

"Where is he? Let me see him."

MacGrearicque called over another officer. "This is a friend of that reporter who got burned. Get him out of here. See if that ambulance is gone. If not, send him off with the victim." The big cop led Mahatma away. They passed inside the police lines, away from the crowds. A light swirled on an ambulance forty yards away. Mahatma saw a stretcher being loaded into it. An attendant ran to the driver's door, jumped in and gunned the accelerator. The siren wailed. Something stuck in Mahatma's throat.

The cop asked, "Friend of yours?" He was supporting Mahatma, whose head bobbed. "He'll be okay. I've seen worse. It's the fireman who really got it bad. I doubt he'll make it through the night."

"What happened?"

"Building was bombed. Blew a hole right out the east wall. That was the wall that came down on your buddy and the fireman."

Mahatma was gathering his senses. "What's your name?"

"Stafford. Corporal John Stafford."

"Thanks."

"Don't mention it. Who are you, anyway?"

"Mahatma Grafton. From *The Herald*."

"Jesus! We're under orders not to talk to you."

The blaze engulfed the building. Mahatma had to see Chuck. He had to contact *The Herald*. Walking to his car, he met FAM president Pierre Gratton and scribbled down his comments. Then he interviewed two bystanders who had seen the building erupt in flames. Then he worked his way back to MacGrearicque.

The cop said, "I thought I got rid of you!"

"I feel better now."

"Yeah, right! You're in shock."

"Just tell me how you'll handle this investigation."

"We assume it's arson. They used a bomb."

"They?"

"Tell you about it sometime. Now get out of here."

"This was motivated by French-English tensions?"

"We'll look into it. Go home, Mahatma. You look like shit."

Mahatma drove to the hospital. While waiting to see a doctor, he called Betts. The city editor was stunned. He asked Mahatma if he had details about the fire. He wanted a story, but Mahatma was in no mood. Then a doctor came out. "You're Chuck's friend?"

"Yes. Is he gonna make it?"

"It's touch and go. Sixty percent of his body has been burnt."

"Can I see him?"

"Not today."

"Is he conscious?"

"He's in and out. We have sedated him."

"What happened to the fireman?"

"He died in the ambulance. The burning beam that hit Chuck's leg caught him on the chest. He didn't have a chance. Look, I've got to go."

Mahatma drove to the office. He wrote the stories on the fire and on Lawson's suspension, and took a taxi home, exhausted. He told his father about it, couldn't sleep, called the hospital, couldn't get any more information and fell into fitful nightmares.

Mahatma hurried to a gift shop and scanned the get-well cards. Humorous or serious? A humorous card might offend Chuck. Mahatma purchased the most sober card on the rack. Helen Savoie was the first to sign it. Together, they circulated in the newsroom, getting ten reporters, the switchboard operator and all three librarians to sign the card. But then they learned the hospital wasn't letting anybody visit Chuck.

"Poor bastard," Norman Hailey said. "Remember how he liked to remind us that *The Herald* doesn't pay life insurance?"

Paul Holtz held up the newspaper. "Somebody ought to show Chuck the front page. He'll want to frame it."

Page one ran a two-column head about the FAM explosion that killed a fireman and critically injured a reporter. A sidebar contained a picture of Chuck and a few more inches of copy. It gave his age, said he'd joined the paper at age sixteen and described him as one of the best-liked reporters on staff.

"He'll be bragging for years about how he got third-degree burns covering a news story," Hailey said. "He'll be telling people it was the number one story of the year."

"Of the *year?*" Holtz said mockingly. "Listen! This was the biggest story of the decade and no ten-alarm fire was gonna keep him back."

Mahatma imitated Chuck's deep voice. " I went after that story and I'm proud of it. As a professional journalist, you have to be committed. You have to be a man of the people. That's what I am." When Helen chuckled, Mahatma squeezed her shoulder.

Chuck was placed in the hospital's burn unit. He was kept naked on a damp, no-stick sheet resembling cheesecloth. Other sheets were suspended over him like a tent. Sedated, he was connected to an electrocardiogram, a respirator and an intravenous unit. He managed, nevertheless, to ask the name of the doctor standing over him and to flirt with the nurse. Later, he kept asking for Hat. Nobody understood what he meant. He also asked for Elizabeth. "Elizabeth who?" someone asked him urgently. "Elizabeth! The Huck Finn lady."

After thirty-six hours, they reduced Chuck's heavy sedation. He asked again for Hat, and this time added, "My buddy. Mahatma. At the paper." Someone at the hospital called Mahatma, who drove to the hospital with Betts.

A nurse met them. "Two visitors?" Betts explained that Chuck had no family. He claimed to be Chuck's closest friend.

"You can see him for five minutes. Put on these gowns, masks, gloves and shoe covers. Don't touch the patient or anything in the room."

It was a private room with no window. A heart monitor, built into the wall above the bed, had several wires running into the tent over Chuck's body. Chuck's face was covered, to protect it from airborne germs. An intravenous unit stood dripping by his bed. A urine bag was empty. Chuck lay motionless in his tent.

"Chuck," Mahatma whispered. "It's Mahatma. Are you awake?"

"Glad you came, Hat. Awful glad. Who's with you?"

"It's me, Chuck. Don Betts."

"Jesus Christ, I don't believe it," Chuck said. Betts laughed loudly. "I didn't think I was gonna make it," Chuck said.

"Sure you're gonna make it," Mahatma said. "We need you back at *The Herald*. You hit the front page, Chuck. Your picture and everything." Chuck grunted. He sounded tired. "We've got a card for you with lots of signatures. We left it with the nurses." Chuck grunted again.

The nurse stepped into the room and held up a finger: they had one more minute.

"Come here, Don," Chuck's voice was weak. Betts stood close to the bed. "Do me a favour."

"You name it, Chuck. Whatever you want."

"Have a heart, next time a reporter fucks up. Anyway, I forgive you. I forgive you for everything. Now get out of here. I want to talk to Hat."

Betts shrugged and stepped back. "He must be delirious," he muttered to Mahatma.

The nurse escorted Betts from the room. Then she came back for Mahatma. "It's time to go."

"Wait a minute," Chuck said. "C'mere, Hat."

"Yes, buddy?" Mahatma said.

"I want you to fuck off."

"Sure, Chuck."

"You're my friend, right? So I'm telling you, as a friend, to fuck off out of *The Herald*. Go do something better. Fuck off to the Greek islands. Crete. Go to Crete to . . ." Chuck gasped. Then he started up again. "Write. Write your ass off. Do some great book. Do it for me, Hat. Do it for you. Go write a novel. A great novel."

"I don't write fiction, Chuck," Mahatma said, stupidly.

"Go write one anyway. You've got one in you, Hat. You've got better things in you. You've . . ." Chuck lost his breath, again.

"You must leave now," the nurse said.

"Bye, Chuck," Mahatma said. Chuck said nothing more.

The next day, hospital staff told Mahatma that Chuck's condition had deteriorated. The doctor advised against visiting. Mahatma called back later but couldn't reach the doctor. The next morning he learned that Chuck had developed an infection. The day after that, the hospital didn't return his phone calls.

Mahatma busied himself with a story on the anti-French backlash—enraged by a *Herald* editorial in favour of the language accord, LAFTOM supporters had flooded *The Herald's* switchboard with phone calls one day, making it impossible for regular business to get through. As soon as Mahatma finished the article, he took a taxi to the hospital.

Mahatma was desperate to see his friend. But he didn't want to jeopardize Chuck's health, barging into the room without sanitized hospital garments. He stood around feeling awkward but when a nurse told him to wait downstairs, he said, "I'll wait right here." This meant more to him than getting any story. This was Chuck's life. "He's my friend. We work together. We are like family! I have a right to know how he is doing!"

An hour later Mahatma raised his head from his palm and looked up to see a nurse conferring with a doctor. Both of them were looking at him. Mahatma got to his feet. "I've been trying for two days to find out about Chuck."

The doctor led Mahatma down the corridor. "I don't think your friend is going to make it."

"He's not?"

"He has developed a pseudomonas bacterial infection, an overwhelming bodily infection. It is extremely hard to stop. The signs look bad. Blood pressure, heart rate, temperature, urination—"

"Can I see him?"

"All right. Ask for garments at the nursing station."

Mahatma changed into the hospital clothes and approached Chuck's bed. "Chuck? It's me."

"Mahatma!" Chuck croaked. "Mahatma!"

"Hang in there, Chuck." That sounded so stupid. It sounded like encouragement to a runner, or a boxer. "Everybody is asking about you."

"Mahatma!" Chuck cried.

"Yes, Chuck."

"C'mere."

"I'm right here, Chuck. Can I do anything? Is there anything you want?"

"Stay here. You're my buddy, right? You never screwed me around, and I never screwed you around. Buddies, right?"

"Sure." Mahatma swallowed hard. "Sure we are." He wondered if he should tell Chuck about the card again. The card and the flowers and his picture on the front page. Chuck grunted. He gasped. He sighed and shivered and then he slept.

The telephone rang in the night. Mahatma jumped up, yanked it from the cradle and mumbled into it.

"Mr. Grafton?" a voice asked. "I'm very sorry. Chuck died this morning."

PART FIVE

Edward Slade hadn't written a decent victim story in a month—no old ladies shooting purse-snatchers, nobody killed by falling icicles, no one crippled saving someone else's life. There wasn't even any police corruption to be found. News was so dead that Slade imagined that cops were behaving well solely to starve the tabloid business. He persuaded his editor to let him take a run at the French rights controversy. Why leave all the good stuff to Mahatma Grafton?

Slade's first story ran under the headline *What's All the Fuss About?*

> The Manitoba government wants to make French an official language of the province. It wants the rights of Franco-Manitobans spelled out in the Constitution. Here's what the government says about the language deal:
> - French will become an official language in Manitoba
> - the province will need 500 bilingual employees within three years to boost services in French
> - Manitoba will translate 450 statutes, or about 10,000 pages, into French

But here's what critics say:
- it's unfair to other ethnic groups to give the French language number one status (right up there with English) when Franco-Manitobans number only 50,000 and rank as the province's fourth largest linguistic group
- it takes jobs from those who don't speak French
- it paves the way for the French to dominate Manitoba

Do YOU want French to be official here? Take part in *The Star* survey by filling out the questionnaire below.

Next, Slade published a report card on the players in the French language crisis. He had used this device on the cop beat once, ranking police inspectors by performance. His readers loved it. And nothing infuriated a police inspector more than seeing the mark "C minus" next to his photo in *The Star.*

Jake Corbett's leg hurt. His foot was swelling. Sometimes, it felt like somebody was hitting his leg with a hammer. The skin was rotting on his lower right calf. The blood wasn't circulating well. His skin there had turned into a charcoal black broken only by the pinkish, coin-sized ulcers of cracked and open flesh. On top of that, his room was too hot. Downstairs in the Accidental Dog and Grill, Frank cranked up the heat too high. His clients liked coming in off Main Street to sit in the warm and steamy café. But all the heat went upstairs, pouring out the air vent in the wall near his bed.

Jake began spending a lot of time in the Flapjack Café, on Main Street just north of the railway underpass. The cook didn't mind Jake spreading his welfare documents all over the table. One day, the cook, whose name was Harry Carson, said, "Hey Jake, how do you feel about eating with black folks all the time?"

Jake looked him in the eye and said, "I don't mind black people, so long as they keep their pamphlets to themselves and don't go putting them on my table." Harry doubled over at that one.

Jake told Harry that his lawyer, a lady named Brenda, was helping him fight the welfare people. She was working on getting Jake a vacation. Everybody else got to take holidays. Why not people on welfare? Jake wanted welfare to pay for a three-week vacation in Toronto and Montreal.

Harry Carson thought, this fellow doesn't have it all together. There was nothing sadder than the sight of a poor white man. Harry couldn't understand it. If *he* were white, he would have made train conductor. Hell, he would have made engineer.

Jake Corbett got lucky. Two days after he read in *The Herald* that some group called the League Against French something was to demonstrate outside the Legislature, the police returned his confiscated loud hailer. Jake took it to the demonstration and wandered through the crowd, looking for a good place to speak.

Edward Slade tapped his shoulder. "Hey Jake, what you doing here?"

"I got something to tell the people."

Slade started scribbling in a notepad that seemed to drop out of his sleeve. "You agree with the league?"

"Sure."

"You think it's wrong to make French official?"

"Sure."

"You oppose constitutional changes, translation costs, et cetera?"

"Right on."

"Why?"

"It's a waste of taxpayers' money," Jake said. He meant to tell Slade that what the government ought to do is scrap welfare and bring in a new idea: Guarantee Annual Income. This was the last hope for poor people in Canada. Jake was going to explain all this but Edward Slade ran off to interview a politician.

Jake pushed through the crowd and reached a platform. There, between columns by the entrance to the building, men and women were arranging microphones and electric cables and chairs and documents. Six men and two women stood on the platform looking down at a thousand people who had surrounded a statue of Queen Victoria and filled a circular driveway abutting the steps of the Legislature. A man with a beard and a deep voice said a few words into a microphone. Everybody cheered and clapped. A second man spoke for a minute. A woman took her turn. When she finished, the speakers took a break. They were caught by surprise when Jake limped up the steps and onto the platform.

Mahatma Grafton arrived shortly after the speeches began. He hadn't had time to talk to Lawson. He hadn't even had time to estimate the crowd size. He only had time to ask himself what Corbett was doing on stage.

"Ladies and gentlemen," Corbett said into the microphone, "I'm gonna tell you straight and true: WE'RE GETTING SCREWED!" The crowd cheered. "The government isn't minding our Charter of Rights. What about poor people? We aren't getting any security like it says in Section Seven! We got to mind our Charter from the roots to the top! We . . ."

Mahatma smiled broadly. Give it to 'em, Jake! People in the crowd began to mutter. Complaining to their neighbours, they drifted off. A man on stage approached Corbett. "Just a minute, I'm still talking," Corbett said. The man persisted. "I SAID JUST A MINUTE!" The microphone belched a chalkboard screech. Hundreds of people were leaving the demonstration. "THE PROBLEM WITH THE WELFARE PEOPLE IS . . ."

Mahatma could see Corbett's mouth working but heard no more sound. Corbett had been disconnected. He stopped, turned and stretched a wide mouth at the man beside him. Two men pulled Corbett away from the podium. Lawson told the crowd the demonstration would continue. But he was interrupted by megaphone-boosted soprano anger: "Down with unfairness. Down with this meeting. Down with poverty! Up with the Charter of Rights and Libidies!"

Shoving broke out behind Lawson. Corbett lost his place on the platform and found himself back in the crowd. He pushed his Blow-Joe megaphone volume button to max and let loose with another speech. Half the crowd wandered away, while others stayed to watch Corbett's tussle. Finally, Lawson took the microphone on stage. Corbett matched him word for word. At that point, the rest of the crowd disbanded.

Ben Grafton had attended the rally out of curiosity. "Who is that man?" he asked his son.

"That's the welfare kook I've written about."

"That man is no kook. I don't care if he's on welfare, I don't care if he sleeps under a bridge, I'm telling you he has power. Took him three minutes to send a thousand people packing. Could the premier of Manitoba do that? Answer me that!"

Mahatma borrowed his father's idea for his lead:

> A Winnipeg welfare recipient accomplished yesterday what Premier Bruce Gilford couldn't have hoped to do: he disheartened and disbanded 1000 anti-government protestors at the Manitoba Legislature.

Slade, in *The Star*, wrote:

> He came, he saw and he messed up the whole works.
> That was what organizers of yesterday's rally against the Manitoba government's French language plans were saying after a $178-a-month welfare man poleaxed the proceedings with an outburst of his own.
> Jake Corbett, who lives in a greasy spoon and lugs around a megaphone to air his beefs about so-called 'welfare injustice' . . .

In his column for *Le Miroir*, Georges Goyette wrote:

> Introducing an unwitting champion of the Franco-Manitoban cause . . .

None of these articles generated any media interest outside Winnipeg. However, by a circuitous route, a fourth article sparked the interest of the international press. For *La Voix de Yaoundé*, Yoyo wrote:

> Winnipeg—A brilliant social strategist has managed to defuse a wave of anti-French bigotry and at the same time attract attention to the plight of the poor in Canada.
> Jake Corbett, a middle-aged man of poverty, no education and ill health, again showed his talents as one of the fastest rising social critics in North America. . . .

Christine Bennie, who had been reporting for *The New York Times* since quitting *The Herald* eight months ago, was covering an assignment in Cameroon when Yoyo's article appeared.

Christine Bennie had a passion for local newspapers. Everywhere she went, she read them. In Tucson, in Tijuana, in Toledo. Bennie could read Spanish, French and German, and she made good use of it with the local press. In Yaoundé, lounging in a bar in the Forum Golf Hotel, scanning *La Voix de Yaoundé,* Christine locked onto a fascinating line in bold face that said, "De notre correspondant à Winnipeg, Hassane Moustafa "Yoyo" Ali." Christine took a long sip of her tonic and asked herself: What's this paper doing with a correspondent in Winnipeg? She devoured the story. Some guy on welfare was turning everybody on their heads in good old Winnipeg. Christine vaguely remembered Jake Corbett. She had intended to do an article on him, but had ended up resigning from *The Herald* before she got around to it. The truth was that for months, Christine had been pestering her new editors to let her return to Winnipeg for a few days. "I could write you some local colour that you wouldn't believe," she told them. Nobody doubted that. Everybody in *The New York Times* newsroom remembered the wire story that had come out of Winnipeg a year or so earlier: *Wild Moose Bolts into Downtown Winnipeg, Causing Panic.* An even wilder wire story had come out of Winnipeg since Christine had left *The Herald*: *Welfare Recipient Pardoned for Sucking Letters from Mailbox.* After that, *Times* reporters began teasing her about the city. "Winnipeg? Where's that?" someone would say. "It's where they suck moose out of mailboxes." First the moose, then the vacuum incident, and now the welfare recipient with more personality than Martin Luther King. Or so *La Voix de Yaoundé* suggested. Christine would see for herself. She'd be going to Winnipeg soon. She felt like scooping the ass off *The Herald*. And she had to meet this Hassane Moustafa Ali! What on earth was he doing in Winnipeg?

Ten days after Yoyo's article appeared in *La Voix de Yaoundé*, Christine Bennie arrived in Winnipeg. She had contacted *La Voix* before leaving Cameroon to obtain Hassane Moustafa Ali's address and telephone number. She flew from Dakar to New York, spent five days at home and then flew to Winnipeg. Mr. Ali was extraordinarily hospitable. A true Cameroonian! She had phoned from her office in New York and he had offered to meet her at the airport. She accepted with pleasure. She would write two stories from Winnipeg: an offbeat piece on a Cameroonian correspondent in Canada, and a piece about Jake Corbett, the welfare hero.

Yoyo met her at the revolving baggage counter. "It is my honour and privilege to welcome you to Winny-peg, even if it is not my city," Yoyo said. The smiling woman had a firm handshake and big, firm hips, like a good Cameroonian woman. She was gregarious. She loved to talk. He liked her immediately.

They chatted all the way into the city, in the back seat of a cab. "You came out here on a *bus* to meet me? I don't believe it. I simply don't believe it!"

"You went all the way to visit my country and read our humble newspaper in Yaoundé?" Yoyo countered. "I don't believe that! I simply don't believe that!"

Yoyo directed her to Frank's Accidental Dog and Grill. She wouldn't go in at first. "Just a minute. Just give me a minute. I just have to get this down." She appeared to be noting the name of the café, the address, the name of Joe's Barber next door, the look of the men in the street.

They stepped inside. She shook the hand of the man behind the counter. "Hello," she said warmly, "I'm Christine Bennie from *The New York Times.*"

"Hello," he replied evenly, "I'm Frank, from an accidental pregnancy."

"Good one. I'll remember that. Is Jake around?"

"Hey. Would you do me a favour? If you're doing a write-up, would you kindly not call this here establishment a greasy spoon?"

She smiled. "Sure. I think I can do that."

"Good. Jake's upstairs. Your friend knows the way," Frank said, indicating Yoyo. "He's been here before."

Christine found Jake Corbett in fine form. He was arranging his files and clippings about welfare when she came in. There was no place for her to sit. The bed and chairs were covered with documents. She noted the documents in his hand, the clothes he wore, the sagging bed, the paint-peeling window held open by a brick.

"Don't tell Frank about the brick," Corbett warned her, "he says I'm burning up his energy. Says he's gonna boot me out he hears that brick's in the window." Christine steered Corbett through his welfare woes, keeping him on track for the story she was framing. Then she went with Yoyo to see Mahatma Grafton. He provided photocopies of his earlier stories on Corbett and explained who Christine should talk to for more details. She phoned a welfare officer who hung up when Christine identified herself. She phoned the deputy minister of Community Services. She phoned Corbett's lawyer. She phoned a professor of social work at the University of Manitoba. She found out about how a judge had ordered Corbett's arrest, how Corbett had gotten beaten up in Polonia Park, how he had turned an anti-government protest into a dud, how he had gotten on the front page of *The Herald* four times in as many months.

Christine wrote the story of Jake Corbett's public life, highlighting the key moments over the last year. She didn't do any more than anyone else had ever done, but she summed it all up in one article. It ran as a colour piece on page one of *The New York Times*. Reporters began calling Corbett from all over the United States and Europe. The American and European interest came at a time when the Manitoba media were ignoring Corbett. *The Herald* noted that *The New York Times* had written about Corbett; it also noted when Corbett was interviewed on U.S. television. But, on the whole, it ignored Corbett. It was too busy following the French language crisis.

The League Against the French Takeover of Manitoba regrouped after the abortive demonstration. It sent delegations to meet six Cabinet ministers. It protested to the federal government. It won the support of ten provincial government backbenchers. It sent a delegation to Mayor Novak, who dismissed them after stating that he believed in minority language rights. Undaunted, the league urged city councillors to hold a civic referendum on the question. It pushed other Manitoba municipalities to do the same. It scraped together 20,000 names for a petition, taking a ten-dollar donation from each petitioner to pay for newspaper ads.

The editors of small radio and TV stations noticed that Edward Slade was raising hell over French. "Why aren't our reporters doing that too?" they wondered. They noticed that Slade was writing the dickens out of the French issue and that *The Star* readers seemed to love it. So they put their police reporters on the French beat too.

His behaviour in the French language dispute did not endear Edward Slade to his police beat competitors. Three days into their dual roles as police reporters in the morning and language-crisis reporters in the afternoon, Bob Stone of CFRL Radio and Susan Starr of CBRT Radio were told by their editors to match a *Star* story carrying the headline *French Activist Has AIDS!!!*

> The killer AIDS disease has struck a French rights activist who works with St. Boniface school children, *The Star* has learned. . . .

Bob Stone balled the tabloid in his fist. "I don't have to imitate that runt! He makes his living poking into things that are none of his business."

"That's what reporters do," Bob's editor said. "You should too."

Over the next weeks, Edward Slade produced a few mild morsels (one of LAFTOM's leading activists was charged with wife-battering; police caught a married Franco-Manitoban leader in a brothel). But he felt dissatisfied. Mahatma Grafton was outwriting him. Every day, Grafton was covering complicated political angles. Slade knew Grafton's work was more serious, but he also knew that almost nobody read it.

Slade opted for the low road. Everywhere he went, he dug for dirt. This approach was based on his belief that behind every news story of any consequence, somebody was running a scam. The harder you looked, the greater your chance of unearthing it. Scams were hard to snag. You missed them nine times out of ten. But Slade lived for the exception.

Judge Melvyn Hill reached two painful conclusions. He would never make the Supreme Court of Canada, or any federal court at all. And he would not be allowed to work past the age of sixty-five. Perhaps he was a man ahead of his time. While many of his race still toiled on the trains, Melvyn had risen in the ranks, become a contributing member of society. But nobody cared. Nobody appreciated him. Years ago, train porters had ridiculed him for wanting something better. And now, he still got no respect. Not from his peers, not from reporters, not even from bums on the street. Melvyn wanted to be seen in his robes by every railway porter in Canada, by every passenger whose shoes he had shined, by every Air Force officer and law partner who had slighted him. But he knew he would never rise above the Provincial Court, and in that court, he would never get out of the Institute of Public Protection, whose endless coterie of cons, ex-cons, to-be cons and their sniffling families made it the worst of all postings.

Nevertheless, he wanted to work past his sixty-fifth birthday. Retirement terrified him. What would he do? His wives had left him. He had no kids. He had always been certain that children would hate him. He was a good person, didn't cheat people and had never betrayed his wives. But he sensed that children would turn against him. So he never had them.

All he had was his job. In the past year, he had written three times to the chief provincial judge, and twice to the attorney general's office, reminding them of his situation and asking for a renewed contract. But Melvyn had received no response.

Melvyn had attended the LAFTOM rally at which Jake Corbett raised a ruckus. That man brought disaster everywhere he went. Corbett's interruption had irritated Melvyn, who believed the government was carrying this French business too far. Why give French people higher status than the rest? The next thing you knew, they would start requiring Provincial Court judges to be bilingual. Just today, Ben Grafton's son had written that the province now intended to provide bilingual services in its courts. Sources predicted that francophones would fill the next several openings on the Provincial Court. Melvyn knew that judges rarely got 'promoted' from a provincial to a federal bench. But he was sure that some new French-speaking judge would be bounced up a notch or two after serving briefly on Provincial Court. This angered Melvyn. He wanted to enter the debate over bilingualism. But as a judge, he couldn't take a public stand. If he got embroiled in another controversy, his chances of working past sixty-five would be shot.

The scoop Edward Slade had been hoping for finally landed in his lap. Slade found the story by scanning letters to the editor that *The Star* had judged unworthy of publication. Perusing them for story ideas, Slade noticed several by the same author that attacked the provincial government for promising to make Manitoba's court system bilingual. The author only left his initials—M.H.— but he often added a postscript: "I am a highly placed legal professional, and I am eminently qualified to examine this issue. It behooves me, however, to safeguard my anonymity, and therefore I only sign with my initials."

"Give me a break," Slade muttered, throwing the letter and others with the same signature in the waste-basket. But suddenly he retrieved them. Slade recognized the initials. He phoned Melvyn Hill.

"Hello, this is *The Winnipeg Star.* We need to clarify a detail concerning the letters about bilingualism that you sent to *The Star.*"

"I'll clarify any detail you'd like, but I don't want my name appearing under those letters. I did write them, but . . ."

Edward Slade had his scoop. His story ran under a photo of the judge.

Provincial Judge Joins Anti-French Movement
Provincial Court Judge Melvyn Hill gives the NDP government and its pro-French policies a licking every day.

For the past week, the controversial judge has been penning livid letters against provincial bilingualism proposals and sending them to the editorial office of *The Winnipeg Star.* . . .

Golden here, burnt there—perfect! Frank slid the hashbrowns onto a plate, crowned them in ketchup and sat down to eat. At the same time, he studied, for the twentieth time, a paragraph in *The New York Times* of March 2. A paragraph having to do with his business: . . . *a cholesterol factory* . . . "The fuck's that?" Frank mumbled, beaming with pride at being written up in the cream of the cream, *The New York Times* . . . *equipped to send the hardiest street bum into diabetic shock* . . . "The hell's that Christine Bennie talking about?" Now came his favourite line: *Frank's Accidental Dog and Grill is a world-class greasy spoon, an Orwellian pillar of down-and-outdome* . . . "Let her have it right in the kisser, I will. Calling my place a greasy spoon!"

"Excuse me, Frank," Jake Corbett said, for the fourth time. "Somebody's gonna be calling for me. Can you say I'm at the Flapjack Café?"

"I'm no answering service. That doesn't come with the room. Speaking of which, keep that brick outa your window. My heating bill . . ."

"Can't you tell 'em I'm at Harry's?"

"No! That simple enough? I'm not helping the competition."

"Just tell 'em I'm at Harry's, okay?" Jake Corbett limped toward the door. Reaching for the knob, he moaned.

"What's the matter?" Frank said.

"My legs."

"It's your imagination."

Leaning on the back of a chair, Jake waited for the pain to subside. Then he went out. It was friendlier at Harry's. The food was cheaper. Harry treated him nice. Never talked to him like Frank talked. Harry's nose looked like it had been flattened by a two-by-four. Thick lips loose and swinging, three chins, silver hair screwed tight on a black head, brown eyes as tired as old shoes, eyes that looked straight through you. Harry was a nice man. Jake felt free to eat there every day.

Yoyo met her at the airport again. The big hug embarrassed him. The smack on his lips embarrassed him even more. North American women were like that. Helen had been that way, now Christine Bennie. Women would kiss you right on the lips, in public! Thoroughly uncivilized!

"Darling," she whispered. She told him she was dying to ball his buns off. Idiomatic speech still caused Yoyo problems. But he still understood, somehow, what she wanted.

"Shall I take your valise?" he said, reaching down.

"Suitcase," she said. "Valise makes you sound like a butler."

"Thank you for the correction."

"You're so formal."

She slapped his bum. Also in public. He did his best to ignore it.

"Let's grab a cab. Is that how you say?"

She screamed with laughter. "Yes, honey, perfect. Grab a cab!"

All that talk in the airport had aroused him. The instant they arrived in her hotel room, he unbuckled his belt. "Not right now, honey. If I get all relaxed and warm and tingly, I won't be able to get going again today. So let's save it for tonight, hummm? We have to track down Jake Corbett."

"Okay." He started to fasten his pants.

"No, wait! Let me see it. Just let me see that darling thing. Oh, it's so cute! It's so, oh oh! Yoyo! . . ."

Frank practically melted when he saw her. Walking in with that skinny African. "No, he's not here," Frank said. "But wait a minute, lady, don't you want to do another write-up on us here? You never mentioned me. You never told 'em about—"

She asked, "Don't you know where he is?"

"Nah," he said. She sure was a good-looker, that *New York Times* reporter. "Siddown. Have a coffee. It's on the house."

"Sorry, Frank, we've got to run. Where do you think he'd be, Yoyo?"

"I don't know."

She wrote a hotel name on her card, gave it to Frank. "If he comes in . . ."

"He's at Harry's."

"Where's that?"

"Up the street. Past the railway trestle. On your right."

They found him eating flapjacks with maple syrup in an empty café where a large, fat black man stood with a smock over his shirt and pants. The man drummed thick fingers on the counter. Jake Corbett sipped from a glass of Coke. Both men had their heads tilted toward the TV.

Harry saw them first. A mighty leggy white woman in a skirt, a good-looking woman at that, tousled brown hair, pretty face, nice smile. Not the smartassed smile of a rich white lady to a poor black man. Just a little smile, said hi there, how're things? Harry was looking her up and down with his left eye, dedicating his right to the fellow beside her. Blackest man he'd seen in years. This stranger was no Canadian Negro. Didn't dress like a Canadian Negro. Not like any Canadian Negro porters, anyway. This man dressed fancy, like a Frenchman. Polished shoes, fancy belt buckle, ivory ring, eyes too dark to read.

Harry liked this couple. He could tell just from looking at 'em, seeing the way they were standing close, aware of each other without any eyeballing at all, that they'd been humping. Harry would bet his fat ass they'd been humping half an hour ago. Good on 'em! It gave him hope for the human race. The more white women and black men and black women and white men mixed it up, the harder it was gonna be to keep coloured people down. One day, *everybody* was gonna be coloured.

The woman went to talk to Jake Corbett. What was a classy lady like her doing with that broken welfare bum?

The brother joined Harry at the counter.

"Aren't you gonna sit with the lady?" Harry asked.

"No thank you. She has to talk with him. Talk about business. May I eat here?"

"Sure you can eat here. What you want, brother?"

"I'll have what Jake has."

"You know Jake?"

"Sure. I have introduced Jake Corbett to all my countrymen."

"And where are they from, your countrymen?" Harry asked as he poured batter onto a hot griddle.

"Cameroon." Seeing Harry look puzzled, Yoyo added, "Africa. Where you from, brother?" Yoyo used the word with pride. He knew that word. He understood its idiomatic meaning.

Harry turned and smiled. "I'm from right here. Raised smack dab in Winnipeg." He served the Frenchman. Leaning his elbows on the counter, he asked in a low voice, "What're they talking about, anyhow?"

"Welfare."

"How come?"

"She's from *The New York Times*. She's writing a story about him."

"No shit?"

"No. No shit, brother." Yoyo smiled. He felt immensely happy. He knew that expression too!

"An article for *The New York Times*!"

"She has already done one. Now she will do another. No shit!"

The New York Times broke the story two days later, scooping every reporter in Winnipeg. Even Mahatma Grafton. He had recently met Christine Bennie for a second time, and had again accommodated her request to photocopy more articles that he had written about Corbett. Mahatma hadn't asked what Christine was working on because he knew she wouldn't tell him. He also knew that journalists never helped their competitors to the degree that he had helped her, twice providing photocopies and detailing Corbett's situation. She was pleasant. She was a good journalist. Why not give her a hand?

The New York Times story revealed that in the socialist province of Manitoba, Canada, a welfare recipient named Jake Corbett, who had several long-standing disputes with the social assistance authorities, had won an administrative battle: he had persuaded the authorities to give him a $2000 "medical vacation fund" so that he could leave town on a holiday.

Don Betts went crazy when he saw the story. So did Edward Slade. Betts and Slade happened to read the story on the wire services in their computer terminals at exactly the same time of day. Both screamed the same thing: "Why don't we have this?"

Mahatma, sensing that he was going to be scooped by *The New York Times,* had been watching the wires more closely than Betts. He saw the story fifteen minutes before Betts, and mumbled to the man, who wasn't doing much of anything, "I think I'll go dig up a story."

"Yeah? Like what?"

"I don't know. Nothing much stirring here. Maybe I'll go see what Jake Corbett is up to these days."

"I don't want to see one more printed word about that twerp unless the story is rock solid," Betts said. "Corbett's been getting too much ink. He doesn't know his ass from a hole in the ground but you know something? He's manipulating us! Not one more word, you got that?"

"Yup."

Mahatma hailed a taxi. He implored the driver to get to the Accidental Dog and Grill as fast as possible. "Wait here," Mahatma said. He raced in, ran upstairs and banged on Corbett's door.

"Jake! We've gotta talk. Got your documents about the medical vacation fund handy?"

"Yeah," he said proudly, "right here in my briefcase."

"Good. Let's go. We have to talk."

"I was resting my leg. It's killing me."

"I'll take you to my place. You can rest there."

Corbett asked suspiciously, "You got any flapjacks?"

"Sure. I'll make you some."

"Do you make 'em as good as Harry?"

Working from the phone at his home, and supplying Corbett with food, Mahatma first matched Christine Bennie's story. That was easy—Jake's briefcase contained documentation for the entire "medical vacation fund" story. Corbett had three doctors' letters saying he had a medical need for rest. He had a supporting letter from a University of Manitoba social work professor saying that welfare people needed holidays too. He had a letter from the welfare office confirming that he would receive $2000 in holiday money. Mahatma called the welfare office and got someone to say that the authorities would pay for a vacation if it were medically necessary.

Mahatma also got comments from Corbett's lawyer. But then the lawyer dropped the bomb. "That isn't the biggest story," she said.

"No? What is?"

"The Federal Court of Canada has agreed to hear our argument that the federal government should stop subsidizing Manitoba's welfare costs until the province stops its overpayment deductions."

"You're talking about cutting off millions of dollars of federal aid to Manitoba!" Mahatma said.

"That's right. The decision came down today."

"Could you send me the decision by courier?"

The Winnipeg Star, three local radio stations and two TV networks ran Corbett's medical vacation story. They lifted the information from The New York Times. The Herald not only improved upon that story, but turned out a new scoop on Corbett's court case. Both stories hit page one. Christine Bennie was impressed. This Mahatma Grafton didn't fool around.

Jake Corbett didn't feel well at all. The busier he got, running around to all the radio stations that suddenly wanted to interview him, the more his legs hurt. Jake had hoped that *The Herald's* two front-page stories on him would help him out. The story about the court case business was fine. But the other one brought him trouble. People started complaining about Jake's vacation. It came up in Question Period in the Manitoba Legislature. "How come this guy on welfare gets a holiday paid by taxpayers?" The minister of social services stepped in and chucked Jake's $2000 vacation out the window. Only Harry was sympathetic: "These folks jumping up and down about their taxes, how much they contributin' to your holiday? About one cent, I bet. I ain't adverse to donating one cent to the cause. A man needs a holiday. You got a doctor's letter, don't you?"

But something else came along. The New Zealand Anti-Poverty Organization wanted him to go over there. NZAPO would pay for him to come and speak.

"Guess what, Harry. I'm going to New Zealand."

Harry Carson was stirring oil in a pan. A drop of water rolled off the spatula and splattered in the oil, spraying up onto his forearm. "Say again, Jake?"

"New Zealand. They're gonna put me in an airplane, buy my ticket, everything. They want me to tell 'em about welfare in Canada."

Harry said nothing. His back was turned. He made a sniffling noise, drawing sadness into his nostrils. Man was a tragic case. His lid had come unscrewed. Black people, he expected them to be in a bad way. When he saw a black person having a rough time, he thought, so what, you think I been laying on moss all my life? But it was *unnatural* for white people to be broken down. Jake didn't deserve to suffer like that! Bad legs, no money, no job, no family. Only friends he had were newspaper reporters. Hunh! Harry could live as long as Methuselah, he could live to the day you could take a bath on the moon, and he still wouldn't trust a reporter. A reporter had to write about things every day. Even on days when nothing happened. Any man who wrote about things whether they happened or not was a man Harry didn't trust.

"Look!" Corbett was opening a newspaper. "They wrote me up on page twenty-three. 'Winnipeg welfare recipient to speak in New Zealand.'"

Harry dropped his spatula. "Lemme see that."

Harry missed the man. He missed giving him flapjacks for half price. Harry bought the paper every day. He saw articles out of Christchurch, Dunedin, Auckland . . . all these places he looked up in an atlas. Places in New Zealand. Articles from Reuter and Associated Press, saying Jake Corbett this and Jake Corbett that. Harry didn't read the details. He just wanted to know how Jake was doing.

The League Against the French Takeover of Manitoba held sixteen public meetings in three months. It held meetings in churches, curling halls, gymnasia and finally in the Winnipeg Convention Centre. It lobbied municipalities. It lobbied every opposition politician in the provincial Legislature and harassed every government member. And finally, it won a major battle. Over the objections of Mayor John Novak, it persuaded Winnipeg city councillors to vote in favour of holding a referendum on French language rights.

The Question: "The Governments of Manitoba and Canada wish to amend the Constitution to extend bilingualism in Manitoba. Do you prefer that the Governments abandon their plans and ask the Supreme Court of Canada to rule on this issue?"

Everybody in the province was talking about French language rights. Mahatma couldn't handle more than a fraction of the stories; *The Herald* had five reporters covering the constitutional crisis.

LAFTOM demonstrators spilled five times into the marble halls of the Manitoba Legislature, the Manitoba provincial police chief had three constables demanding the right to work in French, English parents predicted that their children would be jobless, editorials all across Canada called Manitobans rednecks, Manitobans screamed back 'we are not bigots!!!,' Ben Grafton proudly watched his son struggling to deliver straight information throughout the crisis, FAM president Pierre Gratton moved his family into hiding after receiving death threats, LAFTOM members shouted down the premier of Manitoba at a public meeting, and, in the end, with the referendum two days away, federal and provincial officials decided to hold an urgent and secret meeting with Franco-Manitoban leaders. The meeting was to involve some of the highest elected officials in the country. The premier of Manitoba. The attorney general of Manitoba. The federal minister of justice. The federal secretary of state. Their top advisors. It was scheduled for an April afternoon at the Fort Garry Hotel.

Two dozen reporters, including Mahatma, waited outside the hotel to scrum the politicians after the meeting. But the media's focus soon shifted to the large demonstration assembling outside the Fort Garry. The crowd chanted and hollered. The anger reached the politicians cloistered on the second floor of the hotel, who snuck out a back entrance after their meeting. Mahatma knew then that the provincial government would soon bow to English anger.

The referendum came two days later. Seventy-seven percent of Winnipeg voters opposed the plan to amend the constitution. They wanted the government to kill the accord and let the Supreme Court of Canada decide the matter. The provincial government dropped its French language plans. Mahatma considered the move disgraceful. He was struck by the intensity of his feeling. He wished there were someone to talk to. But Ben was at home, and the phone wouldn't do. Helen Savoie was on holidays. Mahatma would have liked to have seen Chuck, but he was gone.

Everybody would be at the Legislature, battering the premier with questions and scrumming the opposition leader. All the reporters in the city would be over there. What was the point of joining that troupe? What could he possibly contribute that was unique? Mahatma drove a company car to St. Boniface. It was a warm spring day, with nudging sunlight bathing every tree and home in the city. As if his ears had just been unplugged, he noticed the steady whelps of birds in the trees. He saw four chipmunks race in a line across someone's front lawn. He saw an old man hobbling into Chez Luc, a barbershop with two chairs and one barber. Mahatma wandered in and asked the man, a short guy in his sixties, what he thought of the government's decision.

"I knew they'd never give us anything," he said. "All we want is to save our language, but everybody says we want to take over the province. We're five percent of the population! Take over the province? Bah!"

Later, Mahatma found a few people sitting around the offices of *Le Miroir*. They surrounded Yoyo, who was splitting his listeners with laughter. "Cameroonians will never understand what happened today. If I tell them that thousands of people were demonstrating in the streets, they'll say, 'Why? For food? For work? For shelter?' I'll say, 'No, because they didn't want to hear French.' 'Canadians demonstrate because they don't want to hear French?' And I'll have to tell them yes. 'Do they have to listen to French?' 'No.' 'Is the air very cold in that part of Canada?' 'Yes.' 'Can very cold air hurt the brain?' "

Now that Jake was in New Zealand, Harry Carson looked for his name every day in the papers. Rooted it out with his brown index finger. My buddy, Harry would tell anybody who happened to be around. That's my buddy Jake! He takes a stack of flapjacks here every day of the week. He's travelling at this moment. Look— Christchurch! What do you make of that?

The day after the headlines about the government killing that French plan, Harry turned to page eleven and found a two-paragraph bullet:

Winnipeg Man Collapses in Auckland
AUCKLAND (AP)—A Winnipeg welfare recipient collapsed
yesterday while making a speech to the Auckland Anti-Poverty
Organization.

Jake Corbett, 46, touring New Zealand on the invitation of
a coalition of anti-poverty groups, was summarizing a section
of the Canadian Charter of Rights and Freedoms when he
collapsed.

He is under observation at the Auckland Memorial Hospital.

There wasn't much to write about. The provincial government
had dropped the French language issue, deciding to let the
Supreme Court of Canada rule on Franco-Manitoban
constitutional rights. There weren't any sensational crime stories
to report, and had there been any, Mahatma wouldn't have been
involved. He was glad a new reporter was covering the beat. He
didn't want to return to it for any salary on any newspaper. The
police never did find the arsonist who bombed the Francophone
Association of Manitoba. Jake Corbett returned to Winnipeg,
having recovered from his collapse in New Zealand. Melvyn Hill,
Mahatma learned from Ben, had received official notice that his
work contract would not be extended past his sixty-fifth birthday.

In early April, Don Betts handed Mahatma a news release.
"Find out about this. Sounds fishy."

Mahatma studied the sheet.

> The Hon. John Novak will hold a reception for Cameroonian
> journalist Hassane Moustafa Ali on May 2. Mr. Hassane has
> spent the last ten months working for *Le Miroir* and reporting
> to his own newspaper, *La Voix de Yaoundé*. He returns to
> Yaoundé on May 4.
>
> Mayor Novak will present Mr. Hassane with a friendship
> plaque and, via Mr. Hassane, send a card of greetings and good
> wishes to the Mayor of Yaoundé, His Excellency Boubacar
> Fotso.

Mahatma had been so involved in his work that he had neglected to stay in touch with Yoyo. It must have been a lonely year in Canada for Yoyo.

Betts interrupted Mahatma's thoughts. "What I want to know is, what kind of note is Novak sending this African mayor? Is he a communist? And another thing. What do our External Affairs officials think of our mayor contacting a mayor in Africa? Aren't they pissed off that Novak is bypassing diplomatic channels?"

Mahatma wasn't able to reach the mayor that day. He complained about the assignment that night to his father. But Ben perked up. "John Novak is writing to the mayor of Yaoundé?" he said. "Good! How many Canadian mayors show an interest in Africa? Stick with that story, son. Could be interesting."

Mahatma reached Sandra Paquette the next day. She said the note was just a letter of greetings. An External Affairs official said Ottawa didn't object to the mayor's greeting Fotso. Mahatma presented this information to Betts.

Betts frowned. "Find out more about this African mayor."

Sifting through *The Herald* library files, Mahatma learned that Boubacar Fotso had been appointed mayor of Yaoundé in 1982. That same year, various Reuter clippings quoted him as saying that if he had to choose between Ronald Reagan and Moammar Gadhafi for a world leader, he would pick Gadhafi, who opposed South African apartheid.

"There's your story," Betts said. "We can write that Novak is forging ties with an anti-American mayor in Africa. The African's gotta be a communist. Find out about that."

"No," Mahatma said. "If you want that shit in the paper, then you write it. I looked into your idea and I say there's no story. I'm not writing anything. Not now. But I'll cover that reception the mayor's holding, when it comes up."

"You do that, Mahatma. You do that." Betts liked coming up against Mahatma Grafton. Good reporter. But one hell of a smartass. Betts would nail him sooner or later. Give Betts time and he'd get even.

Yoyo was the first to arrive at his own reception. Since his arrival in Canada, the notion of timeliness had been drilled into him repeatedly. Canadians seemed preoccupied with time. If someone were to invite you to dinner, the person would not only state the day and hour but specify even the quarter of the hour: "How about 6:45?" Canadians did not appreciate your arriving late. But the one thing that disturbed them more was to arrive early. It was better to arrive one hour late than fifteen minutes early.

Sandra Paquette took Yoyo's coat—it was the month of May and 12° outside, but he was still wearing a heavy overcoat with a furry, elf-like hood. He was ushered into the mayor's office. Yoyo said, "It is an honour and a privilege to be received like this."

"Oh Yoyo," Sandra said, "you're so formal."

Mahatma arrived just as people were crowding around the food tables in the mayor's reception room. Despite Mahatma's reservations, Betts had been urging him again to play up Novak's connection to a communist African mayor.

Sandra Paquette met Mahatma at the door. She shook his hand. "I'm glad you could come," she said. She had a beautiful smile. Eyes, darkish blue, tinged with green. "The mayor will be making an announcement that might interest you."

They lingered together at the door. "Feel like coffee after the reception?" Mahatma asked.

"Sure." Their smiles met. Just then, the mayor beckoned to Sandra. "Catch you later," she said.

Mahatma headed toward the food table. He approached a stout, red-haired man in running shoes and an old suit. "Jake! What are *you* doing here?"

Jake Corbett brought a card from the same pocket into which he had just deposited two salmon sandwiches. "Sandra gave me an invitation."

"So you're back from New Zealand, safe and healthy again?"

"Yeah. But the welfare people cut off my payments."

"Why?"

"They're calling my trip to New Zealand a gift. A gift in kind. They say I can't have gifts in kind. So they cut me off."

Mahatma asked, "Did they put this in writing?" Corbett produced a photocopy. "I hope you're not going to *The Star* with this story."

"Are you gonna put it on page one?"

"No guarantees. You know that, Jake."

"Well then, maybe I'll call *The Star,* and maybe I won't."

"You've turned into a real bargainer."

"The welfare rights people in New Zealand told me not to put up with any nonsense. They said reporters will get you if you don't watch out."

Mahatma shrugged. "Can I have this photocopy?"

"Yeah. For fifteen cents."

"I thought photocopies cost a nickel."

"I gotta live, you know."

Mahatma gave him a dollar.

In his speech, Mayor Novak said he was sending a note via Yoyo to Yaoundé mayor Boubacar Fotso. Novak was proposing that Yaoundé and Winnipeg become twin cities, that they establish a program of formal ties, with regular visits and contacts and exchange programs for students and teachers and civic officials. This would be the first time a Canadian city had established formal links with an African capital.

Mahatma didn't consider it major news, but it was worth a few inches. He asked Yoyo for information about Yaoundé. Yoyo responded obligingly: Yaoundé, the capital city in the south of Cameroon, had a population of about 400,000. Cameroon was a country of some ten million inhabitants. Shaped like a triangle with the apex at the north, Cameroon shared borders with six countries and had an area of 475,440 square kilometres—about three-quarters the size of Manitoba.

Yoyo was called to the podium. He spoke of Canada and Cameroon, the only two countries in the world with English and French as the two official languages. He spoke of Winnipeg, a city of cleanliness and decency! Winnipeg, at the junction of the two great rivers, the Red and the Assiniboine, whose majesty Yoyo would extol to his countrymen! Cameroonians would hear about Manitoba, its flat and open land, its cold. The cold in

Winnipeg could freeze the moisture in your nostrils, or turn a lake into an airplane runway. Cameroonians would never tire of hearing of Winnipeg. All Cameroonians would think of this great city when they thought of world centres: Rome, London, Paris, Winnipeg. . . . In concluding, Yoyo extended his most heartfelt wish: that Winnipeg's population triple or quadruple, so that its streets would not seem so lonely. A million or two more people was what Winnipeg needed, and that was what he, as a true friend, wished the city.

After a lengthy coffee break with Sandra, which stretched into lunch at the Lox and Bagel, Mahatma returned to the office and wrote the Jake Corbett story.

> Provincial officials have blocked social assistance payments to welfare rights advocate Jake Corbett because he accepted a free airplane ticket to New Zealand. . . .

It wasn't a bad story. Next, Mahatma wrote the blurb about Mayor Novak proposing that Yaoundé and Winnipeg become twin cities. It was a five-inch story that Mahatma expected to find on page twenty-one, or perhaps not find in the paper at all, the next day.

The next morning was beautiful. Sunlight coaxed the buds on American elm trees. Birds fussed overhead. A warm breeze blew in from the south. Mahatma walked peacefully through Wolseley, along Westminister Avenue, past Mrs. Lipton's, past the Wolseley Bicycle Company, past Prairie Books and The New Taste Bakery and Vegetarian Deli, thinking that it was a lovely morning, and continuing to think so until, minutes later on Portage Avenue, he bought *The Herald*.

Mahatma opened the folded paper. He groaned. He didn't recognize his story. It wasn't his story any more. All that remained of his story were a few details about Winnipeg's plans to twin with Yaoundé—but even that information had been perverted. Mahatma looked at the story again.

Novak Forges Ties with African Communist
By Don Betts and Mahatma Grafton

Mayor John Novak has outraged local politicians and federal officials by trying to make formal ties between Winnipeg and the communist-run capital city of Cameroon.

Bypassing the federal Department of External Affairs, Novak is directly contacting the mayor of Yaoundé to propose that the two cities become "twinned" and set up regular student, work and cultural exchanges.

Employing leftist slogans such as "let us promote the solidarity of our peoples" and "let us toil against oppression and unite in transnational, transracial brotherhood," Novak has written directly to Yaoundé Mayor Boubacar Fotso.

"He shouldn't be doing that," said External Affairs spokesman John Scarlatti when told by *The Herald* of Novak's initiative. "The mayor of Winnipeg shouldn't be proposing formal ties with another country without consulting us about protocol."

Scarlatti confirmed that the Yaoundé mayor has advocated the use of violence to destroy South African apartheid. But Scarlatti refused to comment on concerns that the Yaoundé mayor may be a communist.

Winnipeg councillor Jim Read, however, said it was "scandalous" that Novak was promoting ties between Winnipeg and communist Africa.

"First it was Nicaragua, now it's an anti-American mayor in Cameroon. Next we'll be in bed with Moscow," Read said. "Mayor Novak is a threat to his own people."

Mahatma marched into the managing editor's office.

"Great story, Hat! Papers all around the country are picking it up."

"I didn't write that story. Not any of it. All I did was a three-inch bullet that Novak was sending greetings to the Yaoundé mayor. Betts turned it into a controversy. Someone should have taken off my byline. I never would have written that story!"

"You think Betts exaggerated the communist angle?"

"I'm not convinced Ottawa is upset. I talked to a person ranking higher than the one Betts quoted and I was told there was no problem. And Betts is probably wrong to call the Yaoundé mayor a communist. Cameroon is a non-aligned country with western leanings. Its mayors are appointed. The national government would never appoint a communist mayor. Communists have had to stay underground in Cameroon until very recently. So what does all this trash mean?"

"I don't know. Give us a better story and we'll look at it."

The local and national media pounced on the story. Novak was Canada's only communist mayor. Winnipeg was vying to become the first Canadian city to twin with an African city. Yaoundé had a mayor who had spoken favourably of Moammar Gadhafi and of anti-apartheid forces in Africa. At a recent conference in France, Boubacar Fotso had blasted Reagan for his weak-kneed approach to apartheid. Fotso had said he supported the anti-apartheid struggle in Africa, including that by the Soviet-backed Libyan leader. "I don't see the Libyans or the Soviets as a threat in this matter," His Excellency had stated. "I share their outrage over apartheid." At the conference, an American participant branded His Excellency a communist. Reuter and Associated Press picked that up. Subsequent articles referred to Boubacar Fotso as "the communist mayor of Yaoundé." Betts had found these references in *The Herald* clipping files. This is what Mahatma learned as he researched another story.

Mahatma caught up with the mayor outside a committee meeting at City Hall. Mahatma explained he hadn't written the story in *The Herald*. And he asked why Novak had contacted the Yaoundé mayor.

"Mayors should seize every chance to promote world peace. And as for the political leanings of the Yaoundé mayor, I would urge you to do more research."

Mahatma tried to call the African mayor, but Yaoundé was seven hours ahead of Winnipeg, and His Excellency had gone home.

The Canadian media continued to refer to Fotso as the communist mayor of Yaoundé. More reporters pestered John Novak. How hard was he willing to push this twinned cities idea? Did he plan to travel to Cameroon? Was he prepared to ruffle Ottawa's feathers over this disagreement about diplomacy?

Such was the excitement over this issue that editors lost interest in Corbett and the French language question. In the confusion and hustle about the twinned cities story, even Mahatma failed to notice at first that *The Herald* never ran his story about Corbett.

It took a few days, but Mahatma finally reached Boubacar Fotso.

Yaoundé Mayor Denies He's a Communist
By Mahatma Grafton

Yaoundé Mayor Boubacar Fotso has vehemently denied that he is a communist and has invited Winnipeg Mayor John Novak to visit Cameroon.

In a telephone interview yesterday, Fotso said recent statements that he is a communist are false.

"Communist sympathies? Of course I have communist sympathies. I also sympathize with capitalists, Jews, Christians, Moslems, black people, white people and Asians. Does that make me all of those things too? Let me state unequivocally: I am not a communist. I am the mayor of the capital city of a country which is non-aligned in world politics.

"Furthermore, I am not anti-American. Cameroon values its diplomatic and economic ties with the United States. In the past, I merely stated that the American president wasn't doing his part to fight apartheid."

Fotso expressed pleasure at having received recent greetings from Novak and said the Winnipeg mayor would be welcomed with "classic Cameroonian hospitality" if he agreed to visit Yaoundé. . . .

Three weeks passed. Mahatma received a letter from Yoyo.

Mahatma, my dear friend and brother, every day I dream of your splendid land, of the friendly people in your wondrous country, second largest in the entire world.

Winnipeg, city of open spaces, so few people, cold, freezing winds that chase people into their vast, brick homes, Winnipeg, how I miss you, and your people, such as you, brother Mahatma, you who pulled me from the Polonia Park riot and visited me in the hospital and made my stay in a foreign land meaningful, you I will always remember and thank.

Please, dearest friend, write immediately, write this very
minute! Tell me about yourself, tell me what has happened to
the city since I left. Quickly! Tell me everything! I wait anxiously
for your reply, which absolutely must come within the month!
Already I long for Winnipeg, my adoptive city.

Yours, Yoyo
P.S. Come visit Yaoundé. Come soon.

The enthusiasm in Yoyo's letter astonished Mahatma.

"It's just the style," Ben said.

"What do you mean?"

"Africans write like that."

"How do you know?"

"Your old man has lived through a thing or two, you know."

PART SIX

Mahatma improved the story about Jake Corbett losing his welfare because of the free trip to New Zealand, but *The Herald* wasn't interested. "That retard has had enough coverage," Betts said. "He's been manipulating us for months." Mahatma complained, in vain, to the managing editor. *The Herald's* intransigence infuriated Mahatma. He spoke of it to his father, who encouraged him to keep writing. "Don't give up. They'll turn down one article, or two, but keep working away, and they'll take the next one."

A news release was issued in late June:

> Mayor John Novak has the pleasure to announce that Winnipeg and Yaoundé, the capital of The United Republic of Cameroon, are to become twin cities.
>
> The mayor and his counterpart, His Excellency Boubacar Fotso, take pride in initiating the first formal and regular series of educational, cultural and professional contacts between a Canadian and an African city.
>
> Mayor Novak has accepted an invitation from His Excellency Boubacar Fotso to visit Yaoundé for one week in July.

At that time, the mayors will sign a friendship pact and plan future contacts between the two cities.

Members of the news media should contact Sandra Paquette if they wish to accompany Mayor Novak on his trip to Cameroon.

Four Winnipeg news outlets decided to send reporters to cover the event. They rarely sent reporters anywhere, but this story was national news. *Canada's only communist mayor forges ties with anti-American leader of Yaoundé.* . . . In a telephone interview, Edward Slade got the mayor of Yaoundé to say, "Capitalist trade with South Africa must be defeated so that common people may lead decent lives." The next day, *The Star* ran the headline *African Mayor Says Kill Capitalism.* Slade's story began: "Capitalism must crumble to give working stiffs a chance in South Africa, says Yaoundé Mayor Boubacar Fotso."

Slade frightened his editors into sending him. "What if some nut knocks off Novak over there? You wanna miss that story?" After learning that *The Star* was sending Slade, *The Herald* did decide to send somebody. Betts wanted to go, but Van Wuyss chose Mahatma, whose bilingualism would help in Yaoundé, where French was predominant. CBRT Radio sent its crime and City Hall reporter, Susan Starr. She had always wanted to see Africa and was considerably more enthusiastic about the assignment than Bob Stone of CFRL Radio, who was also being sent. "Who wants to travel with Slade?" Bob grumbled, but he finally agreed to go. He had his eye on Susan and thought that she might return his glances in the tropics.

Sandra Paquette was finding it impossible to work. After Edward Slade had written that the mayor would be selling communism in the darkest of Africa, City Hall was bombarded by the media calls. Local reporters scrummed the mayor whenever he left his office. Others were phoning from Vancouver, Calgary, Toronto, Montreal and the U.S.

The office of His Excellency Boubacar Fotso had also been swamped by phone calls. At first, this stroked his vanity. Reporters calling all the way from Canada! But one impudent reporter named Edward Slade had provoked him with questions about communism. Mayor Fotso lost interest in the call. This reporter was a boor. No other reporter was quite so bad—indeed, the mayor had a delightful chat with Mahatma Grafton, to whom Hassane Moustafa Ali had frequently referred in *La Voix de Yaoundé*. But the calls interfered with His Excellency's work. He was obliged to dispense with African hospitality and have his secretary unplug the phone.

Mahatma wrote to Yoyo. He mentioned that Jake Corbett was still fighting to recuperate his welfare, but that *The Herald* editors felt Corbett had burnt up his credibility over his welfare holiday and for that reason hadn't let Mahatma write about it. Mahatma said he was looking forward to seeing Yoyo soon.

Ben was proud that his son was following the mayor of Winnipeg to Africa. It deserved an entry in Ben's "Negro History Appreciation" book. The boy was terribly busy now, writing around the clock, getting vaccinations, compiling information about Cameroon. Ben hardly saw him. It didn't matter. Ben slept well at night, knowing that Mahatma was there with him, under the same roof. Ben watched his son coming in at night, leaving early in the morning. He noticed that Mahatma had become too busy to dwell on himself. He actually showed an interest in the world. He had escaped the curse of his generation.

The entire Winnipeg contingent, including Mayor Novak and Sandra Paquette, arrived in Yaoundé on a steamy July afternoon. Walking off the airplane, Mahatma felt as if he had stepped inside a car that had been baking in the sun. For a moment, the heat seemed pleasant, like lying in bed under too many blankets. But within a minute, his armpits grew wet. He hurried toward the shade of the airport terminal.

Waiting for his luggage in the hot, humid terminal, Mahatma studied the crowd forming in an adjacent room. Through the glass, he saw many people staring at him. Children too. Why were all those children at the airport? Shoeless, shirtless, they certainly weren't there to travel. He saw them clapping; he could hear them singing some strange and happy song; he could also hear the drum of tam-tams. Finally, he spotted Yoyo, waving wildly. Mahatma waved back. Yoyo pounded the window.

Mahatma touched Sandra. "Look. There's Yoyo!" She jumped up and waved in a funny motion that only North Americans make, moving the hand like a windshield wiper. The children's chanting grew louder. Mahatma grabbed Sandra, who leaned against him excitedly. "Those kids! They're here to welcome us!"

"No way," said Edward Slade, who had already entered into his notebook that beggars had jammed the airport.

They were swept past customs. In the next room, two men rushed up to greet the mayor and Sandra. Yoyo pumped Mahatma's hand. "Mon ami, welcome to Cameroon, which is my country and yours!" Yoyo greeted the other Canadians with equal warmth. Slade said he needed to get to a phone immediately. "A telephone?" Yoyo repeated. "A little later, my friend."

"I have a deadline and—"

"Soon, Edward, very soon," Yoyo promised. He skipped ahead to welcome the mayor.

A man on a platform silenced the crowd. Yoyo led the mayor, Sandra and Mahatma onto the platform with three Cameroonian officials. Hundreds of people surrounded the platform. Barefoot children. Men dressed in large African *boubous*, women wrapped in multicoloured *pagnes* and bearing platters of fruit and drinks on their heads. Mahatma counted one hundred heads in a section that he judged to be one-tenth of the entire crowd. He scribbled: "1000 people greet Novak at airport." Someone introduced the mayor to the crowd. "Un très très grand canadien, Son Excellence le Maire de Winnipeg!" The crowd exploded with applause and tam-tam drumming. The man motioned again for silence, which followed immediately. "Et son assistante, Mademoiselle Sandra Paquette!" Again the crowd exploded. "Et le célèbre journaliste canadien, Monsieur Mahatma Grafton!" Again the crowd went nuts.

Edward Slade knew little French, but he understood that this guy had just called Grafton "a celebrated Canadian journalist."

Hundreds of children broke out in a song. They sang at the top of their voices, wonderfully pitched, laughing, loving little voices, singing something whose message of friendship any foreigner could divine:

Bokele, bokele bo,
bokele, bokele bo, Canada!
bokele, bokele bo.

Bokele, bokele bo,
bokele, bokele bo, Cameroon!
bokele, bokele bo.

The African officials on stage began singing. The mayor joined in. So did Sandra. Mahatma saw a clutch of radiant children waving at him and, despite the piercing stare from Slade, Mahatma sang. He sang along with his thousand hosts. It was a delightfully happy melody. This contrast, more than any other, would stay with Mahatma during his week-long stay in Yaoundé. In Canada, airport crowds fought for taxis and luggage carts. In Cameroon, they sang.

They sang another song. And a third. A man on stage welcomed the Canadians in the name of His Excellency the Mayor Boubacar Fotso, the city of Yaoundé and the entire country of Cameroon. The man then conferred with his colleagues, the crowd grew talkative and boisterous, the Canadians on stage fidgeted and waited, and nobody seemed to know what would happen next. Suddenly the emcee broke out of a huddle with his colleagues and called out in French for the other Canadians to come up on stage. Yoyo translated. Susan and Bob mounted the platform, but Edward Slade refused.

An official in a long blue *boubou* approached him. "You don't wish to join your colleagues on stage?"

"They're not my colleagues. They're my competition."

The African scratched his head. "You don't like Cameroon?"

"It's not that. I'm here as a reporter. That's all."

A second official conferred with the first.

"He doesn't wish to go onstage?"

"No. He says he's a reporter and that he doesn't like Cameroon."

The second man clucked with his tongue and led the first one away.

Slade watched them go. It wasn't his fault if they couldn't understand English. Look at them! Slade whipped out his notepad. Two men walking hand-in-hand. Not even ashamed! Slade saw other men doing the same. He wrote, "Homosexuals uninhibited in Yaoundé airport!" He underlined this observation. He had a great idea! He could write about sexual diseases in Yaoundé. AIDS in Africa.

Leaving the stage, the Canadians were mobbed by children. Susan scooped a little boy up in her arms. "Isn't he a darling!"

Something tugged at Mahatma's leg. Engaged in conversation with an official, he ignored it. The tug made itself felt again. "Papa!" cried a little voice. Mahatma looked down. A shirtless, shoeless boy with a bald head and ebony disks for irises again closed his fist around Mahatma's pant leg and called up, "Papa!"

Before Mahatma and the other Canadian journalists were led from the airport, four Cameroonians—including two local reporters—stunned Mahatma by asking him about "the famous" Jake Corbett.

John Novak and Sandra Paquette snacked with His Excellency, a corpulent, middle-aged man with a booming laugh and quick eyes. Afterwards, the mayors retired to another room, leaving Sandra to wait in His Excellency's office. Sandra yawned. She tried reading, but her eyes hurt. She wondered what the reporters were doing. Sleeping, probably! Sandra put her book down and fell asleep on a couch. She was awakened by His Excellency's baritone chuckle.

"She's a lazy one, a real sleepyhead," His Excellency joked to Novak.

Sandra stared at her boss. Novak said, "We're both quite tired."

"Absolutely," said His Excellency. "My driver will take you to the Hotel Kennedy. He'll pick you up in time for the press conference."

The Hotel Kennedy, however, had only reserved one room for the mayor of Winnipeg. It had not been informed about his assistant and had no room for her. Nor did any other hotels in town. Sandra was put up with the reporters in the university dormitory.

Murmurings, excited squeals and hissing sounds slowly drew Mahatma out of his nap. At first, he didn't know where he was. Then he did. The hissing resumed. Every few seconds, it came like a brief rush of water. Between each rush came the murmurings and squeals. It was a delightful chain of sounds: water, laughter, then water again. Mahatma climbed out of bed, swept aside the curtains and leaned out his window. He saw a valley of brilliant green and a red clay road connecting earthen, box-like homes.

Directly below his second-storey window, boys conferred under a mammoth tree. It was pregnant with mangoes. Every few seconds, a boy would hurl a stone up into the foliage, aiming for the peduncle linking a fruit to a branch. Mahatma stood at the window for fifteen minutes, mesmerized by the boys, their excited gestures and their strange language, which he couldn't understand, except for numbers of felled mangoes, which were called out in French. *Deux. Trois. Quatre. Cinq mangues!*

Somebody knocked at his door. Yoyo had brought food for Mahatma and his fellow journalists. He brought baguettes and spicy chunks of goat meat bundled in paper, and short, thick bananas twice as thick and tasty as those sold in Canada—and four bottles of Sprite. The Canadians devoured the food and pumped Yoyo with questions.

Edward Slade asked, "Where are the phones?"

Susan asked, "Who is that cute guy across the hall?"

Mahatma asked, "What do we do next?"

"Bananas make me constipated," Bob mumbled.

"Would you all shut up and let Yoyo talk?" Slade said.

Yoyo said he would take them later to the bank. Then they could file their stories from the telecommunications building. Then, time permitting, they could sight-see. Then attend a press conference. Then attend a banquet and dance at the mayor's residence.

"Couldn't we just file our stories and come back here to sleep?" Bob whined.

Yoyo was amazed. "But you can sleep in Canada, my friend! Surely you didn't come all this way to sleep?"

Slade asked, "Where's the mayor? Where's Sandra?"

"The mayor is sleeping at his hotel. Sandra has a room in this building . . . she came in while you were sleeping."

Mahatma flung open his windows to let in the sunlight and the sound of stones skimming through mango trees. Then he activated his portable computer and wrote two articles. The first described Cameroon's recent political history. Mahatma mentioned that former president Amadou Ahidjo had steered the country into independence in 1960 and led it for twenty-two years, handing over the reins subsequently to the current leader, Paul Biya. And that Biya, who had quashed an attempted coup in April of this year, now sought visits from foreign dignitaries to reaffirm the government's credibility. Mahatma tied this into John Novak's visit, mentioning the welcome at the airport.

Mahatma wrote a second story about enthusiasm in Cameroon for Jake Corbett.

> In Canada, he has been jailed, refused service in restaurants and publicly ridiculed.
> But in Cameroon, Winnipeg welfare activist Jake Corbett has a hero's following.
> Articles about the 46-year-old anti-poverty crusader have frequently appeared on the front page of the biggest newspaper in Cameroon—to which Corbett has never travelled. And local journalists are anxious to discuss 'the Corbett case' with visiting Canadians.

Having finished his work, Mahatma chatted with Jean-Paul Gribi, the building janitor, until it was time to go to the bank and the telecommunications building. Speaking to Yoyo as he left the dormitory area, Mahatma expressed surprise that Gribi had such a wide range of interests. In a ten-minute exchange, Gribi had wanted to discuss Castro's revolution in Cuba, problems facing Canadian wheat farmers and Sino-Soviet relations.

Yoyo asked, "Does he have a transistor radio?"

"Yes! He was holding one while we talked."

"Then he has been listening to Radio Yaoundé. It has explored all those themes lately."

Yoyo hailed a taxi and the reporters crowded in. Mahatma, who sat up front with Yoyo, looked out at the women grilling fish and corn cobs over roadside fires. They passed a woman in a *pagne* of red cotton swinging an axe into a log held by her bare foot. They passed a man repairing sandals under a sign proclaiming him a shoe doctor. The driver, who avoided potholes with great care, grew excited when Mahatma told him they were Canadians.

"So you know the great Canadian, Jacques Corbeil?"

Yoyo tapped his friend on the shoulder. "He means Jake Corbett."

"Yes, of course," Mahatma responded in French, "I know him well."

"Tell us what you know of him," Yoyo told the driver.

For the rest of the trip to the mayor's office, the cab driver recited facts about Jacques Corbeil.

They got out at the bank. Yoyo helped them change their money. Then he took them to the phone building, where they filed stories to Winnipeg. Later, they went to meet his Excellency the Mayor. The reporters were greeted there by the mayor's deputy executive assistant. This gentleman—a tall, thin fellow wearing a jacket and tie and leather sandals—introduced himself as Pierre somebody. He quickly began, in French, on the rules of protocol. Edward Slade cut him off. "Can't you do this in English?"

The executive assistant spoke no English. Mahatma translated for him, laying down the rules: His Excellency would entertain questions about friendship between Winnipeg and Yaoundé; he would answer questions about how the two cities intended to deepen ties in the future; and he would accept statistical and historical questions about his country. He would *not* tolerate questions about his political ideology. And one other thing. The journalists were to write down all their questions now. The mayor would review them, answering as he saw fit.

Bob began writing hurriedly. So did Susan. And Mahatma followed suit. He hoped to get on the agenda and then slip in some extra questions once the mayor loosened up.

Slade growled, "This is bullshit."

Two mayors entered the room holding hands. His Excellency Boubacar Fotso wore a magnificent African *boubou*. "Honourable and Esteemed Canadian Journalists," he began, reading in English from a prepared script. It lasted ten minutes and contained no facts or promises.

Now it was John Novak's turn. He said he hoped to renew ties with a visit to Winnipeg by Yaoundé's mayor next spring or summer. He outlined a proposed student exchange program. Slade cut him off.

"Mayor Fotso, will communism solve poverty in Africa?"

The mayor of Yaoundé conferred with his assistant, who spoke to Sandra, who translated for Slade. "You are requested," she said, "to accord His Excellency due respect."

"I'm a journalist! I don't have to kowtow to anybody."

The mayor of Yaoundé passed another message to Sandra, who said, "I'm sorry, Mr. Slade, but you are asked to leave the premises immediately and not return."

Slade blanched and walked out silently.

A taxi left him at the Yaoundé police headquarters. He wandered inside, met a uniformed man in the first office and explained what he wanted. The officer said, "Have a seat. My name is Ibrahim Somo. I am the assistant superintendent of police. It's a pleasure to meet you."

Slade fired away, "What sort of crime do you get around here?" He scribbled the answer at a furious pace. Thirty-seven voodoo murders had eluded homicide detectives for years. Also, a lucrative white-slave-trade market involved the kidnapping of foreign diplomats and tourists and, in particular, journalists. The victims were routinely enslaved for five years and then beheaded. And there was more barbarity. . . .

Slade filled half a notebook. What a scoop! What a story! But the assistant superintendent could only spare fifteen minutes.

Slade phoned in his story and decided to follow it up with several more articles under the theme Bloodbath in the Tropics. In one story he could examine the penal system, in another, African techniques of murder detection, and so on.

Don Betts studied the words forming on the computer screen as Mahatma Grafton dictated his stories by telephone to a reporter in *The Herald* newsroom. So a thousand people sing at the airport! And who wanted to read background on Cameroon? Betts watched Grafton's second story come onto the screen. Jake Corbett, famous in Africa? Betts waited until Grafton had completed his dictation, then flattened the tape recording suction cup against the earphone of the receiver and picked up the telephone.

"Hi, Hat, Betts here! . . . Great stuff. . . . First rate. . . . So tell me, what's going on over there? What kind of place are you staying in? . . . A run-down university residence? Really! And the mayor's in a three-star hotel? And the city, what's it like? God, I wish I could see it! . . . Pretty, magnificent trees, potholed roads? Potholed roads, huh? You see a lot of poverty in the streets? . . . Women cooking fish right on the roadside? Really! . . . Selling to passers-by! Anybody buying? . . . No kidding!

Betts didn't tell Mahatma he was rewriting his copy. He didn't say he killed the story about Corbett's fame in Cameroon. He stayed pleasant on the phone. But he exploded the next morning when he saw Slade's Bloodbath in the Tropics scoop. He left a message at the Yaoundé mayor's office for Grafton to match Slade's story immediately.

The previous night, the Canadian contingent—minus Edward Slade—had been invited to a feast at the home of the Yaoundé mayor. Children crowded outside a locked gate to the three-storey residence, staring at the white guests and the perfumed Africans. One lighter-skinned boy latched onto Bob's leg. "Papa, Papa!" he called out. Bob looked down at the kid hanging onto him. Shaven head. Shirtless. Shoeless. Whites of the eyes catching light from the door. "Papa, donnez-moi dix francs."

"He wants ten francs," Mahatma said.

"Ten francs?" Bob said. "What is that, about three cents?" He found a coin in his pocket and handed it down.

"D'ou êtes-vous?" one older boy, around twelve, asked the group.

"Canada."

Lawrence Hill

"We know all about Canada," the boy said. He and his friends went into a huddle, their animated voices ringing out in French and Bamileke. Then they burst apart and began clapping in unison and shouting out a roll call, led by the first boy: "Le Président, Pierre Trudeau. Son Excellence le maire, Monsieur Novaque. Et le grand héro canadien, Jacques Corbeil!!!"

His Excellency's chauffeur ran to the scene, kicking the children.

"Hey, take it easy," Susan shouted at the driver.

He ignored her. "Allez vous-en, foutez-nous la paix!" The youngsters scattered.

Inside, the Canadians were escorted up to a balcony overlooking a valley. Mahatma, the mayor and Sandra were placed at a table with the mayor of Yaoundé and the elder of his two wives. A visiting mayor from the city of Bafoussam joined them later at the table, shaking hands with Mahatma and asking if Sandra were his wife.

Mahatma, embarrassed, said no.

"Alors vous êtes des amants comme ça?" the Bafoussam mayor asked.

Sandra cleared her throat.

The mayor of Yaoundé corrected his colleague. "This is Sandra Paquette. She is Monsieur Novak's assistant."

They were given a feast of the likes that Mahatma had never seen. They started with braised fish fillets in an explosive chili sauce. The mayor of Bafoussam jokingly dubbed the spices "des piments de crocodile." In an aside to Mahatma, he nodded suggestively downward and said that eating lots of them would give him strength "en-bas, vous comprenez, là où vous êtes un homme." The mackerel was followed by plantains fried in palm oil and served up as hot chips, which were sweeter than bananas. After the plantains came chicken breasts served in peanut sauce, rice wrapped in vine leaves, cassava sticks, lettuce smothered by tomatoes and avocado. Finally, they had coffee, madeleines and liqueurs. The feast lasted three hours. Conversation flowed between each course; indeed, each mouthful. The Cameroonians expressed great interest in Mahatma.

"You know, good sir," said Boubacar Fotso, "that you bear the name of a great man."

"Ah yes, the name but not the fame," Mahatma said, provoking a round of laughter.

"But how did you get that name? Why was it given to you? There must have been a reason. I have met many North Americans, but never anybody with the name 'Mahatma'."

"It means 'Great Soul' in Hindi," Mahatma said.

"A difficult name to live up to."

"It must have been an error. It would have been easier to go with 'Great Appetite'."

The Cameroonians laughed.

"You have an odd pigmentation," the mayor of Bafoussam declared. "Your father, is he a black man?"

"Yes."

"So your mother, she is a white woman?"

"My mother passed away when I was a child. But she was black too."

"Impossible!" declared the mayor of Bafoussam.

"Why?" John Novak asked. "She was black and his father is black, but lighter toned than you."

"You know his family?" asked His Excellency of Yaoundé, pouring Beaujolais into his guests' glasses.

"Yes. I know his father well."

The Yaoundé mayor asked, "Is Mahatma's father a journalist too?"

"No. He worked on the railroad. He had a labourer's job. He and his fellow workers were all black. It was practically the only work they could get. This was in the late 1930s and '40s. They had horrible working conditions. One of their colleagues, a fine man commonly called the Rabbi, died needlessly in a fire. The railroad tried to cover it up. Mahatma's father risked his job by coming to me. I was a young lawyer, anxious to make my reputation. We raised an awful stink."

"But," the mayor of Bafoussam exclaimed excitedly, "you must tell us more about this! A black Rabbi on the railroad!"

Mahatma told that story.

The Cameroonians countered with a few of their own. They told of the misfortunes of foreigners who had cut down sacred baobab trees. And they told of the newly arrived Canadian foreign aid worker who, just last week, had to bribe four people to get a visa problem straightened out. By the time the aid worker got around to his fourth bribe, he had no pocket money left. The man with the visa stamp actually sent the aid worker off to the bank. And the Canadian actually said "thank you" after he came back, made his payment and got his problem fixed.

After the talk and the many courses, came the dancing. It had a great deal to do with the pelvis and very little to do with conversation.

Bob and Susan met Mahatma and Sandra beside the dance floor.

"I feel like such an idiot, not speaking French!" Susan said. "All these officials speak English, French and two or three other languages, and all I speak is English. But what a feast! I ate enough for a week!"

"Think we can go back soon?" Bob said. "I'm beat."

"I feel like dancing!" Susan said. "Listen to that music!"

Makossa music blasted from stereo speakers. It was such earthy, happy music that Susan felt she had known it all her life. A man swept her onto the dance floor. She moved happily, swaying and thrusting her hips like any relaxed Canadian would do. Hardly moving his feet, the Cameroonian ground his pelvis rhythmically. His arms were bent at the elbow, held just above his hips, with the hands turned out slightly; quite unlike Susan, who brought her arms up high, even above her shoulders.

Somebody pulled Sandra onto the dance floor. She disappeared in the crowd. Mahatma watched the dancing, loving the music, thinking of the good food he had eaten, but thinking also of filing a story about the street children outside.

Mahatma chatted with a crowd of men for fifteen minutes, then moved on. He came upon Sandra and Susan, standing in a corner, fending off invitations to dance.

"Some guy just put his hand right on my tit!" Susan said. "You should have seen it, Hat. He put his hand right here! And he pulled me against him. I swear, that guy had a boner as big as a horse!"

Sandra laughed nervously. She, too, had been grabbed during a few slow dances.

Bob joined them. Susan pulled him onto the dance floor.

Mahatma touched Sandra's elbow. "May I?"

"I thought you'd never ask."

They played three slow dances, back to back. Mahatma and Sandra stayed on the floor for all of them.

Bob heard Mahatma and Sandra laughing. The noise kept him awake. Much later, he heard Sandra moaning. Was she ill? Crying? Maybe she needed help. Bob rose from his bed, opened his door, then slammed it shut. Suddenly he understood what kind of moaning it was!

In the morning, he was awakened. Swish, swish. Like water being tossed over rocks. It was impossible to sleep in this country. People made too much noise. And what was it now? It was coming from outside.

Bob opened his window and leaned out on the sill. He saw a stone hurtling toward a huge mango tree. It swished through the leaves and a mango fell into the hands of a shoeless boy. He and several friends had a pile of fruit at their feet.

Bob looked to his left and saw Mahatma and Sandra standing side by side, shoulders touching, elbows propped the same way on the window sill, leaning out and looking down at the boys. He went back to bed.

Someone pounded on Mahatma's door. He rinsed the suds off his body, tied a towel around his waist and opened the door.

"I'm starving!" Bob said. "Want to get some breakfast?"

They walked up the hill and found a food stand in the shade of a baobab tree. Men clustered around it, drinking coffee and tea and eating scrambled eggs sandwiched in baguettes. The cook called out to Mahatma and Bob, "Messieurs! Voulez-vous un petit déjeuner camerounais?"

"And why not," Mahatma replied in French, "your eggs look good."

"Monsieur!" the cook said. "These eggs are more than good. They will make your mouth water. Your stomach smile. Your entire being, Monsieur, will be at peace with these eggs."

"In which case," Mahatma said, "I'll have one order of eggs à la baguette. With fried tomato and onion. And if those eggs are as good as you say, I shall spread the word throughout my country."

"And which country is that, Monsieur?"

"Canada."

"Ah! Canada!" The cook twirled his spatula, broke two large eggs on the side of the frying pan and addressed a young African man eating next to Mahatma. "You, lazy student," the cook jested, "why don't you speak to Monsieur le Canadien? Is it because you know nothing of his country?"

"Bah! I know about Canada."

"Then tell Monsieur le Canadien something about his country!"

The student put his baguette down. He stood tall, chin up, chest out, and began: "Canada is a great country! It has the second largest surface area in the world. It shares a southern border with the United States of America. It has been led until recently by Prime Minister Trudeau."

"Pof!" the cook snorted. "You, a university student, and that is all you know?"

"No," the student replied, "I know more. Much more. Canada has a great sprawling city with an extremely low population density, and this city is called Vinn-ee-peg. There is a famous poor man there. A poor white man. His name is Corbeil. Jacques Corbeil. So there! You see! I do know about Canada. And I know more. A delegation of Canadians is visiting our city right now. His Excellency the Mayor of Vinn-ee-peg is visiting! And journalists."

"And you, my friend," the cook asked Mahatma, "what is your name?"

"Mahatma."

"I thought so," cried the student. "Mahatma Grafton! The famous journalist! We know all about you. Humble cook, open the newspaper!"

The cook shook open a newspaper. Its front page carried a picture of Mahatma at the airport with the mayors of Yaoundé and Winnipeg.

"Humble cook, crack open more eggs for this man, and feed his shy friend!" The student shook Mahatma's hand vigorously. "Two breakfasts for the Canadians, on me! Welcome to Cameroon!"

Mahatma had a busy day. He interviewed a Canadian diplomat about trade relations between Cameroon and Canada, and talked to another official about Cameroon's economy. He wrote one story based on those notes and arranged to visit a rural hospital developed with Canadian funds. Then he booked an appointment to interview Mayor Fotso. The mayor's secretary told Mahatma to call *The Herald* immediately.

Betts answered the phone. Mahatma asked about his stories.

"They came out just fine. But why didn't you get that scoop on the Bloodbath in the Tropics?"

"What are you talking about?"

Betts described the story and provided the name of Ibrahim Somo, assistant superintendant of the Yaoundé police force. "Match Slade's story! Find a new angle. Dig into the white slave trade."

"I'll see what I can do." Mahatma preferred not to fight on the telephone. He would be calling Betts every day; the man could make Mahatma's job impossible.

"I have a story for you now," Mahatma said.

"Yeah, about what?"

"Economic relations between Canada and Cameroon."

Betts said politely, "Okay. Let it roll."

Mahatma had no intention of following Slade's story. But he wanted to know what Slade had written and how he had researched it. First, he spoke to Slade. "Hear you got a big scoop. Now that it's out in Winnipeg, can you show it to me?" Slade unfolded the handwritten copy he had dictated by phone. Mahatma noted the details and ran to find a taxi. At the Yaoundé police station, Mahatma asked for the names of the two most senior officers. But neither the superintendent nor his assistant was named Ibrahim Somo. Nobody on the force had that name.

Mahatma went to see the superintendent, who had heard of the arrival of the Canadian journalists and recognized Mahatma's name.

"Do you have anyone on staff named Ibrahim Somo?"

"No."

"Was your assistant superintendent here yesterday?"

"No. His child died on the weekend. He is in mourning."

Mahatma explained what had appeared in *The Star*.

"Someone has made a fool of that journalist. We have no such crimes on record. They must have been conjured up by someone who knew your friend would like such a story."

Mahatma asked Slade how he had come across the source named Ibrahim Somo. Slade told him. Then Mahatma said what he had discovered.

"That bastard!" Slade yelled. "And I believed him! He was in uniform and everything. You're not going to write about this, are you? I hope you can keep this between us!"

"Sorry." Mahatma wrote down everything Slade had just said.

Slade stared at him. Then he smiled, a little. "Fucking Mahatma Grafton. I underestimated you. Sucking me in like that. You're just as slimy as me."

Mahatma's story began:

> The Winnipeg Star published "complete falsehoods" about barbaric crimes in Cameroon after being spoofed by an imposter posing as a senior police official, says Yaoundé Police Superintendent Paul Beti.

Mahatma raced back to the telecommunications office to phone in the story. Then he returned to relax at the dormitory. He felt like seeing Sandra. He wanted to tell her about the story he had just filed. He wanted to ask her what she had done today. Had she seen much of Yaoundé? Did she want to go for a stroll? Mahatma knocked on her door. No answer. He knocked again. She opened it. Her eyes were red. A hand was on her hip.

"Look who," she said. "And what's up for tomorrow's article, a detailed description of the mayor's assistant?"

"What do you mean?"

She produced a piece of paper with five handwritten paragraphs. "This is the top of your page one story today."

> Communist Mayor John Novak booked himself into a luxury hotel but checked his female aide into a bug-infested dormitory after arriving yesterday in Cameroon's poverty-stricken capital.

It went on and on. People living off roadside fish, potholed roads all over the city, the misery of communist Africa. . . . Not a word about the twinning project. Not a serious word about Cameroon.

"I didn't write that. Not one word of it."

"Then how did they get details like that, three-star hotel, bug-infested hovel, mayor's aide, potholed roads?"

"I filed two stories, neither of which made any such references. I talked to Betts on the phone. He drew things out of me in conversation. He twisted them around."

"But how could you even mention things like that to him? How could you say 'mayor takes luxury hotel and dumps his aide in hovel' when you know there were no other rooms available? And why would you even *mention* such things?"

"I didn't say it at all like that. Betts sucked me into chatting about Yaoundé. I had no idea what he was up to. I mentioned my room had a lot of bugs and that you were staying with the journalists, and you can see how he used it. He asked how the roads were, I said okay, but there were a few potholes, and you can see how he used that."

"How disgusting!" Sandra said.

Mahatma called *The Herald* from the mayor's office. Helen Savoie answered the phone. "Good thing you called when I was here," she said.

"What's going on with my stories?"

"Betts has butchered them," Helen said. "He's gone wild. If I were you, I'd refuse to file another story from Africa."

"Let me talk to Van Wuyss."

Van Wuyss was out of town and had left Betts in charge.

Mahatma's article about Jake Corbett never ran. The piece he had filed about the Cameroonian economy and bilateral trade with Canada might never see the light of day. Mahatma sighed and dictated his story about Slade's screw-up.

Don Betts turned on his computer. *This* was something to write about. Far better than that no-news mush Mahatma Grafton kept trying to peddle on the phone. Betts had sources everywhere. He was friendly with some cops. He knew one or two well-placed politicians. He even knew the guy who ran the civic dog pound. And he had a contact with the U.S. Immigration and Naturalization Service. Betts phoned his contacts monthly to see if something was stirring. He had checked in with his U.S. Immigration source two days before Mayor Novak was scheduled to fly back from Cameroon via New York.

And this source had turned up gold.

"Somebody in the Canadian group in Cameroon is not going to be permitted to enter the United States."

"Why?" Betts had asked.

"Suspected communist sympathies."

"Fantastic!" Betts had howled. "Who?"

"Draw your own conclusions," the source had said.

Betts had left several messages with the Yaoundé mayor's office for Mahatma Grafton. But the reporter didn't call back. He hadn't called or filed a story for twenty-four hours.

Betts got another reporter to call Novak's office in Winnipeg. They put the message through to the mayor, got his response and fed it back to the reporter: "In response to *The Herald*'s query, Novak

stated that he does not believe *The Herald's* story, has no difficulty
with the U.S. Immigration and Naturalization Service and will not
change his plans to fly to Canada via Dakar and New York."

Betts bashed out the story:

> United States immigration officials will detain and deport
> Mayor John Novak if he lands in New York on the return flight
> from his visit with a leftist leader in Africa, *The Herald* has learned.
>
> A U.S. immigration official—who spoke on condition that
> he remain unnamed—implied that the mayor would be refused
> entry into the country because of "communist sympathies."
>
> Novak, a long-time member of the Canadian Communist
> Party, has previously had his name in the U.S. Immigration and
> Naturalization Service's lookout book. It contains thousands of
> names of foreigners barred for being terrorists, anarchists,
> homosexuals or communists.
>
> Novak used his political office to have his name struck from
> the list several years ago. The source would not explain why it
> appears that the mayor has again become a persona non grata. He
> refused comment on Novak's current visit with Boubacar Fotso,
> the left-wing, anti-American mayor of Yaoundé.
>
> In a statement released through his Winnipeg office, Novak
> told *The Herald* . . .

Mahatma heard about the immigration story the morning it
came out. Waging a silent strike, he hadn't been in contact with
his editors for thirty-six hours. But he spoke every day with Helen
Savoie, who told him in whispered French what was going on.
Mahatma thanked Helen, wound up the phone call, met Sandra
and walked up the hill with her toward the omelette-maker who
knew all about Canada.

She said, "You're going to get fired, Hat."

"I doubt it. Suspended, maybe. I wouldn't mind a long
suspension. Especially if you got one too. I wouldn't mind staying
here for a few months," he said. "Mangoes. Makossa music."

"Boys throwing rocks through the fruit trees."

Mahatma asked if she wanted to know about Betts' latest coup.
"Shoot."

"He says the mayor's going to be detained by U.S. immigration
in New York."

"We know all about it. Betts had someone calling our Winnipeg office yesterday on that. We issued the standard denial."

"Is there any chance Betts could be right?" Mahatma asked.

"No. We straightened all that out years ago."

It was a quiet afternoon. Susan and Bob had only had one story to file and they had already done that. Susan was resting in her room. Bob was bickering with Slade, who had nothing to do, having found himself cut off in Yaoundé. The problem was that he couldn't speak French and most people in Yaoundé didn't speak English. He, too, had gone thirty-six hours without filing a story. Mahatma Grafton had landed him in deep shit. The story about the Bloodbath screwup had run on page one of *The Herald*. Other papers had picked up the story. *The Star*'s managing editor had gotten on the phone with threats. That was thirty-six hours ago. Now Bob was giving him a hard time about it. "So you walked in there and just took that guy's word for it and wrote all that stuff without—"

"Knock it off, Bob," Slade said.

Mahatma and Sandra walked into the residence and spoke with the other two about plans for the rest of the day.

At that moment, Yoyo ran into the residence. "I am sorry, my friends, but I have very very sad news."

Everybody stared at him.

"Our very great friend Jake Corbett died this afternoon."

Tears sprang from Yoyo's eyes. Mahatma gulped. Bob simply gaped at Yoyo. Sandra said, "Oh my God, how'd he die?" Slade shrugged but stayed to listen.

Mayor Boubacar Fotso had planned a reception for the Canadian journalists, but he cancelled it upon the news of Jake Corbett's death. Instead, the mayor and his assistants came to express their condolences. The mayor of Yaoundé clasped Mahatma's shoulder and kissed his cheeks. He said Cameroonians sympathized with Canadians about the loss of a great humanitarian, a leader, before his time. "It must hurt you to lose a brother like that," the mayor continued. "I am told that you wrote of him often."

The mayor and his entourage left. Yoyo raced off to write a story for the evening edition of *La Voix de Yaoundé*. Mahatma felt numb. He tended to think of the event as news: Jake Corbett died . . . that's worth a story. How did he die, what were his latest struggles with welfare authorities, what were his greatest victories . . . these things should be included in Corbett's obituary. Mahatma wondered who would write it. Under Betts' reign, nobody would write anything about it. Mahatma felt he *had* to write something. Newspapers featured famous bankers, politicians, academics, athletes. Why not take a long look at a man who was turning the welfare system on its head? Who was the poor bastard with a bad leg and a confiscated megaphone who slept in a lousy bed over Frank's Accidental Dog and Grill? What had his life meant?

Bob and Susan sent news clips to Winnipeg, quoting the reactions of Mayors Novak and Fotso to the death of Jake Corbett. Slade didn't write a word.

Mahatma went for a walk in the evening. Darkness came early to Yaoundé. The hills were dark shapes in the distance and dogs howled miles away. Shopkeepers waved as Mahatma passed by.

The omelette-maker, whose name was Janvier, stood alone at his food counter. He shook Mahatma's hand and said he was very sorry about their friend Jacques Corbeil. He also said he was out of eggs but he would be honoured to serve Mahatma coffee and a croissant. Mahatma said that would be fine. Janvier handed over the evening edition of *La Voix de Yaoundé* and said he would be back soon. He ran down the road, his thongs slapping the dirt. Mahatma opened the paper and saw the headline on page one: *"Décédé, Un Grand Frère Canadien."* Yoyo's long obituary described how he had met Corbett, how they had shared a banana in a park before both of them were beaten up in a demonstration, how Corbett scrounged for meals and fought welfare authorities to maintain his dignity and a decent standard of living, and ended up—almost—with a hero's status across the country. The article mentioned Corbett's struggle with phlebitis and said he had died of a pulmonary embolism. A massive blood clot had dislodged from his leg, entered the heart and blocked an artery to his lungs.

Janvier came back with croissants and two coffees. They ate together, leaning against the counter and watching the sky darken until the clouds were no longer distinguishable.

"Was he a very great friend of yours?"

"I knew him. I had a strong feeling for him but I couldn't say we were really friends."

"Here in Cameroon, we had a strong feeling for him. A white man, poor in America. Poor but with dignity. As long as you have your dignity, you're still a man. He was a good man, Jacques Corbeil."

Janvier wouldn't let Mahatma pay. "We have eaten tonight as friends. Friends don't pay each other for food. One gives to another, who, in turn, gives to yet another. This humble offering of mine, give it in turn to a Canadian. Give it to someone like Jacques Corbeil."

Mahatma led off with a description of the anguish in the face of a Cameroonian journalist who had come to know the man in Winnipeg. He mentioned the many times Corbett had been featured on the pages of *La Voix de Yaoundé,* how roadside cooks and building janitors and taxi drivers all knew about Corbett, and admired his struggle for dignity and decent treatment in the face of poverty and abuse. He wrote about the man named Janvier who had given Mahatma a meal and asked him to return the favour to a needy Canadian. He wrote about sitting with Corbett above Frank's Accidental Dog and Grill and hearing the phone ring constantly downstairs for him. Journalists swamped him during moments of big news, but poor people phoned him every day for advice. Concluding his piece, Mahatma wrote that Yaoundé buzzed with the news of Jake Corbett's death. Neither the beautiful African capital nor its twin city in Canada would be the same without him.

They argued on the phone. Betts asked where he'd been for the last day and a half. Mahatma ignored the question and said he wanted to file an obituary on Corbett. Betts said *The Herald* already had an obit.

"I want to file another one, from Africa, about Corbett's life and death, as seen from here."

"Let us have it, then, and I'll take a look," Betts said. He assigned another reporter to take down Grafton's dictation.

Mahatma told Sandra about the argument with Betts. "If they don't use my obit, I'm selling it elsewhere. And let me tell you something else. I'm *going* elsewhere!"

Sandra stroked his hand. "You really care about this, don't you?"

"Yeah. And it surprises me," Mahatma said. "A year ago, I could hardly have imagined myself caring about anything to do with *The Herald.*"

"Show it to me," Sandra said.

> One year ago, Jake Corbett hollered outside the Winnipeg City Hall until police arrested him.
>
> At the time, the ailing welfare recipient hoped somebody would notice him. Little did he imagine that his death, which was already imminent, would touch men and women thousands of miles away.
>
> But here in Yaoundé, mere mention of the welfare rebel sparks debate in taxis and at roadside food stands. . . .

Helen Savoie read the story on the computer screen. She shook her head in admiration. *Maudit!* Mahatma was wasting his talents. He could move onto something better. He could do something great. This was the best obit Helen had ever read in *The Herald.* But the paper didn't use it.

Flying back across the Atlantic, Mahatma interviewed the mayor about future relations between Yaoundé and Winnipeg. He also asked about Don Betts' article predicting that Novak would be detained by U.S. immigration authorities at the John F. Kennedy airport.

"My situation with U.S. Immigration was straightened out years ago," the mayor said. "I won't have any problems in New York."

Mahatma took careful notes. But it seemed pointless. Why should he stay on with *The Herald* and continue to let Don Betts ruin his stories?

Mahatma wanted very much to cover Jake Corbett's funeral, and use it as a hook to write about the man's life and death. But what was the point? Betts had killed both stories Mahatma had filed on Corbett from Cameroon. When Helen Savoie had said so by telephone, Mahatma realized that he couldn't write about Corbett's funeral for *The Herald*. Could he write about anything for *The Herald*?

The Air Afrique flight arrived in New York at 7:30 a.m. The mayor was the first off the plane. Sandra was right beside him. But the reporters were at the back of the airplane and they disembarked several minutes later. Edward Slade began running when he stepped off the plane.

Bob asked, "What's the big hurry?"

"He wants to see what happens at Immigration," Susan said.

Bob started race-walking. The mayor was already out of sight in the airport terminal. If they did stop him, every media outlet in Winnipeg would want the story. And if Bob missed it, while Slade got it . . . Susan also began to run—and more quickly than Bob. Mahatma, too, gave into it. He had to see this. Just in case.

The corridor turned at a right angle and fed into an escalator. It opened into a room with ten United States Immigration officers, each in a booth, each facing a line-up of travellers.

Mahatma was the last of the Winnipeg group to get there. He saw Sandra near the front of one line, with the mayor behind her. Slade, with a pen and notepad ready, stood behind the mayor. Seven other travellers separated Bob and Susan from Slade. Mahatma placed himself in the same line, three places back from Susan. He watched Bob approach Slade.

"Hey, Edward, can I stand in front of you? I want to catch this with my microphone." When Slade told him to screw off, Bob walked to the back of the line—directly behind Mahatma.

"Don't worry, you won't miss anything," Mahatma told Bob.

Sandra approached an immigration officer and was let through quickly. The mayor stepped ahead. Slade sidled forward. The mayor gave the officer his passport. The officer stamped it and waved the mayor through. Slade was interrogated for a few seconds and then let through.

When his turn came, Mahatma stepped up to the officer, thinking about his connecting flight in two hours from LaGuardia airport. If Mahatma made that connection, he would reach Winnipeg in time to cover Corbett's funeral later that day. *The Herald* wouldn't want the story. But he would write it anyway and sell it to another paper.

"Name?" the immigration officer asked.

"Mahatma Grafton."

"Nationality?"

"Canadian."

"Occupation?"

"Journalist."

"Where are you coming from?"

"Cameroon."

The officer checked every page of the passport. He asked, "Are you involved with any communist organizations?"

"No."

"Bringing any literature into the United States?"

"No."

Looking again at Mahatma's passport, the officer typed something into his computer keyboard. Then he walked away with the passport, saying nothing. Mahatma leaned over the counter and peered at an opened black binder. He saw the initial 'G' at the top of the page. Mahatma grasped that he was getting a rare view of the famous "lookout book." He spotted his picture. A recent picture. It was the very picture he carried in his passport! In small print, he saw his full name. Leaning further over the counter, he could see the computer screen. He saw his name and address in the U.S. immigration computer system! Then, near the top of the bright green screen, he read: "Non Grata/INA

Sections 212(a)27, 212(a)28, 212(a)29." At the top of the screen were the words: Automated Visa Lookout System.

Mahatma's mouth dropped open. Writing last year about the mayor's situation with American border authorities had taught him that INA was the U.S. Immigration and Naturalization Act and the cited sections were those invoked to bar communists, among others.

"Psst," Bob Stone whispered, "he's coming."

Mahatma jumped back. The immigration officer returned to his station. He read from a typed sheet.

"You are barred from entering the United States of America. If you have the funds on your person, we would advise you, in the company of one of our escorts, to book a flight out of the country immediately. If you lack such funds, we will be required to detain you until you obtain them."

"I don't want to enter the United States. I'm going to Canada."

"You can't fly to Canada. Not from New York."

"Why not?"

"Flights to Canada leave from LaGuardia Airport. Going to LaGuardia means entering the United States. You have to go to a country that can be accessed from this airport."

"You're joking! If you're worried I want to stay, escort me to LaGuardia. Walk me right onto the plane!"

The officer refused to discuss it. Or to say why Mahatma was barred entry. As an alien, he had no right to information.

Don Betts yelled at everybody to shut up. He cranked up the radio in the newsroom, in time to hear the words: ". . . a special report from CFRL correspondent Bob Stone, who is travelling with the mayor."

> Moments after Mayor John Novak breezed past a United States immigration check in New York this morning, authorities detained a Winnipeg reporter travelling with the politician.
> A U.S. Immigration and Naturalization Service officer at the John F. Kennedy airport grilled *Winnipeg Herald* reporter Mahatma Grafton about whether he was involved with

communists. Mr. Grafton, who was last seen being led into a closed room, failed to retrieve his luggage or to make his connecting flight to Canada.

Ironically, Mr. Grafton has written in the past about the communist mayor's delicate relationship with U.S. border officials. And only yesterday, Mr. Grafton's newspaper quoted an immigration source who predicted that the mayor would not be allowed to enter the United States on his return trip from Africa to Winnipeg.

Asked about the incident, the mayor said . . .

Don Betts answered the phone.

"Let me talk to Van Wuyss," Mahatma said.

"Mahatma!" Betts said. "What's going on? Where are you?"

The managing editor picked up the phone. "Van Wuyss here. Hat! Is that you?"

Mahatma said the U.S. authorities were making him fly to a third country. He needed *The Herald* to buy him a seat on the next British Airways flight to London and a seat aboard Air Canada the next day from London to Toronto.

"Do they have you in a cell?" Van Wuyss asked.

"No, but they are watching me closely. I can't stay on the phone long. Could you get me on those flights? The payment will show up in the airlines' computers here at JFK. Then they'll give me the tickets and let me out of here."

"We'll get to it immediately," Van Wuyss said. "But wait a second." He read another note from Betts, who had snapped a recording device onto the telephone. "Why did they stop you? What reasons have they given?"

"They're not telling me anything. And they're making me get off the phone now. Bye."

Betts wrote a story for the newspaper's second edition. It ran as the flare on page one.

U.S. immigration authorities detained a *Winnipeg Herald* reporter at John F. Kennedy Airport in New York this morning and refused to let him make a connecting flight to Canada.

Returning from Africa to Winnipeg with Mayor John Novak, reporter Mahatma Grafton . . .

Mahatma boarded a flight to London three hours after arriving at JFK. He booked himself into a hotel for the night and called his father.

"If any reporters contact you, tell them I'm arriving at 3:00 p.m. tomorrow and that I'll have a statement to make."

"Don Betts already called," Ben said.

"What'd you tell him?"

"I told him I wasn't inclined to help someone who had been messing up my son's writing."

Arriving at the Winnipeg International Airport at 2:45, Harry Carson spotted Melvyn Hill. He waded through the crowd to shake the man's hand. "Well well, if it isn't His Honour, himself," Harry said, in a friendly tone. He clapped Melvyn on the back.

"His Honour no longer," Melvyn said, grinning. "They made me retire."

Harry smiled. "Well, in my mind, you'll always be 'the judge'."

Melvyn asked, "So what are you doing here?"

"I have something to tell young Mahatma Grafton. And you?"

"My days are free now. I just felt like seeing the lad."

"Lookit, there's Ben!"

Ben Grafton approached the duo. The three men carried on boisterously, waiting for Mahatma to arrive.

Ben asked Melvyn, "So they made you retire, did they?"

"I wish I could have stayed on. But what can you do? They let me go. But I'm okay. I have a pension. And my house is paid off. You know what? I may even take a long, fancy, first-class train trip."

"Halifax to Vancouver," Harry whistled, "feet up the whole way."

"No, try Paris to Moscow," Ben said. "Do that and I may come too."

A crowd of journalists jostled the three men. Mahatma's flight was due to arrive.

"I'll call you sometime, Harry," Melvyn said. "And Ben, I want you to tell your son something for me."

"What's that?"

"Tell him he has a good mind. Tell him he ought to leave *The Herald* and do something with his life!"

Harry Carson also had a message for Mahatma. He wanted to tell the reporter how highly Jake Corbett had spoken of him. Three days earlier, Jake had come into Harry's café and ordered flapjacks, and suddenly keeled over. He had a fork in his hand when he hit the floor. Jake had tried to speak. It sounded as if he had food in his mouth. Harry pried open the mouth and used two fingers to scoop out the food. He didn't want Jake choking. Harry withdrew a large, unchewed piece of flapjack. It was covered in bright red blood. Jake was trying to tell him something. But he was short of breath.

Harry put a coat under Jake's feet. He dried his friend's sweating face. He touched Jake's hand. Curling his fingers around Harry's thumb, Jake whispered his last words and gasped. A thick line of blood dribbled down his chin. Harry called an ambulance. But Jake Corbett was gone before Harry heard the siren.

The mayor asked her to go to the airport. He wanted to know what Mahatma had to say about his troubles in New York. Sandra was to take careful notes if Mahatma made a public statement.

"I'd go myself, but it would be unseemly for the mayor to appear so curious. Besides," he said, grinning, "you might want to see him alone."

When she lowered her eyes, he continued, "I want you to know that I don't mind you seeing him. I know you'll guard the privacy of my office."

Waiting for Mahatma at the airport, Sandra avoided the crowd of journalists and camera technicians. When reporters were hungry for a story, they would scrum anybody. Sandra didn't want to be scrummed. She didn't want to be followed and badgered. She wanted thirty seconds alone with Mahatma. She had done something crazy in New York. She had picked up Mahatma's suitcase and brought it home. "It's at my place," she planned to tell him. "Want to get it?"

They were standing in a bar at the airport. Everybody was drinking. Bob Stone, however, stuck to orange juice. He hadn't been planning to be back on the job the day after his trans-Atlantic return from Cameroon. But this was his story. He had broken it. He wanted to follow it through before taking any time off. A CBC-TV reporter had a word with Bob. "All right," Bob said, striving to sound nonchalant. He was told to face the camera. Lights shone down on him.

"Bob Stone," the TV reporter asked, "tell us what happened when Mahatma Grafton was stopped by immigration officers at the John F. Kennedy Airport."

Bob assumed his radio voice. This was his third interview that day.

Don Betts and Lyndon Van Wuyss stood at a coffee counter opposite the door through which Mahatma would appear. A pack of reporters pressed in on them. "Come on, Don, tell us about it," one journalist said.

"Not on your life," Betts said. "You're wasting your time. Mahatma Grafton isn't going to talk to you, either. We're taking him straight to the office for a debriefing."

Camera lights shone on Van Wuyss. Someone called out, "Can you tell us about the detention of your reporter in New York?" Reporters stuck microphones close to the M.E.'s face.

"*The Herald* is outraged by the blatant harassment of one of its best reporters. We did everything in our power to make Mr. Grafton's detention as brief as possible."

"Sir," another reporter said, "we have sources saying that Mahatma Grafton was denied entry to the United States because his father was a socialist and labour activist in the 1950s. How do you respond to that?"

"I'll have to discuss that with Mr. Grafton."

Another reporter spoke up. "A spokesman for the U.S. Immigration and Naturalization Service admitted this morning that Mr. Grafton was detained under Section 212(a)28. That is the section barring communist aliens from the U.S.A. Mr. Van Wuyss, is your reporter a communist?"

Van Wuyss ignored the question.

"Here he comes," someone shouted.

Twenty-five journalists, seven camera technicians and thirty onlookers pressed toward the arrivals door. Betts fought to the front of the pack. Sandra was hit on the head by a television camera. She dropped her tape recorder. She knelt to retrieve it, but the crowd surged forward, knocking her over and leaving her at the outer edge of the scrum. A hand touched her shoulder. Softly. An old, lined, brown hand with long, slender fingers. From behind her came a melodious voice. "Let me help you."

Ben Grafton gently took her elbow. Sandra felt dizzy. Her forehead was sticky.

"You've got a cut on your face. Come sit down." The smiling man led her to a bench and sat beside her. He pressed a tissue against Sandra's temple. She moaned. "You'll be just fine. I looked after cuts and bruises for forty years on the railway."

Flying west over the Atlantic for the second time in two days, Mahatma no longer felt impatient about getting home, or irritated about missing Corbett's funeral. He felt calmer. He ate a little but skipped the wine. After the meal, he prepared a statement. He practised reading it until he had it memorized. Then he slept until the plane landed in Toronto. He made a connecting flight and slept most of the way to Winnipeg. As the plane began its descent toward the prairies, Mahatma shaved in the john, washed his face and picked out his hair. He wished he had a clean shirt.

The first person he saw was Don Betts, pressed against the side of the glass door which had been swung open for arriving travellers. Mahatma shoved past him and through the humming pack of journalists. He stood up on a bench to be seen and heard better. He thought he saw his father sitting with Sandra. But a cameraman on a stepladder blocked his view.

Mahatma said he wanted to make a statement. The scrum grew silent. He described his experience in New York.

"The measures were intended as harassment. The authorities knew I wasn't stopping in the United States, but only attempting to fly to Canada. Why they harassed me, I don't know. I'm not a communist. I belong to no political party. I sat on the student council of my high school ten years ago, and that's as political as I've ever been.

"But there is something else I wish to say. I am resigning from *The Herald*, as of this moment. I am resigning because reports I filed from Yaoundé were distorted and falsified by *The Herald*." Mahatma added that Don Betts had twisted two of his stories and killed others outright.

A reporter asked, "What are you going to do now?"

When Mahatma stepped off the bench to answer, Betts shoved him. Three reporters jumped into the fray. Betts punched one of them. Airport security officers ordered Betts from the terminal. Lyndon Van Wuyss, bombarded by questions, left of his own accord.

It took Mahatma an hour to conduct all the interviews. He didn't care how the journalists presented his border trouble. He just hoped they let people know that he hadn't written the stories from Africa that had run under his byline.

A thin, pale man approached Mahatma after the last interview. "I'm Frank, 'member me? Jake lived in my place."

"Yes, I remember."

"How'd you like to come clean out Jake's room?"

"I beg your pardon?"

"He's got all sorts of diaries and papers and documents and suchlike and if you don't want 'em I'm junking 'em on trash day."

"Don't throw them out. I'll come see you in a day or two."

"I'll give you a hot dog. Deluxe. On the house."

Mahatma walked up to his father, who stood beside Sandra. He would have hugged them both, but the cameramen would have filmed it. He winked at her and shook his father's hand. "Did I get the message out to enough media stations?" Ben asked. Mahatma smiled. Ben introduced his son to Harry Carson. Mahatma put his hand in Harry's big palm.

"Jake Corbett loved you a whole lot," Harry said. "He wanted me to give you a message. It was the last thing he said. I wrote it down so I wouldn't forget. But my spelling's awful bad, and I'm sorry about that."

Mahatma read the note. "Jake says you're supposed to write a story on him. A big story or a book. On the life and time of Jake Corbett." "I'll come see you soon," he told Harry.

"Do that. I make good flapjacks. Jake liked 'em, anyway."

Lyndon Van Wuyss tacked two announcements to the message board at *The Herald*. The first read: "Mahatma Grafton resigned from *The Herald*, effective July 25, 1984." The second read: "Don Betts has been suspended for one week, effective July 25, 1984, for unbecoming conduct at the Winnipeg International Airport."

Mahatma could go to Crete. He could live in Spain. But he didn't want to. Cameroon was more appealing, but he didn't want to go back there. Not right now. For the present, he wanted to be involved with his own country. He wanted to *do* something.

Jake Corbett must have been some kind of saint or something. Frank could tell. He had never seen Jake do one bad thing. But beyond that, Jake had done something unique. Twice, without even being there, he had drawn couples to the Accidental Dog and Grill. Frank had seen these couples come looking for Jake, in body or in spirit. Couples *never* came to the Dog and Grill. Bums, yes. Bums and winos. And guys out of work. But couples? First, that African journalist had come to Frank's with that woman reporter from New York. And now, upstairs, there was Mahatma Grafton with a woman called Sandra. There was something special about these two couples. In both cases, the man and the woman were hot on each other. They weren't clinging or kissing or carrying on like horny kids; they just gave off a certain feeling. There was something going on. They were *discovering* each other. They were discovering Jake Corbett. It could only mean one thing if such distinguished people were running after Jake, even when he was dead. It meant he was a saint.

Jake Corbett had kept a diary. It spanned several years. On the first page, he had written: "This journal is dedicated to Section Seven of the Charter of Rights. And to telling things straight and true."

Mahatma flipped through the pages. Certain lines caught his eye. Mahatma lingered over the entry for July 11, 1983—that was the day he had joined *The Herald*. "I been going to Burger Delight on Osborne Street but today they wouldn't let me in. The man at the door said try Robins Donuts across the street. I never seen anyone else stopped in a restaurant. Except some Indians, one time. Robins let me in. I had two crullers."

Corbett had documented everything he had ever done. The day he flew to New Zealand. The day he learned his welfare would be cut off to compensate for his trip to Christchurch. The day he was arrested for vacuuming mail from a letter box.

He had boxes and boxes of welfare-related documents. Court decisions, news clippings, booklets setting out welfare rates, letters from welfare officers, notices that his benefits were being curtailed, doctors' certificates . . .

Sitting on Corbett's concave mattress, Mahatma said, "It's going to take weeks to go through all this stuff. But there's a hell of a story in it."

Sandra, who was sitting behind him on the bed, rested her chin on his shoulder. "Write it, Hat. I'll kill you if you don't."

Mahatma and Sandra visited Harry Carson at his café. They sat at the counter and ordered coffee. Harry served up stacks of banana flapjacks with hot maple syrup. He served juice and pie and coffee. And he wouldn't take a cent.

After the meal, when Mahatma went to the john, Harry leaned over the counter and whispered to Sandra, "You're his girl, aren't you?"

"I wouldn't put it quite that way," Sandra said.

"I'm too old to put things the right way," Harry said, pouring her another cup of coffee. Mahatma and Sandra sat with Harry for two hours, past the closing time of the Flapjack Café. Mahatma took notes and said he also wanted to write about the Rabbi one day. Harry said, "Yes, come back. I'll tell you all about the Rabbi, 'cause he's worth a book just like Jake."

It was a Saturday morning, three days after his return. They were in a simple room, with a big window and a big bed and one big pillow. Sandra was still sleeping. Columns of sunlight poured through her window and burst against the mirror. Mahatma heard the breeze. He heard the leaves conversing. He rose, slipped on his clothes and stepped outside. He bought *The Herald, The Star* and *The Toronto Times,* held them under his arm and crossed the street to a deli. There, he bought two large cafés au lait and, in memory of Jake Corbett, two crullers. He brought them back to Sandra's room, and then ate and drank and read in bed until she rolled over and opened her eyes and laughed.

Mahatma devoured the news, pausing over weak articles to calculate what he would have added, deleted or improved. Reading *The Herald* and *The Star,* four story ideas came to him. He wondered who he could sell them to. But then his thoughts skipped to something else. He sifted again through *The Star.*

"Hey," he asked Sandra, "where's Slade's byline?"

"He was fired for his Bloodbath in the Tropics screwup."

Ben was out. But he had scribbled a message and a telephone number on a piece of paper.

"Son, call Christine Bennie at *The Toronto Times.* Urgent."

Christine Bennie asked about Yoyo, of course. Mahatma told her Yoyo had given him a gift to pass on to her. Christine was glad to hear that. And she wanted to know more about Mahatma's border troubles. Mahatma said he planned to sell an article about the incident to a newspaper. She asked if he knew that she had left *The New York Times* to take a new job as city editor of *The Toronto Times.* Christine said she had given her boss several of Mahatma's clippings about Jake Corbett. The managing editor liked them. Could Mahatma come for an interview in two days?

EPILOGUE

Edward Slade moved to New York City. He proved himself on *The New York Sun*, the raciest tabloid in North America. He broke apart some major scams. He liked New York and respected its tabloid reporters. They hated cops and cops hated them. But after two years there, Slade began thinking beyond New York. He branched out. He studied French at night school. Two hours a night, five nights a week, for a year. His teachers, at first, were taken aback by his questions: "How do you say slash? How would you translate bullet hole? What about rape?" Slade listened to French radio, watched French TV, went to French movies, met French women and devoured all the French tabloids that he could buy.

After his year of study, Slade became *The New York Sun*'s first foreign correspondent. He moved to Paris, where he demonstrated a remarkable ability to dig out news about French lovers and their fits of jealousy. He became the first reporter in North America to tap the exotic crime beat. New Yorkers ate it up. They constantly phoned and wrote to *The Sun* to complain about the revolting stories from Paris. Slade's salary doubled. He became the world's most famous tabloid scribe.

Helen Savoie lobbied until Lyndon Van Wuyss finally agreed to let her drop the horoscopes and return to reporting full time. She covered municipal politics from a press office at City Hall. Helen strove to build up an impressive portfolio. She worked harder than she had in years and paid careful attention to her writing. Within a few months, she had ten solid articles to her credit. She mailed them and a résumé to *The Toronto Times*. Mahatma Grafton put in a good word on her behalf. Helen was called for an interview and she got the job. And she requested a slight change in her byline. At *The Times,* she would be known as Hélène Savoie.

Mahatma Grafton found a scoop and gave it to Hélène.

"You don't have to do that," Hélène said.

"I know. But this will make it easier for you. They're looking for you to break The Big Story. You know how editors are. So here's the scoop." Mahatma had researched every fact. He had prepared a list of all his sources. All that remained was for Hélène to double-check the details and write the story in her own words.

"I owe you one," Hélène said.

"We're friends, remember?"

Hélène's story appeared on page one of *The Toronto Times.* It was picked up by the Canadian Press and printed on front pages all across the country.

> United States immigration authorities reactivated John Novak's name on a computerized list of unwelcome aliens the day he retired as the mayor of Winnipeg.
> Novak, a long-standing member of the Communist Party of Canada, learned Monday that . . .

Mahatma was close to completing a long feature about the life and death of "Rabbi" Alvin James. *The Toronto Times* was going to publish it in its weekend magazine. Two months earlier the same magazine had printed another long piece by Mahatma Grafton, called "Straight and True; the Life and Times of Jake Corbett."

Someone put his hand on Mahatma's shoulder. Mahatma swivelled in his chair to face a copy editor. The stocky, middle-aged man had hazel eyes and dark hair.

The Toronto Times had hundreds of employees and Mahatma hadn't met this man, although he had often noticed the man looking at him. Mahatma now looked back for the first time, studying the thick lips, the loose, black curls and the skin colour, which was faintly brown.

The man coughed nervously. "I've been assigned to edit that story you're working on. I just took a look at it on my computer screen, to see what it was about."

Mahatma nodded, patiently.

"My name is Alvin James."

"Alvin James? Alvin James was the Rabbi!"

"Yes, I heard he was called that. He was also my father."

Mahatma jumped up. His mouth fell open. He pumped the hand of the Rabbi's son.

"I know about your father and what he did for my family," said Alvin James, Jr. "My mother told me all about it."

Mahatma nodded and smiled. He had learned, through his research, that the Rabbi's wife had died in Winnipeg fifteen years ago. But, scouring the Winnipeg telephone directory, Mahatma hadn't been able to find any relation to Alvin James.

"I have pictures and some old railway documents if you'd like to see them," James said. Mahatma gaped at the man. "And my wife and children would love to meet you. They always ask about my father, and I can never tell them enough. Why don't you come to dinner tomorrow night?"

Mahatma clasped the man's shoulder. "Tomorrow night will be fine."

Ben Grafton bought a subscription to *The Times*. Each day, he unfolded the paper and scanned it for his son's byline. Seeing Mahatma's name made Ben feel closer to his son. He would read the story line by line, imagining his son's voice, wondering which parts were truly Mahatma's and which parts had been modified by editors. "Did you write it the way it came out, son?" he would ask later, on the telephone. Mahatma liked it at *The Times*. He told Ben that he wanted to stick with journalism. He wanted to see what he could do.

Mahatma came home for Thanksgiving. Ben baked a turkey and stuffed it with chicken livers, home-made croutons, onions and herbs. Sandra loved it. She and Mahatma spent most of that weekend together. Ben didn't mind. Just to see Mahatma's suitcase in the hall, to hear him in the shower and to chat with him in the kitchen were enough to make Ben happy. He had a son, and his son loved him. He also had a daughter-in-law who loved him. Well, she wasn't a daughter-in-law yet, but she was heading that way. What else did a broken-down old former railway porter need?

Over the next year, Ben visited Toronto a few times. He considered moving there. But what was the point? Mahatma had a whole career in front of him. And he had started writing a novel at night. He said he was looking forward to showing it to Ben. Wouldn't talk about it, though, wouldn't even give the name of the title, except to say that it had something to do with one of Ben's favourite lines.

Ben stayed in Winnipeg. It was his city, it was his home and it became his final resting place.

The Cover Artist

Scott Barham is a freelance artist who was born in Manitoba and received his Bachelor of Fine Arts from the University of Manitoba. For twenty years he has designed and illustrated for a wide variety of clients, including numerous magazine and book publishers. He has been a contributing artist to *Quill & Quire*, *Books in Canada*, *Canadian Forum*, *Border Crossings* and *Cycle Canada*. His illustrations have been included in books published by Talonbooks, Blizzard Publishing, Peguis Publishers, Hyperion Press and Red Deer College Press, among others. His work has been shown throughout Europe as part of a travelling exhibit of children's book illustrations, and won a silver medal in Stuttgart for design and illustration of the book *The Lion in the Lake*. Mr. Barham currently lives in Winnipeg.

Recent Fiction by Turnstone Press

The Pumpkin-Eaters by Lois Braun

Black Tulips by Bruce Eason

Raised by the River by Jake MacDonald

Fox by Margaret Sweatman

The Canasta Players by Wayne Tefs

Murder in Gutenthal by Armin Wiebe

Tell Tale Signs by Janice Williamson